Secrets of the Heart

Secrets of the Heart

A Michael Moreland Story

Brad Lussier

RESOURCE *Publications* · Eugene, Oregon

SECRETS OF THE HEART
A Michael Moreland Story

Resource Publications
An Imprint of Wipf and Stock Publishers
199 W. 8th Ave., Suite 3
Eugene, OR 97401

www.wipfandstock.com

PAPERBACK ISBN: 979-8-3852-6506-0
HARDCOVER ISBN: 979-8-3852-6507-7
EBOOK ISBN: 979-8-3852-6508-4

VERSION NUMBER 12/01/25

Secrets of the Heart is a work of fiction, and any resemblance to actual events or persons, living or dead, is entirely coincidental. While the author enjoyed making some events and locations in the story historically accurate, he made up a lot of things, too. For example, Prohibition on Prince Edward Island was in effect from 1901 until 1948. In this book, however, it ended sometime before 1937.

Chapter 1

"The damnable Nazi U-boats are here, Michael, deployed up and down the east coast, and if they navigate to Montreal, the war is over for us," Sir Richard said as he paced in his study, reviewing an overnight SIS communique from London. "We knew a pair of U-boats sank a British freighter and a Dutch freighter in the Gulf of St. Lawrence this spring, and some weeks later another U-boat sank three more freighters there. But U-boats are appearing in our waters more frequently now, and they've grown bolder. If they find their way beyond Quebec, the war could be over for us."

"Over?" Michael asked.

"Yes, over. Millions and millions in gold and negotiable securities, all the British wealth shipped to Montreal and Ottawa for safekeeping when the war began, could be plundered within days. Without it, all our banks will fail, and the British economy will be in ruin. Britain will be unable to pay foreign vendors for essential raw materials required by our war industries. We will be unable to finance the manufacture of essential weaponry in British factories. Without that wealth, our fate is sealed," he said.

Clearly distressed, Sir Richard paced behind his desk and paused a moment before going on.

"The world hasn't yet fully recovered from the US stock market crash in 1929," he said. "That economic recession will seem like a picnic compared to the disaster the free world will face if the Nazis find their way to Montreal and Ottawa. History will change forever. The UK will fall, and our people will become Germany's slaves, just as the Nazis are making the Poles their slaves now. Hitler is already marching toward Moscow, where he intends to inflict the same horrors on the Soviets. Without the UK to defend the rest of Europe, all our allies on the continent will fall to the same fate."

"We must take heart, though," Michael said, "for if the Nazis knew that Britain's wealth was stored here in Canada, the Kriegsmarine would already have launched a relentless attack."

Taking a moment to breathe, Sir Richard replied, "True."

"So, they must assume that Britain's wealth remains at home within the boundaries of the United Kingdom," Michael said.

"True again," Sir Richard nodded, his eyes still cast down toward the floor.

"And despite their best efforts, plan after plan to make a strategic land invasion on the UK has failed," Michael said.

"Correct," Sir Richard said, as he propped himself on the corner of his leather-topped mahogany desk and allowed his shoulders to relax. "We can assume our secret has not been discovered. The locations in Montreal and Ottawa are not under immediate threat."

After a quiet moment when neither man spoke, Michael pointed to the report in Sir Richard's hand and asked, "Where does the SIS communique indicate the U-boats have already attacked?"

"The reports have been gleaned from sources in the United States in part, but they're months old. They've been kept undercover since January," Sir Richard said as he left his desk, walked to the globe next to the fireplace, and pointed. "U-boats have been patrolling the east coast of the United States as far south as the Gulf of Mexico, here," he said. Then, pointing to the East Coast on the globe, he said, "Here, on the coast of North Carolina, they sank a merchant ship in an overnight raid more than two months ago. That sinking was completely avoidable. It appears that most American ports on the East Coast have failed to adhere to coastline blackout protocols. Sadly, they feel it will discourage tourism."

"And the result?" Michael asked.

"Bright city lights backlit that first Nazi target, a merchant ship leaving the harbor. The captain of that U-boat must have been smiling as he fired his torpedoes at a perfect silhouette on the horizon. He couldn't have found an easier target. What's worse, it appears the Americans haven't learned much from that first attack. Since then, there have been scores of others just outside American ports."

"Scores?" Michael asked, amazed. "Have they attacked US Navy ships as well?"

"It seems they have stayed away from military targets thus far," Sir Richard answered. "US intelligence indicates that Nazi targets-of-choice have been oil tankers sailing from Texas, here," he said as he pointed to the globe again. "The tankers sail across the Gulf of Mexico before they reach the Atlantic and set a course for European harbors."

"So, now the US is fighting a naval war not only against the Japanese thousands of miles away in the Pacific, but also here at home against the Kriegsmarine just offshore on their east coast," Michael said.

"Yes, and sadly, it's not the first time in history that German U-boats have attacked the US," Sir Richard said. "In 1918, near the end of World War I, a German U-boat fired on the coastal town of Orleans on Cape Cod in Massachusetts. Within months that year, U-boats began sinking shipping vessels on the entire US eastern shoreline. Few people remember that Germany deployed more than 375 U-boats during World War I."

"I wasn't aware of U-boat attacks on this continent during that war," Michael admitted. "I've always thought of World War I solely in terms of Britain's involvement in Europe."

"It was primarily a European war, of course," Sir Richard said, "but it spread to the Middle East, Africa, and parts of Asia. For the United States, it was the first time a foreign enemy had attacked their home soil since the War of 1812, when Britain was her enemy. Shortly after the US entered World War I to support Britain in 1917, U-boats proceeded to sink over 200 US ships in US waters. With the ever-growing size of the Nazi fleet, it's very possible that military targets in the US and Canada could be next."

"How large is the Nazi U-boat fleet today?" Michael asked.

"SIS intelligence reported Germany had 57 U-boats in 1939 when they started the war," Sir Richard said. "Today we know they have more than 350, and, at the rate their naval shipyards are producing them, they'll have launched at least 400 by the end of the year."

"But none have attacked targets like Bell Island in Newfoundland, and, to our knowledge, none have been discovered roaming the St. Lawrence to attack inbound and outbound shipping from Quebec. Is that correct?" Michael asked

"Correct," Sir Richard said as he walked toward the study window. "However, with the sad state of the Royal Canadian Navy, we remain inadequately defended. So, our only immediate hope for the safety of the gold and securities hidden farther up the St. Lawrence is Nazi ignorance. Our secret *must* remain secure."

"Thankfully, our convoy system, with help from the US, has provided some protection for shipping in waters near Halifax and farther east," Michael said.

"True," Sir Richard nodded, "and there are no vital military targets close by. Only the iron mines at Bell Island would prove a worthy target for the enemy."

"Then we must pray that they remain ignorant of the British treasure stored up the St. Lawrence beyond Quebec," Michael said, "because we also face a concern closer to our home here on Prince Edward Island."

Looking at Michael with knowing eyes and nodding, Sir Richard didn't need to speak.

"We know that Ernest Duncan, once a German spy, but now serving the Allied cause in Germany," Michael began, "fulfilled Nazi orders two years ago to chart landings at three remote shoreline locations here on Prince Edward Island."

"Yes," Sir Richard said. "He buried maps, money, and other supplies for future invasion parties that were to be deployed from Nazi U-boats. But remember, even though we've retrieved everything he buried, the Abwehr, Germany's intelligence service, still has maps to those three sites, and probably a map to Highfield as well."

"True, but meanwhile, we can take heart and attend to the preparations we made from the beginning," Michael said. "Highfield is equipped with a supply of weapons and armaments safely stored in our basement survival bunker, where our loved ones can remain secure during an emergency."

"Correct," Sir Richard answered, "and now would be a time for us to relocate some of those weapons to our attic, where the windows offer sight lines to every compass point. We'll need to take other precautions as well, as I am sure you understand," he said quietly, "but to prevent undo concern among our family members, I suggest we work surreptitiously. Let's schedule our work for times when our ladies make their shopping expeditions to Charlottetown. What do you think?

"My thoughts exactly," Michael agreed.

Sir Richard's angst had softened, and he returned to the leather chair behind his desk. As he sat, he said, "When I take time to consider it, a single major German failure in long-term strategic planning continues to comfort me here."

"What failure is that?" Michael asked.

"The Kriegsmarine has failed to deploy a single aircraft carrier since the war began," he said. "Japan sent six carriers 3,500 miles to launch their fighters and bombers to attack the American fleet at Pearl Harbor. If the Kriegsmarine were equipped with a similar fleet of carriers, they could make similar attacks on this coast. This single strategic oversight allows us to live without fear when we hear the drone of aircraft overhead. Every engine we hear in the sky is one of our own, and most are training aircraft flown by pilots and crewmen preparing to fight in battles abroad."

Sir Richard sat silently for a moment and looked into the distance before saying, "I still believe I made the right decision."

"Right decision?" Michael asked.

"Yes," Sir Richard answered. "I began searching for a place like Highfield in Canada after assessing SIS intelligence reports from Germany, intelligence that many others lacked. I knew that Nazi Germany was much better prepared for war than the UK. After World War I, the people of the UK, like all of Europe, craved peace. When Hitler came to power, however, many of our leaders remained attached to those outdated hopes. We watched as Germany, violating the Treaty of Versailles, laid the keels for scores of U-boats, assembled an air corps second to none, and built hundreds and hundreds of Panzers. At SIS, we could see what was coming, and I did my best to advise those who had the power and authority to prepare our military forces to meet that ever-growing danger, but to no avail."

"So," Michael began, "why are you questioning your decision to purchase Highfield?"

Sir Richard thought for a moment before beginning, "I suppose it's because the UK hasn't suffered a German land invasion. Our Chain Home radar sites on the East Coast have proven their ability to protect us from the worst the Luftwaffe can offer. To the Führer's disappointment, all his plans for a land invasion have been foiled. Yes, parts of Suffolk and other cities and towns on our east coast have been bombed, but our home at Clifton Manor has remained untouched. My logical side, the part that I inherited from my father, sometimes wonders if I really needed to tear my family away from their home in Suffolk to come to Canada."

"You forget several other factors, however, Richard," Michael said.

"Such as?" asked Sir Richard.

"Your personal safety, for one," Michael began. "Although SIS headquarters in London still stands, you could have been killed in any number of bombings during the Blitz as you walked the streets or slept in your flat."

"True," he agreed.

"And Lady Moncrieff," Michael added. "You must not forget how she began to find healing from her poor health almost immediately after she arrived here. That factor alone was worth your investment, I would argue."

"True again," Sir Richard nodded.

"And then there are your grandchildren, Case and Reed," Michael said.

"What do you mean, Michael?" asked Sir Richard. "They hadn't yet been born when I decided to purchase Highfield."

"Correct," Michael said, "and they wouldn't have been born if Susan and I hadn't been reunited and discovered that our marriage was meant to be, a marriage that Lady Moncrieff foresaw many years earlier. Remember, it was Lady Moncrieff who ultimately secured your approval for our union."

Sir Richard raised his hands in surrender and began to smile.

"I've second-guessed myself most of my life, Michael," he said. "There's no question that Highfield was meant to be. Thank you for calling me on it this time." Then, looking at his watch, he noted, "My playtime with my grandsons is scheduled to begin in just a few minutes. I know a half hour with those two will erase any suggestion that purchasing Highfield was an error."

Just then, the door opened, and Susan entered with Case and Reed. Moments after she and Michael left the room, Sir Richard was on hands and knees, romping with two giggling boys on the plush oriental carpet in his study.

Chapter 2

During the winter months, nothing on Prince Edward Island had claimed Michael's attention more completely than the house plans spread out on the library table at Highfield this morning. The first page elevations revealed a large, handsome structure in a modified Greek revival style. The rectangular two-and-one-half-story home, some sixty feet wide and forty feet deep, had a gable roof populated with five attic dormers on both the front and rear elevations. Everything about the style fit in well with historical PEI architecture. The south-facing home boasted a massive central chimney with flues for five fireplaces on the first and second floors, while both the east and west gables had chimneys serving the central heating and hot water systems located in the basement. A fully enclosed breezeway on the east gable led to an attached two-car garage so that Susan would never need an umbrella when taking the boys to Charlottetown in her cabriolet or when returning with bags and boxes after shopping. The north face, the "back" of the house, offered two ells, each twenty feet wide and twenty-eight feet long. One was labelled 'Susan's Studio' while the other was labelled 'Michael's Shop'. Between the ells was a stone patio with planters surrounding three sides.

Bill McCauley, arguably the most accomplished architect on the island, had never worked with a more enthusiastic client than Michael Moreland. Before he bought the 190-acre parcel across Suffolk Road from Highfield's driveway, Michael invited Bill to walk the site and offer his thoughts on the placement of the proposed home the Morelands were considering. Michael and Bill were able to agree almost immediately on the best location and settled on Michael's design for the south-facing front facade. While Bill got started on the initial drawings, Michael was already clearing the building site and its six-hundred-foot driveway. With the tree stumps removed and the gravel construction driveway completed, Bill and the Morelands were able to locate the house and garage for the team of excavators and masonry contractors who poured the concrete footings and ten-foot-deep foundation walls three weeks later. Michael couldn't wait for the first floor to be framed so the foundation could be backfilled and rough graded.

With over twenty years of experience in residential, commercial, and several industrial designs, Bill McCauley was not one to settle for anything but the best in every aspect of the project. While Michael was enamored with Bill's insistence on only the best in engineering and materials, it was one of Bill's long-term relationships with a well-experienced contractor that brought his design to life and made the Morelands' new home a reality.

Building a new home during wartime presented a host of challenges unknown to architects and building contractors before the war began. Many builders faced labor shortages as their employees answered the call to serve in the military, both in Canada and abroad. Building materials such as copper, steel, and iron were in short supply, especially those required by manufacturers of armaments, machinery, vehicles, and aircraft, which were essential to fulfill military needs. Without Bill McCauley's long list of contacts, Michael had nowhere to turn to find both the labor and materials to complete the job.

When building crews on PEI weren't to be found, Michael and Bill looked to the mainland. One crew with whom Bill had worked on several occasions, the McLeod Brothers Construction Company from St. John, New Brunswick, was ordinarily contracted at least a year ahead. However, when Bill telephoned them, he found that they were facing a sudden and unexpected vacancy in their schedule. A client ready to begin construction of a new home in St. Andrew had been called to serve in the RCA and was forced to cancel his contract with the McLeods. Thankfully for Michael and Susan, the McLeods had also been left with a warehouse full of building materials, everything from framing lumber to slate for the roof. With that cache of framing, roofing, and siding materials, the Moreland house could be tight to the weather by summer's end.

With manpower on hand, the McLeods were ready to start work almost immediately. Fortunately, they had also stockpiled a supply of copper and cast-iron pipe, as well as supplies of copper cable and electrical fixtures. No lack of materials would delay the plumbers and electricians from completing their work once the framing was finished. Finding those materials once the war began might have been difficult if the McLeods hadn't had two more warehouses in New Brunswick stocked for their former client's house.

"In the US," Bill McCauley said, "March 31, 1942, was the last day that manufacturers could use tin, steel, copper, aluminum, nickel, or chrome to create their products. That would affect the plumbing and electrical systems in your house, as well as every household appliance – refrigerators, freezers, kitchen ranges, hot water heaters, and even the locksets and knobs on your kitchen cabinets. I have two projects in the States that are currently on hold indefinitely. Thankfully, in Canada, those restrictions don't exist, but finding some of the materials we need would be difficult if it weren't for folks like the McLeods. Gus has always kept his warehouse full. I'm confident he'll be able to supply just about everything we need for your new home. While home construction in the US has been halted to support the war effort, here in Canada, we're still building."

The Morelands had a ten o'clock appointment with Bill to begin sorting out the interior finishes, including the kitchen cabinets, appliances, and bathroom fixtures. Bill had promised to be ready with details for the mantles, stairs, and the remainder of the millwork, including mouldings, paneling, and doors. When Michael drove home from his errands in Charlottetown this morning, however, Susan met him in the library with a surprise.

"I can't go to another meeting with your architect today," Susan said as she turned away from the blueprints on the library table and walked to the window. "I'm not sure I want to go to another any time soon, either. I'm tired of the entire process."

Michael could hardly believe his ears. "I don't understand, Susan," he began. "Bill McCauley isn't *my* architect. He's *our* architect. We've spent months and months with him, the finest architect available on PEI. You've never expressed any hesitation since we first discussed building a new home. Now, when we have the final framing plans in hand, the building site is ready, the concrete foundation has cured, and hundreds of board feet of lumber are on site, you want to abandon construction of our new home?" he asked. "The McLeod Brothers are scheduled to arrive from St. John in a week to start framing. We scheduled our meeting to confirm the interior millwork with Bill over a week ago. The meeting is at ten o'clock, and now," Michael said, looking at his wristwatch, "now you're telling me you're not sure you want to go on?"

"I can't stand the thought of sitting another two hours while you two hunker down at a drafting table to discuss 'bearing walls' and 'wind shear,' Michael. I don't want to look at any more sketches or catalogues with pictures of newel posts, balusters, and handrails. I need to see them with my own eyes and put my hands on them. It may be easy for you to be excited. You love all these details, but I don't need to be there. Besides, Dr. MacMillan telephoned while you were away this morning. He has the results of the tests he took during my physical examination last week. I made an appointment to meet with him after lunch. One trip to Charlottetown is all I can face today."

Michael said nothing but stood looking down while shaking his head.

"We can talk about this later today when you return from the architect's office. For now, however, please excuse me. I need to settle Patrice with Case and Reed before I start the laundry," Susan said.

Why Susan was suddenly so conflicted about moving forward with construction was a complete mystery to Michael. It wasn't like her, but as he sat a while longer, he recalled that she hadn't been herself for the last week or so. She'd seemed distracted and short with him and their boys. Michael was more than concerned. He was beginning to get worried. He decided to drive to Charlottetown early enough to stop at St. Peter's to talk with Fr. Hunt. When he arrived, he was happy to find that Fr. Hunt had a few minutes to spare.

"So, Susan hasn't been herself lately?" Fr. Hunt asked.

"No," Michael said, "but I'm afraid I didn't think much about it until today."

"I suspect you've been busy, then," Fr. Hunt said. As Michael nodded, Fr. Hunt continued, "When we get busy with our own pursuits, we often fail to notice those who need our care."

"But it was details concerning the new house I was chasing. I wasn't trying to ignore her," Michael said.

"I'm sure you weren't, Michael, but Susan was probably already showing some signs she was unhappy, some signs you missed. Do you think that's possible?" he asked.

Michael thought for a moment before answering. "Yes, I do," Michael said. "You're right. She has seemed irritated with me and with our boys lately; she's been short-spoken and impatient."

"Has she felt physically unwell or been ill recently?" Fr. Hunt asked.

"No, at least not that she's mentioned," Michael answered. "She saw Dr. MacMillan for her yearly check-up just last week, and he was running the usual tests as he always does. She's skipping our meeting with the architect this morning, but she's planning to see the doctor this afternoon."

"Well, you're in town and the hospital is not far away. Would it be worth a call or a visit to see if the good doctor could ease your mind?" Fr. Hunt asked.

"I suppose it would," Michael said, "but I'm due at the architect's office in a few minutes. I'll have to call the hospital when my meeting is done."

"Of course," Fr. Hunt answered, "of course."

Chapter 3

When Michael left Bill McCauley's office at the end of their morning meeting, it was almost 11:30. Bill had confirmed the scheduled arrival of Gus McLeod's framing crew for the following Monday. Because the crew would be traveling from their homes in St. John, Gus had been happy to accept Michael and Susan's offer for his men to bunk in the guest cottages at Highfield during the work week. When the workday ended on Friday afternoons, they planned to return to St. John to spend the weekends.

Michael had his first chance to speak with Gus McLeod by telephone from Bill's office a few days earlier. A fifty-year-old Scot with an appropriate brogue had said, "Your cottages will be a boon, Mr. Moreland, and much appreciated. The short walk across the road to work each morning will help move things along, too. Because my men aren't used to working this far from home, I'm sure they'll be happy to work longer hours each day so they can finish the job as soon as possible. They'll be eager to be back with their families on more than just weekends when the job is complete. I already overheard them planning to start work early each morning and stay longer each afternoon before quitting for the day."

"I understand, Gus," Michael said. "I'm a family man, too, and my wife and I appreciate the sacrifice you and your men are making. On a practical note, please keep in mind our offer to store your materials and equipment. We've got room in the barn and my workshop at Highfield whenever it comes in handy for you."

"In that case, Michael," Gus added, "we'll be bringing two trailers along behind our trucks. One is enclosed and stays at the jobsite. We keep tools, ladders, and scaffolding in it. The other is an open trailer for lumber and such. If we can back it in at your barn, it will remain a handy tow from across the road."

"Then we'll be looking forward to both," Michael said.

"And I'll confirm all the details with you and Bill within forty-eight hours," Gus said.

Before Michael drove home at the end of his meeting with Bill Mc-Cauley, he thought back to his conversation with Fr. Hunt earlier that morning. He called Dr. MacMillan from Bill's office and arranged to stop on his way home to discuss his concerns about Susan. It was a short drive to the hospital, and just a few minutes before noon, Dr. MacMillan's receptionist escorted Michael to the doctor's office.

"Michael," the doctor said as he stood and offered his hand, "it's good to see you. Please sit down."

"Thank you for taking the time to see me, Doctor MacMillan," Michael said. "I know it's probably nothing, but I'm concerned about Susan."

"First," Dr. MacMillan said, it's 'Andrew,' and secondly, I'm glad you're concerned for Susan. Every husband should be concerned about his wife's health." Picking up a folder in front of him, he continued, "I have the results from the tests we did last week. Susan scheduled an afternoon appointment with me today to review them."

"Yes," Michael said. "She told me this morning. I hope you've found nothing out of the ordinary. I can't point to anything specific, but she just hasn't been herself lately."

"I've seen nothing to alarm me," Andrew said as he put his glasses on and looked through several pages. "Let's see. Red blood cell count, white blood cells, and hemoglobin are all normal."

"Anything else?" Michael asked.

"Nothing in particular," Andrew answered. "Her lungs are clear, she showed no abnormal weight changes, blood pressure is normal, and reflexes are normal."

"Is that it, then?" Michael asked?

"Not quite," Andrew answered. "She said she'd been feeling impatient at home, even moody sometimes. She seemed concerned enough that I suggested one more test we could do, a simple one that required no needles," he said, smiling. "All we needed was a second urine sample."

"What kind of test?" Michael asked.

"It's called a 'Hogben' test," he said. "We send her sample to the laboratory, and the results are usually available within a few days. I have them right here. I was going to call Susan to give her the results before her appointment today, but since you're here, I could call her now, and you can hear the results together. I think that would be best. Agreed?" Andrew asked.

"Of course," Michael answered, "but it's not bad news, is it?"

"Not at all," Andrew said, "not at all."

As Andrew dialed the telephone, Michael sat quietly, but on the edge of his chair, clearly concerned about Susan despite Andrew's reassurances. Finally, Michael heard Andrew say, "Hello, this is Dr. MacMillan calling. Is Mrs. Moreland available?"

Andrew motioned to Michael to come closer so they could both hear Susan's voice through the telephone receiver. A moment later, Michael heard Susan answer, "Hello?"

"Hello, Susan. It's Andrew, Andrew MacMillan calling. I'm at the hospital and Michael is here with me. Are you free to speak for a moment?"

"Yes," Susan answered, but continued, "Michael is there with you? Is he all right? He's not injured, is he?"

"No, Susan, he's fine. We're in my office. He stopped to ask about your test results from last week, and I suggested I report them to both of you. Michael is listening at the telephone with me right now."

"Hello, Susan," Michael said as he leaned in to speak.

"Hello," she answered. "This is an unusual way for three of us to meet."

"Please don't be worried," Andrew said. "To begin with, all your test results are normal for a healthy woman your age. The one additional test I ordered, however, showed some results I prefer to share with both of you. You may remember that I told you that the test would take several days before we had results, Susan?" he asked.

"Yes," she said, "but I'm afraid I can't recall if you mentioned what the test was for."

"Well, a few comments you made about mood swings and impatience with Michael and your boys convinced me this test was advised, and I hope you'll be happy to learn that the test results proved positive," Andrew said, smiling.

"Positive?" Susan asked.

"Positive for what?" Michael asked.

"Why, pregnancy, of course," Andrew answered.

"I'm pregnant?" Susan asked, surprise and excitement overflowing in her voice.

"Then that explains why..." Michael began as he turned to look at Andrew.

"It explains that a woman's body, mind, and spirit," Andrew began, "are wonderfully inseparable, and the physical changes a woman experiences when she is pregnant need the special care and concern that only her husband can provide. You were right to be concerned when you saw the emotional changes Susan was experiencing, Michael. I'm so pleased you came to discuss her health and that you will be available to support her and enjoy the next seven months together until your third child is delivered." Before handing the telephone to Michael, he added, "I'm needed in the operating theatre just now. I'll leave you two to talk about whatever is next."

Susan and Michael's conversation was short. Michael couldn't wait to get home to her, and she could hardly wait for him to arrive. They had a great deal to plan and discuss, especially concerning some immediate changes to their new home's floor plan.

Chapter 4

Re-naming the second-floor bedroom east of the Master Bedroom, "Nursery," and labelling the bedroom to the west of the Master Bedroom, "Boys' Bedroom", was a simple matter for Michael as he sat at Highfield's library table with a set of open plans. What brought him a smile, however, was telling Susan about his idea to eliminate the second-floor laundry chute and replace it with a dumbwaiter. When he finished sketching the changes, the plans included a dumbwaiter shaft extending from the basement with stops at the first and second floors and terminating in the attic.

"No more carrying diaper pails downstairs to the laundry," Michael announced proudly. "In this house, they will ride to the laundry at the touch of a button, and," he continued, "at Christmas, we won't have to carry all our decorations down the attic stairs to the first floor. When we send them downstairs in the dumbwaiter, we'll still have enough energy left to decorate our tree."

"And in a couple of years, Case and Reed will be riding from attic to basement whenever we're not looking," Susan added knowingly.

"That didn't hurt you years ago at Clifton Manor when you were young and your brothers were having their fun, shipping you upstairs and down in the dumbwaiter," Michael smiled.

"Not until the day the rope jammed," she said, "and I was left between floors for the best part of an afternoon."

Michael's smile wilted as his memory took him back to that day. He remembered how Nigel and Boyd were in a panic, desperate to rescue their sister before their parents returned from their tennis match and discovered what their sons' mischief had caused.

"Well," Michael said, "Nigel was pulling you up from the pantry while Boyd ran upstairs and pulled with him to make the ride faster for you. However, he pulled too fast, and the rope leapt off the pulley."

"Yes," Susan began, "and they got you to run to your father's workshop to get a tool to pry the rope back into place. I remember the long, sad story my brothers told Mother and Father when they returned from their match."

"They meant no harm, Susan, just boys being boys, you know," Michael said.

"Perhaps," Susan said, "but you weren't the one who was folded into that little box like I was, waiting in the dark after trusting their promises for a fun ride."

"Remember, though," Michael said, "I did run as fast as I could and made it back to the attic and freed the rope. Your mother made you thank me, remember?"

"I wasn't ready to let you be my hero then, Michael Moreland," she said, a smile beginning to form on her face, "but I may someday."

"Well," he said, taking her into his arms, "if it's any comfort, our dumb-waiter will be chain-driven, so there won't be any ropes to tangle. It will also be electrically powered, with up and down switches at each landing, and it will be equipped with an emergency switch *inside*. And," he added, "I'm sure our boys will prove to be trustworthy lads, not at all impish like their uncles."

"Then I suppose I'll have to rely on you to train the imp out of them early so that the little brother or sister I'm carrying won't suffer the same treatment their mother endured," she said through her ever-growing smile.

"I wouldn't have it any other way, Darling," Michael said as he wrapped his wife in his arms, and her face melted into his shoulder. "I only want our home to have every convenience available for you, and if I seem over-eager to move ahead, it's only because we need to get any changes or additions on paper before the framing starts in a few days. If you approve, I'll take these marked-up drawings to Bill McCauley's office this afternoon."

"I will be happy to trade stairs and diaper pails for a dumbwaiter any day," she said. "Right now, though, while our boys are napping and the little one within is quiet," she said with her hand on her tummy, "I'm going to take a nap, too." One quick kiss later, Susan turned toward the stairs leading to their bedroom while Michael rolled up the plans and added them to those in his briefcase.

Two weeks later, the early April weather had warmed, and clear skies gave the McLeod Brothers just the opportunity they needed to get started. Working from early morning to late afternoon, they began framing the first floor of Michael and Susan's new home. The crew took the few changes

Michael had made in stride. One detail they had not encountered before was a concrete floor in the garage and breezeway link over the full-depth basement below. A garage didn't generally have a basement. Still, like the safe room in Highfield's basement filled with survival supplies and weaponry, the Moreland house included an equally elaborate plan for the Moreland family's security. Of course, nothing in the plans revealed the future use of the space. Not even the architect was privy to that information.

As Michael watched Gus McLeod's masonry crew pouring the concrete floor, he thought back to his first days on Prince Edward Island. When a retired Royal Navy Rear Admiral purchased the estate and sent Michael Moreland, Highfield's superintendent, to finish the interior carpentry and prepare the estate for its new owners, curiosity on the island was palpable. Michael's British accent identified him immediately with Highfield wherever he went. Knowledge of Sir Richard's senior role at SIS needed to remain concealed. That information was shared only with SIS agents in Canada—Michael, Armand Verrier, and Armand's daughter, Michelle. Thankfully, as far as the local population was concerned, it was only Sir Richard's retirement that brought him and his family to the safety of Prince Edward Island, three thousand miles away from the danger of Luftwaffe bombing raids in England. No one here had reason to suspect that he maintained a relationship with Britain's SIS and was in regular contact with the Prime Minister. One of Michael's responsibilities was to make sure no one had reason to suspect Sir Richard was employed at anything more than gardening and enjoying ocean breezes at the shore.

While the masonry crew was polishing the concrete floor to give it a smooth finish, Michael turned to see Armand Verrier's truck pull up the hill to the construction site. It wasn't like him to be away from his hardware store in the middle of the morning on a weekday. Michael was sure this visit wasn't a social call, and his curiosity brought him immediately to the truck door. When he got there, Armand motioned toward the passenger door for Michael to get in. No doubt, Armand was concerned about something serious.

"I telephoned Highfield to speak with Sir Richard and you this morning, but I found he was away. Lady Moncrieff offered a number where he could be reached, but I didn't want to call him to discuss the news I needed to tell both of you," Armand said. "Telephones on the island offer no security."

"Understood," Michael said, nodding. "He left for a meeting with the RCN command in Halifax this morning. He won't be back until tomorrow afternoon," Michael said. "Can your news wait until then?"

"For him, yes. For you, no. I need to tell you now," Armand said.

"Say on, then," Michael said.

"You'll remember the three landing sites that we visited last fall after you received a note from Ernest Duncan?" Armand asked.

"Yes," Michael said. "They were sites he had prepared for Nazi landings from U-boats. Once he abandoned his Nazi allegiance to serve the Allied cause, he provided maps and coordinates so that we could retrieve everything he had been ordered to hide there."

"Correct," Armand said. "Well, Jacques Boucher was at the hardware store last week. He happened to mention seeing something odd from the *Lady M* when he was on the north shore near Alberton."

"I know Jacques was out on the *Lady M* for her first outing this spring. He told me he made a trip around the island," Michael said.

"Well, after catching some suspicious unidentified radio chatter earlier this week, and after hearing what Jacques had to say, I took a drive to those sites on a hunch. One of them was near Alberton, remember?" Armand asked.

"Yes," Michael said, "I remember that now. What did you find?"

"More than I expected," Armand said. "All three sites showed signs of recent activity - signs of digging in the same places we found everything Duncan had buried two years ago."

Armand had Michael's full attention. "No one could have known the coordinates of those three sites unless Duncan had provided them, Armand said. "I don't believe there's any accident or coincidence here. It could only prove a Nazi presence, as Duncan warned us."

"Then it's as we expected," Michael began, "and we both know the RCN is not adequately prepared to encounter the Kriegsmarine, even in our own waters. Furthermore, we must assume that landing parties at those three sites could be roaming the island even now."

"True," Armand said, nodding, "or they may have recovered all the intelligence they need and have moved on to targets of greater strategic importance. Let's face it. PEI offers targets of no military significance aside from the aircraft at the RCAF training fields. I'd have to wager the Germans are looking at targets in Quebec."

"Well," Michael said, "one thing is sure."

"What's that?" Armand asked.

"If the Nazis had any doubt that Ernest Duncan had abandoned their ranks, they have no doubt now," Michael said.

"And lacking an agent here on the island to welcome them," Armand began, "is one more reason they would probably look for more valuable targets – those with strategic shipping, industry, or an RCN presence."

"I'd have to agree, but let's fill Sir Richard in as soon as he returns," Michael said. "I'll call you when he arrives. He'll want to hear about everything you saw at those three sites. Who knows? Maybe the RCN brass will have further intelligence to share on the subject."

As Michael climbed out of the truck, Armand assured him, "I'll be waiting beside the phone."

Walking back toward the masonry crew working on the concrete garage floor, Michael suddenly had mixed feelings. He was pleased he had specified the concrete floor, so essential to the security of the safe room in the basement below. At the same time, though, Armand's news had brought the reality of the enemy's presence to the quiet village of Suffolk on Prince Edward Island.

"I hope we never need to use that safe room," Michael said to himself.

What Michael didn't know was that the Abwehr had already initiated Operation Grete. A Nazi U-boat was scheduled to sail for Canada on May 1, 1942, with a German spy aboard. A landing party had orders to row him to the Canadian shore exactly as Ernest Duncan had described more than a year earlier. Furthermore, this spy was not the only German agent scheduled to reach Canadian soil in this manner.

The SIS intelligence reports that Sir Richard brought home from Halifax the following afternoon included the Abwehr's plans for yet a second agent's infiltration. When and where the U-boat planned to make its landing, however, remained unknown.

Nothing in Sir Richard's intelligence reports helped to allay Michael's concerns about his family's safety. Instead, they confirmed his worst fears.

Chapter 5

March and April had brought PEI milder temperatures and less precipitation than usual. With the weather on his side, Luc Boucher had made the most of those months, completing the remaining exterior work on the two houses that he and his brother, Joseph, owned on Suffolk Road. By the end of April, Luc was eager to complete the inside finish work needed at both houses. Of course, Michael's help had been essential to Luc's rapid progress. Together, they were a good team.

Today, they were finishing the crown moulding in the parlor of the old farmhouse, the house that Luc and Lois would make their home when they were married in the fall. With the help of Michael's mitre box and their coping saws, the two men had persevered in making all the moulding joints tight.

"Not a single wall, ceiling, or floor in an old farmhouse like this will be straight, plumb, or level, Luc," Michael said. "Still, it's our job to minimize the quirks so that nothing offends the eye of even the most casual observer. You and I will know where we battled her imperfections, and our eyes may travel to those places whenever we enter this room. However, no one with an untrained eye needs to know."

"I understand that a whole lot more now than I did when we started the wainscoting, casings, and chair rails," Luc said. "Now I'm trying to convince Lois that we need to avoid choosing wallpaper with an unforgiving vertical pattern in a room like this. If we do, every corner where the walls intersect will be a monumental challenge!" he laughed.

"Well put, Luc," Michael nodded with a smile, "well put, and I hope Lois will agree."

"Also," Luc began, "the plumber and the electrician have promised to be finished by the end of the month. Then it's up to Lois and me to finish the painting and hang the wallpaper. Her artist's eye sees colors and patterns that my mechanic's mind just can't comprehend. Between us, though, I'm sure we'll work it out."

At that moment, the men heard the kitchen door close and heard Lois call out, "I'm back, Luc, and I have a sack full of wallpaper samples."

"In the parlor, Hon," Luke called. "Michael and I have just finished."

As she entered the parlor and looked up at the crown moulding that surrounded the room and bordered the stairway to the second floor, she said, "That's just what we needed, isn't it now?"

"Once it's primed and I've been able to putty a few holes, it will be ready for finish painting," Luc said as he took the bag from her arms.

Walking around and inspecting the corners, she said, "And where is there room for putty, Luc? It looks lovely to my eye."

"And may it ever be so," Luc laughed as he looked back at Michael and put his arm around her shoulder and squeezed.

"I'm just gathering my tools," Michael said, "so you two can get to choosing your wallpaper. "I'll be back tomorrow so we can finish the mantle, Luc."

After Lois said her goodbyes, she took another look around the parlor.

"So, like Joseph and Ingrid's house next door," she said, "we have only some painting and wallpaper to finish, right?"

"That's right, Hon, but you know how much I hate painting," he said as he took her into his arms, "and the kitchen and laundry appliances will be here in a week, so we'll need to concentrate on those rooms first."

"I'll be glad when we can be rid of these work lights when we've installed the ceiling fixtures and finish the rest of the outlets and switches," she said as she turned in his arms, enjoying his chin on her shoulder and his arms around her waist. "I know you don't worry about them, but there are so many of those metal boxes in the walls with all those scary wires sticking out."

"Well," Luc began, "remember, it's 1942. Electrical standards have changed since this old house was built. I wanted you to have all the outlets you'll ever need in each room. One isn't enough anymore, so every room has at least two, and our bedroom has three, he boasted, "as well as a light switch at the door for the ceiling fixture. No more walking into dark rooms or pulling on strings for us."

"That's certainly more than we had in London," she said. "I feel like a princess when I look around here."

"You're *my* princess," Luc whispered in her ear as he squeezed her waist, "and soon you'll be my queen."

She turned in his arms, looked up into his eyes, and met his kiss with her own. Their kisses lasted longer and seemed hungrier as the days on the calendar drew closer to their wedding day.

As their lips parted, she said, "I'll get the brushes and a bucket of primer for the crown moulding. If we can finish a first coat and putty those other spots, I'll be able to get out of these painting clothes before dinner," she said.

"That sounds like a plan," Luc agreed, "but I have another appetite that needs satisfying before I think about dinner."

Once again, their lips met, and Luc's embrace was even tighter this time. A long moment later, when they opened their eyes, Lois began to turn away, but Luc stopped her, saying, "What, no dessert?"

Lois had to laugh as she pushed herself away. "Dessert will be served after the priming is done and the brushes are clean."

"Then, my princess," he smiled, "prepare to watch the fastest painter in Suffolk break all known speed records for priming."

"And I'll start on the other side of the room and meet you in the middle," she laughed. "Dessert will be waiting for you there," she winked.

Although Luc may never have enjoyed painting before, the smile on his face told Lois he was undoubtedly enjoying it today.

Chapter 6

With Armand Verrier and Michael sitting opposite the desk in the study at Highfield, Sir Richard nodded as Armand described his discoveries at the three shore locations he had explored several days earlier.

"I'm not surprised," Sir Richard said as he stood to indicate a map on the wall behind him. "The Kriegsmarine has gotten bolder since the war began nearly three years ago. Until recently, their U-boats have been content with their convoy hunting a good distance offshore. With a host of fast convoys sailing out of Halifax and the slower convoys out of Sydney, U-boats have paid little interest to the waters farther up the St. Lawrence. Also, because Halifax and Sydney are better equipped and better fortified with RCN artillery stationed on their coasts and are supported by radar and searchlight installations, U-boats prefer the easier targets that lone ships farther at sea present. With regular strict blackout practices and anti-torpedo nets at their harbor entrances, U-boats have chosen to do their hunting elsewhere. Until recently, that is," he added.

Although neither Armand nor Michael spoke, their faces asked questions Sir Richard could not ignore.

"The Canadian government's wartime secrecy policies have kept some incidents out of the public's general knowledge," Sir Richard began. "As a result, few are aware that in February this year, the *Empire Spring*, an unescorted 6,900-ton British freighter, was torpedoed and sunk just fifty miles from Sable Island, Nova Scotia. Furthermore, at the end of March, the *Hertford*, another British freighter, was torpedoed and sunk just south of Halifax."

Armand and Michael sat silently as Sir Richard continued.

"Since U-boats have grown bolder and have begun pursuing targets closer to shore," he said, "and with the Gulf of St. Lawrence defended by only four aging RCN warships, we have every reason to expect more U-boat attacks on RCN targets and commercial shipping in the Gulf."

"As I understand common U-boat tactics," Armand said, "once a U-boat locates its prey, it pursues its target and waits for the most opportune moment to launch its torpedoes. They're used to spending a great deal of time submerged and hidden, only surfacing as necessary to better identify a target and to aim their torpedoes," Armand said.

"That is their standard protocol," Sir Richard said.

"So, the likelihood of us spotting one in the Gulf is small," Michael said, unless we are within view of a potential target they intend to attack."

"Correct," Sir Richard said as he lifted a folder from his desk, "but we have new SIS intelligence of an Abwehr operation concerning U-213 that is due to arrive here sometime soon. If we can verify when they plan to land, we may have an opportunity to intercept them. Our best information tells us that part of their mission is to land a German spy on Canadian soil."

"I'd have to say," Armand began, "that were I planning to insert an operative in Canada somewhere up the St. Lawrence, PEI would not be high on my list of destinations."

"And I'd have to agree," Michael said. "I'd be looking for a site near Quebec, a city where a spy could melt into a crowd, or somewhere farther away, like New Brunswick, where he'd encounter fewer people asking questions."

"And those, gentlemen," Sir Richard said, "would be my conclusions as well. However, I have another bit of information to share with you, one that potentially complicates the issue."

"Say on," Michael said.

"Perhaps you'll remember the name Brenda Kimble, also known as Brenda Ilse Kimmel?" he asked.

"Yes," Michael said. "She was Ernest Duncan's accomplice. She was captured with him and imprisoned in Halifax."

As Armand nodded in agreement, Sir Richard dropped a bombshell.

"She escaped from her cell in Halifax ten days ago. It appears she charmed one of the guards and, following their familiarities, he found she had escaped, leaving him handcuffed to the bars of her cell. With the help of his keys and uniform, she made her escape. As of this morning, her whereabouts remain unknown."

"She could have been the mystery visitor to three sites here on PEI," Armand said.

"Perhaps," Sir Richard answered.

"Or she could be somewhere on the coast or in Quebec preparing to greet an Abwehr operative," Michael added.

"True, as well," Sir Richard said, "or she could be anywhere else she chooses. Nonetheless, she was once a known enemy. She must remain an enemy until we are convinced otherwise."

Standing, Sir Richard added, "Gentlemen, please forgive me, but Nurse Mary Clark should be finishing her visit with my dear wife presently. I am charged with the delivery of a tea tray that should be arriving here at any moment."

As Michael and Armand stood, the men heard a quiet knock at the study door and watched as Sir Richard retrieved the tea tray from Patrice and turned up the stairway toward Lady Moncrieff's dressing room. Only seconds had passed when Michael and Armand heard a crash on the staircase. Hurrying to the study door, they found the tea tray at the bottom of the stairs, its contents strewn on the stairs above. On the center landing, Sir Richard lay sprawled on his back, one hand gripping a baluster. Only his grip and one foot on the plush carpet runner provided the slim tethers that prevented him from tumbling to the bottom of the stairs.

Rushing to his side, the men met Nurse Clark, who had sprinted from Lady Moncrieff's dressing room. Lady Moncrieff was close behind, calling, "Richard? Richard?"

Michael and Armand carried Sir Richard to the divan on the landing at the top of the stairs. Conscious but clearly not himself, he lay quietly while Nurse Clark prepared to perform an examination. Susan arrived from the Nursery to comfort her mother, while Patrice cleared the tea tray and remnants of tea and scones from the stairs. Doris arrived a moment later with several ice packs, ready to offer whatever help she could.

It was some time before Sir Richard was ready to sit up. Though weak, he was fully conscious and heartily embarrassed by the whole episode. Lady Moncrieff sat in a chair next to him as Nurse Clark explained the results of her brief examination.

"Sir Richard," she began. "We have good news. I see no evidence of broken bones, although you do have several bruises, and I would expect several strained muscles. There is evidence of a contusion at the back of your head, which will require an examination by Dr. MacMillan so that he can rule out a concussion."

Breathing heavily, Sir Richard said, "I understand. Thank you." Shakily, he attempted to stand, but Nurse Clark stopped him, saying, "No, Sir Richard, not yet, not yet," and helped him to sit once again.

"You reported some chest pain, sir, and a numbness in your left arm. Coupled with your elevated heart rate and blood pressure, I must insist that we transport you to the hospital at once." Turning to Michael, she said, "Mr. Moreland, would you please call Dr. MacMillan and report what I've just explained and advise him that you will arrive at the hospital with all due haste?"

"Of course," Michael said. "I'll make the call and have the sedan at the front door, ready and waiting."

"Thank you," she said. "Mrs. Moreland, will you please help Lady Moncrieff pack a light bag for Sir Richard, whatever will make him comfortable for a short stay in the hospital?"

"What do you mean by 'short stay'? I don't need to stay in the hospital," Sir Richard growled.

"I'm afraid Dr. MacMillan will have to advise you on those matters, Sir Richard. We simply want to be prepared in the event of such an eventuality," the nurse said.

Minutes later, Michael and Armand helped Sir Richard down the stairs, a few at a time, allowing him to catch his breath before going on. While Michael drove, Nurse Clark rode in the back of the car with Sir Richard, keeping watch on his vital signs for the short drive to the hospital. Susan left Case and Reed in Patrice's able hands while she drove her mother to the hospital in her cabriolet.

Upon their arrival at the Accident Room, Dr. MacMillan assembled his team, ready to do a complete examination. Knowing Sir Richard had never been a fan of doctors, Dr. MacMillan was not surprised to find that parts of Sir Richard's medical history had not been updated since he was discharged from the Royal Navy twenty-four years earlier. Nonetheless, within two hours, Dr. MacMillan, with Lady Moncrieff, Susan, and Michael at Sir Richard's bedside, was able to make his diagnosis.

"Sir Richard," he began, "you seem to be feeling much better since your arrival. Besides the bruising to your back and thigh where you encountered the stairs when you fell, are you experiencing any other pain right now?"

"No, not right now," Sir Richard began.

"No chest pain?" the doctor asked.

"No," he answered.

"And the numbness in your arm?" he asked.

"It's gone away," Sir Richard said.

"Wonderful," Dr. MacMillan said.

"Then I can go home, correct?" Sir Richard said as he began to raise his shoulders from the bed.

"No, no, not yet," the doctor said. "You see, we need to keep you under observation for a while longer before we can rule out a concussion. We can't have any bleeding in your brain."

"Oh," Sir Richard said quietly as he lay back into his pillow.

"Just as serious," Dr. MacMillan said, "is that we suspect the pain in your chest was caused by angina. Angina is a precursor to the possibility of a myocardial infarction. We'll need to keep you under observation for a few days."

"Angina? A myocardial what?" asked Sir Richard.

"A myocardial infarction, commonly known as a heart attack," Dr. MacMillan said.

"Oh," Sir Richard said quietly.

"The angina, the chest pain you experienced," the doctor continued, "is a signal that your heart is not getting all the blood it needs to continue beating while it is busy pumping blood through the rest of your body. Thankfully, we have medicine, nitroglycerine, which can treat the angina and lessen the pain it causes. However, you will need to consider some changes in your diet, your physical activity, and limits on anything stressful that might tend to worry you and interfere with your ability to rest."

Sir Richard only nodded.

"Now, I've already spoken with your wife and daughter about ways they can help adjust your diet and exercise regimen to help you avoid another episode like this. But you need to bear in mind that you have a serious, but treatable condition. I will need you to take our recommendations seriously. Once we discharge you from the hospital, we hope you never have to return because of a similar episode."

"I see," Sir Richard said. "So, it seems I need to hand over my sword and relinquish my command?"

"Sir Richard," Dr. MacMillan replied, "I could not have said it better."

A few minutes later, after Lady Moncrieff and Susan said their goodbyes and left Sir Richard to his rest, he asked for a moment with Michael and Armand.

"Please use the radio in my office to update London regarding the status of my health as of this morning," he said to Armand. "Brevity in our communications rules, so the simple facts of my anticipated short hospitalization should suffice. I'll leave it to you to encrypt the communication appropriately."

"Understood," Armand said.

"Regarding the anticipated arrival of an Abwehr operative by U-boat," he continued, "I have these thoughts."

Michael and Armand leaned in closer as Sir Richard lowered his voice.

"Ernest Duncan, the last German operative we encountered, arrived in the US years before we met him on PEI. During that time, he trained in linguistics in the US and learned to mimic local dialects after hearing them for mere days. I doubt the man the Abwehr has sent will arrive with Duncan's language skills. Rather, his accent, though not entirely German, may be immediately apparent. Furthermore, his journey across the Atlantic in painfully close quarters, sharing a bunk in eight-hour shifts with two young sailors, breathing diesel fumes, and enduring limited rations will probably compromise his training. Upon arrival on shore, he may very well seek to satisfy bodily comforts, seeking good food and comfortable lodging."

Michael and Armand nodded as Sir Richard finished.

"Please suggest these thoughts in a second communique to London and relay them to our appropriate local contacts, especially those in New Brunswick and Quebec," he said, as he relaxed into his pillow and closed his eyes for a moment.

"Done, sir," Armand said as he and Michael turned to leave. As they reached the door, Sir Richard made a last request.

"Michael, please notify Fr. Hunt of my whereabouts. If he can spare a few moments, I should enjoy speaking with him."

Michael nodded his ascent, adding, "I'll be stopping at St. Peter's on my way home."

Chapter 7

Many who still resisted using the label "World War II" for the current conflict in Europe, begun by Nazi Germany in 1939, changed their minds a few days after Japan's Emperor Hirohito sent the Imperial Japanese Navy and Air Service to attack the US naval base at Pearl Harbor on December 7, 1941. What seemed to be an attack solely on the United States soon proved to be an attack on the UK and many of its allies.

Within forty-eight hours, the newspapers reported accounts of further attacks in the Pacific that grew more alarming each day. All of Prince Edward Island learned that while the Japanese were bombing Pearl Harbor in Hawaii, the remainder of the Japanese fleet, along with scores of Japanese land-based bombers and ground troops, had begun a series of long-planned and well-executed surprise attacks on Chinese, British, US, French, and Dutch targets in the Pacific. In that single day, Monday, December 8, Japanese bombers attacked Thailand and Singapore while the Japanese Imperial Army attacked the Shanghai International Settlement, hijacking the USS *Wake* and sinking the HMS *Peterel*. Those unprecedented attacks were but the beginning. On the same day, the Japanese also attacked Malaya, the Philippines, Guam, Hong Kong, Wake Island, and the Dutch East Indies. Two days later, Imperial Japanese Navy bombers attacked and sank the Royal Navy battleship HMS *Prince of Wales* and the HMS *Repulse* while the ships were at sea and returning to defend Singapore.

Within a week, virtually every British and American interest in the Pacific had become victims of unprovoked attacks by Imperial Japanese forces. Only their distance from Japan kept Australia and New Zealand unharmed by the Japanese, but enemy forces were moving closer to those targets each day. Before the month was over, the Imperial Japanese Navy proved that distance was no obstacle for their ships. Less than two weeks after the attack on Pearl Harbor, the IJN found its way to the west coast of the

United States. There, on December 20, Japanese submarine I-17 torpedoed the American tanker *Emidio* off Cape Mendocino, California.

Statistically, the naval prowess of the Axis powers was no match for that of the Allies. The simple facts were these: In 1939, the Royal Navy boasted the largest fleet in the world, with over 1,400 vessels, including battleships, battlecruisers, aircraft carriers, cruisers, destroyers, and 60 submarines. By comparison, the German Kriegsmarine entered the war with only 95 ships fit for battle, including 57 U-boats, and lacking a single aircraft carrier. Although Germany continued to build and launch more U-boats at a remarkably rapid pace, Royal Navy ships, many of them veterans of WWI, never failed to outnumber the Kriegsmarine.

In 1941, when the Japanese attack on Pearl Harbor brought the United States into the war, the US Navy had 345 ships in service, among them battleships, cruisers, destroyers, 66 submarines, and seven aircraft carriers. By comparison, their principal enemy at sea, the Imperial Japanese Navy, was the third most powerful navy in the world, equipped with only 222 vessels, among them 63 submarines and 11 aircraft carriers.

While Emperor Hirohito ordered his emissaries in Washington in the early days of December 1941 to continue to negotiate peace terms with President Roosevelt, the Imperial Japanese Navy, Air Service, and Army had already mobilized their forces to execute attacks on multiple Allied targets by land, sea, and air. The execution of their long-laid plans during the first few days of the war in the Pacific brought them remarkable early success, threatening the entire Pacific theatre. Though quickly entrenched, well-equipped, and ready to defend the territories they had gained in the initial days of their conquest, Hirohito's appetite was not yet satisfied. The emperor immediately turned his eyes toward targets farther from home in the Indian Ocean, where British interests had reigned unthreatened for many decades.

At Highfield, the Moncrieff family's Royal Navy history had long kept them familiar with the Atlantic, the North Sea, and Mediterranean waters. Now, however, the Moncrieffs were following Nigel and Boyd as their ships patrolled the less familiar waters of the Indian Ocean, waters heretofore ruled comfortably by Britain's Royal Navy. Sadly, those waters had become the hunting grounds of the Japanese. Although familiar with the threats that Nazi U-boats offered, the Moncrieff sons and their comrades at sea now faced Japanese threats even more deadly than those of the Kriegsmarine. In addition to the perils the Imperial Navy provided at sea, the

Imperial Air Service offered a second and often more dangerous threat. The sinking of the HMS *Prince of Wales* and the HMS *Repulse* off the coast of Singapore five months earlier marked the first time Royal Navy ships had been sunk from the air. Furthermore, British and American reconnaissance had discovered that a primary Japanese goal when occupying any coastal territory on the mainland or on an island was the immediate construction of airstrips, most of which were large enough to accommodate their heavy bombers, ready to target British and US ships at sea. No ship could outrun a Japanese land-based bomber, nor the many squadrons of dive bombers and fighters the Japanese could send from their eleven aircraft carriers.

Today, Sqd Ldr Nigel Moncrieff was leading his squadron of Fleet Air Arm aircraft aboard the HMS *Formidable* in the Indian Ocean. In the past, Lady Moncrieff would have been happy to know that the *Formidable* was no longer a target of German U-boats. Sadly, however, she became keenly aware that in the waters off Madagascar and Ceylon, the enemy arrived not only in Japanese submarines, but also aboard enemy aircraft carriers and battleships.

Meanwhile, Lt. Boyd Moncrieff was in Colombo, Ceylon, aboard the battleship HMS *Revenge*. As might be expected, Sir Richard had a special place in his heart for the *Revenge*, the same ship on which he had served in World War I. The Moncrieff family knew her as his "grand lady." Now, however, almost twenty-five years later, the *Revenge* was more of a grand *old* lady. Compared to the ships in the Japanese fleet, she was slower, less maneuverable, and inadequately armed to meet the Japanese at sea. With her limitations, Sir Richard hoped the *Revenge* would soon be relegated to escort duties, perhaps patrolling off the east African coast.

Now, on a spring morning in 1942, Lady Moncrieff was writing to her sons. She desperately wanted to keep them informed concerning Sir Richard's health, not to worry them, but to encourage their prayers.

A year earlier, it would have taken weeks for Nigel and Boyd to learn of their father's heart episode and hospital stay. However, thanks to the new British Airgraph Service launched by the British Post Service and Kodak Limited in 1941, Lady Moncrieff was confident that the letters she posted to her sons could arrive aboard ship in less than a week. Of course, she couldn't write on her favorite stationery, because Airgraph letters were written on special forms that were photographed and transferred to microfilm. When they arrived at their wartime destination, they were enlarged, printed on paper, and delivered. Because Airgraph microfilm was so much lighter than canvas mailbags filled with letters, RAF aircraft were able to carry additional wartime essentials.

As she finished her writing, Lady Moncrieff sighed and sat back in Sir Richard's chair at his desk in the study. "There can be no doubt that this is a world war," she said, tiredly. "I'm not posting letters to my sons in the North Sea or three thousand miles across the Atlantic any longer. No, these two letters will be traveling more than eight thousand miles to the Indian Ocean and perhaps beyond. I pray they will find our boys safe at sea."

Chapter 8

Brenda Kimble chose to hide in plain sight. Following her escape from her imprisonment in the RCN brig in Halifax, she found lodging in a rooming house on the outskirts of the city. With her blonde locks cut short and hidden under a sailor's cap, she melted into the busy street traffic of the town, completely unsuspected of being the escaped war criminal she had become.

She smiled as she walked to the train station, her thoughts turning back to the night she left the jail wearing her jailor's uniform, his keys in her hand. "These sad, lonely sailors," she said to herself, "they're so easy." During her first several months behind bars, she learned that all she had to do to compromise a guard was to tie her chambray blouse in a tight knot behind her back to reveal just a hint of midriff. Then, while posing with her back to the wall of her cell, she would make a plaintive call to capture her guard's attention. She knew what to do to guarantee his prompt arrival with the cup of water or whatever else she needed. With one extra button unbuttoned, she would stroll forward to the locked cell door, never allowing her eyes to leave his. Then, suddenly discovering an untied shoe, she would bend to tie it. Looking up to the sailor's eyes, now no longer focused on her face, she would tilt her head and offer a look that said, "Tsk, tsk, shame on you, you naughty boy," before bending even lower to reward her captive's hungry eyes again. "Easy prey, these sailors," she thought, "easy prey."

While the RCN command changed jailers regularly, rotating personnel every six weeks, Brenda waited patiently for just the right man. The casual familiarity she initiated with each guard never went unrewarded. Still, Brenda knew she needed to wait for one who lacked confidence, had little or no experience with women, and who lived with a well-bruised ego.

It took several months, but he finally appeared. His name was William Townsend, but everyone called him "Little Billy". Everything about him

34

was exactly what she had been waiting for. He was a man full of apologies, eager to earn even a hint of acceptance. Brenda knew she needed only to listen to him, feign a personal interest in him, let him know she understood everything about him, a kindred spirit. Soon, he would convince himself that she, too, was an injured soul, just like him. In time, he would persuade himself that she understood him as no one else ever had. Only then would she allow him to touch her, first with his eyes, then with her fingertips when he delivered her meals. Brenda was careful to offer those touches sparingly, a treat she taught him to covet, then crave, but not take for granted. She didn't want him to grow bold before the time was ripe.

It wasn't long before Billy began to reward her patience. He started bringing her gifts, sometimes a pack of chewing gum, a chocolate bar, or a ripe piece of fruit. Their talks grew longer and more personal. She listened intently to all his woes. Then, on the final night of his six-week assignment in the brig, he brought her a special gift, one she had suggested, and he had promised - a pint bottle of Gordon's gin.

Together, they drank from their Navy issue tin cups, but for the first time, they sat on the floor, back-to-back with their shoulders touching between the bars of Brenda's cell. As the gin stole Billy's senses, they giggled like school children, and Brenda let him hold her hand for the first time. To his surprise, she began to squeeze his fingers, one by one, gently stroking his wrist, caressing his arm while the gin took its toll on him. Of course, Billy never noticed that Brenda regularly tipped the contents of her cup into the open drain on the cell floor. When the bottle was empty, though, she surprised him.

"Billy," she said as she released his hand and stood to face him, "stand up for me, Billy." Unsteadily, Billy stood and turned toward her, his face inches from the bars outside and directly opposite hers. There was something different about the way she looked at him. She wasn't looking *through* him as so many other women did, as if he weren't there. No, Brenda's half-open blue eyes were warm and inviting, and they were begging him to look into hers. He found himself helpless and elated at the same time, a prisoner of her gaze.

After what seemed like a long moment, she moved her face closer to his, her eyes inviting him to do the same. Smiling at him sleepily, she slowly and deliberately reached between the bars to take his face in her warm hands, drawing him toward her, closing her eyes and kissing him, long and warm and deep. When she eventually released him, he was completely overcome. Helpless and unable to do anything else, he reached through the bars for her, hungry for more. To his disappointment, though, she stepped back unsteadily, as if the gin was in charge. She looked down, shaking her head.

"No, Billy," she said. "No. No more kisses through these bars. No, I need more than that. I deserve more, much more, don't I, Billy?" she asked, taking a step back and reaching up to release the top button of her blouse. As he nodded helplessly, she said, "I need you to come in here, Billy. Come in here where we can share all the kisses we want."

It was as if he no longer had a will of his own. Stumbling backward, he hurried to get the ring of keys from the rack down the concrete corridor while Brenda turned to sit, posing on her bunk, unbuttoning one more button while she waited for him. After one longing look at her through the bars, Billy began fumbling with the ring, searching for the one key that would open the cell door. As he did, Brenda stepped forward from the darkness. When his gin-clouded vision finally allowed him to extract the key from the open door, it was too late. In a single motion, Brenda lunged toward him, grasped him around the neck with both arms, and turned her back to the bars. Before Billy knew what was happening, she propelled his head like a battering ram into the concrete wall at the back of the cell, where he wilted to the floor, half-on and half-off her cot.

While Billy lay unconscious, Brenda stripped him of his uniform, wallet, and keys, leaving him on the floor with the knot of her chambray blouse jammed in his mouth. Deftly, she tied the blouse's sleeves tight around the back of his battered and bleeding head. After handcuffing his hands to the lowest bar of the cell, she donned his uniform, pulled his hat down to hide her face, and made her escape.

Although Brenda knew that Ernest had escaped his cell months earlier, she wondered if his flight from Halifax had left him time to recover the cache of goods they had hidden in the dark basement of the second-hand furniture store where she had worked for a short time. Amongst the furniture and boxes, they had hidden a small suitcase that held an Abwehr S-90/40 radio set, a change of clothes, identification cards, and a sum of money - everything they would need in the event they had to make a quick escape. To Brenda's delight, when she broke into the store late that night, she found the suitcase exactly where they had hidden it. Its contents were intact.

All her efforts to contact Ernest by radio over the next few days proved fruitless. "No doubt he fled the area and is beyond the range of a radio signal from Halifax," she concluded. Less than 48 hours after her escape, however, she was able to get a message to three of their former contacts. They had learned of her escape through other sources and had been waiting to hear from her. Within hours, they informed her of the expected arrival of an Abwehr agent aboard a German U-boat scheduled to arrive off the coast of New Brunswick in the Bay of Fundy. Her assignment was to contact the agent once he made his way to Halifax. Once secure there, his goal was to continue the work that Ernest and Brenda had begun in the port, tracking and reporting shipping in and out of Halifax. The arrival of a second agent was planned in Quebec later in the year.

Everything appeared to be going according to plan until a large part of the city, including Brenda's rooming house, lost power during an electrical storm. When electricity was eventually restored, a power surge wrought havoc with the radio transmitter. Brenda could receive messages, but she could no longer transmit them. Searching for a local repairman for a German radio was not an option. She needed access to a radio as soon as possible. Only one solution came to her mind. It would require two days of travel, but she had no better option.

"I know where there is a radio whose signal will reach all of my contacts," she said aloud. "It's waiting for me atop an abandoned fire tower on Prince Edward Island. Dark of night will suffice for my cover. Although the enemy knows I was bitten there once, I doubt they will expect my return."

Chapter 9

All Lt. Boyd Moncrieff knew about her was that her name was Kathleen. A mere slip of a girl with blonde hair and the kind of blue eyes that could capture a young man's attention with a single glance, she had enlisted in the Women's Royal Naval Service soon after the war began. Commonly known as "Wrens", thousands of young women had enlisted when the war started, freeing British men to abandon office jobs at home to serve their King aboard ship. Many young women who enlisted also trained at the Royal Naval College. Though they didn't serve at sea, some trained to perform vital clerical and secretarial functions, while others qualified as radio operators and meteorologists. Still others, like Kathleen, filled positions intercepting and decoding both German and Japanese communications.

While strict regulations kept a cordial distance between Wrens training at the Royal Naval College and the Royal Navy male population, those rules could not deter a young Royal Navy officer from being captured by an innocent glance from a blonde beauty. Two weeks of training together at Gosport had given both a few minutes now and again to learn more about each other.

Her family, the Balfours of Windermere, had always lived in the Lake District, a part of the country Boyd had visited with his family as a boy. Boyd learned that he and Kathleen had been born only three years apart, he being the elder. An only child who had enjoyed four years at Girton College in Cambridge, she chose at the start of the war to follow her mother's example by enlisting in the WRNS as her mother had in World War I.

Kathleen had no particular aspirations for meeting a charming Royal Navy officer when she enlisted. She'd met enough young men during all the social events required of a young woman of means in her twenty-two years. When no young man appeared who could capture her interest during that time, her parents had begun to worry that they had a spinster on their hands. Neither dared push too hard, remembering that pushing Kathleen had never worked with her as a child. Both also knew that when something captured Kathleen's interest, her pursuit to acquire it often proved relentless. When the right young man found her, he might find himself chasing her until she caught him.

Kathleen didn't know what it was about that first glance that stopped her mid-breath. She didn't understand why she couldn't stop herself from offering a second glance. She knew only one thing: if this was what being smitten felt like, she hoped it wouldn't end.

He was charming, this young officer, mainly because he wasn't trying to impress her as too many other young men had tried in the past. He was genuine, observant, and caring, able to give her his full attention while requiring nothing particular in return. Everything about him spoke of quality, but he found no need to boast. "Boyd," she said to herself, for repeating his name entertained her. "Boyd sounds like a man who will never age. Perhaps he'll always enjoy a life that clings to his youth." Try as she might, she couldn't picture an old man with the name Boyd. She smiled and shook her head when she finally had to admit to herself that she was quite taken with this young officer.

Boyd and Kathleen found ways to "discover" each other by chance on sidewalks in Gosport whenever they weren't in class or otherwise supervised. Those walks became the high points of their days, closely guarded moments that they treasured. When their two weeks of training together ended, both found themselves quietly distraught. The war ended budding relationships daily and, too often, permanently. With Boyd aboard the *Revenge* in the Indian Ocean and Kathleen soon shipping out to Egypt in the Mediterranean, Boyd knew it was possible he wouldn't see Kathleen again for as long as the war lasted. In the meantime, their letters would have to keep their hopes alive.

In mid-March of 1942, the *Revenge*, recently refit with new radar in Durban, South Africa, had been nominated for service with the 3rd Battle Squadron of the Eastern Fleet. Late in March, while the fleet was patrolling south of the island of Ceylon, Royal Naval intelligence intercepted an enemy radio signal indicating imminent Japanese plans to attack Ceylon to destroy the British fleet. The ports of Colombo and Trincomalee Harbor were their prime targets.

As part of a defensive maneuver, Admiral James Somerville planned to split the fleet, reserving the aging WWI vintage HMS *Revenge* along with three other Revenge-class battleships and the aircraft carrier, *Hermes*, for future duty securing shipping routes and escort convoys in the Indian Ocean. The newer and better-equipped members of the fleet, including the HMS *Formidable* on which Boyd's brother, Squadron Ldr Nigel Moncrieff, was serving, continued their search for the enemy to the south of Ceylon. Admiral Somerville hoped to surprise the Japanese fleet in the cover of darkness north of the Addu Atoll. However, the Japanese were able to avoid the British fleet. They had arrived in the waters of Ceylon aboard four aircraft carriers and three battleships, attacking Colombo in the early morning of April 5, Easter Sunday.

The Japanese goal was to destroy the Royal Navy Eastern Fleet at Colombo in a surprise attack akin to the Pearl Harbor attack against the US three months earlier. However, the 91 bombers and 36 fighters that flew from the Japanese carriers found the port void of the prime targets they sought. They were met by a meagre squadron of RAF and FAA fighters, which were supported by land-based anti-aircraft fire. Sadly, the losses at the Port of Colombo were considerable. Three remaining ships were sunk, and forty-seven aircraft were destroyed. The Japanese lost only seven aircraft during the attack, and later that afternoon, they were able to sink two cruisers, the *Cornwall* and the *Dorsetshire*, at sea, claiming more than 400 lives.

Four days later, on April 9, the Japanese attacked the port at Trincomalee. Early detection of the approaching Japanese fleet the previous day permitted the British forces to clear the harbor. Only 23 RAF fighters met the Japanese strike group of 132 aircraft. The port was severely bombed, but the worst British losses of the day were yet to come. The aircraft carrier HMS *Hermes* and the destroyer HMS *Vampire* were 65 miles south and returning to Trincomalee when they were attacked and sunk. More than 300 men perished.

As Chief Communications Officer aboard the HMS *Revenge*, Lt. Boyd Moncrieff was among the first to hear the reports of the attacks on Colombo and Trincomalee and the sinkings of four British ships at sea. Although the *Revenge* was sailing away from the immediate confrontation posed by the Japanese fleet, he and his shipmates shared the same grief and frustration they always knew when fellow sailors perished in battle. Still aware that Japanese submarines sought them day and night, they remained ever vigilant.

As the *Revenge* sailed toward Kilindini Harbor in Mombasa, British East Africa, Boyd spent every waking hour at his radio console. Following the attacks on Ceylon, he knew that the strategic importance of Kilindini to the British Eastern Fleet had risen overnight. Frustrated with their inability to cripple the British fleet in Ceylon, the Japanese could already be eying Mombasa as their next target.

Among the most recent communications that reached Boyd's post concerned the code-breaking work of the British Far East Combined Bureau in Colombo. Following the Japanese attack, the bureau was moving its operations from Colombo to Mombasa. Ordinarily, that kind of news would have held little interest for Boyd. However, the report contained another bit of news that proved *very* interesting. A number of Wrens, more than forty in all, had just been evacuated from Egypt to continue the work formerly done in Colombo. The Wrens were due to arrive in Mombasa within days, concurrent with the arrival of the *Revenge* at Kilindini.

Boyd hadn't forgotten that Kathleen had begun training in code-breaking when they were together in Gosport. When she shipped out for the Mediterranean, he suspected her destination was Alexandria, a suspicion confirmed in her last letter when she wrote of meeting two new friends – *Alex and Maria*, whom she called "*Ria*" for short. There was a possibility that Kathleen would be among those landing in Mombasa soon.

"I may have to spend some time birdwatching once we're tied up at the harbor in Kilindini," he said with a smile. "If I'm lucky, I'll find someone to direct me to the Wrens' Nest – wherever it happens to be."

Chapter 10

The progress of the construction at Susan and Michael's new home was nothing short of remarkable. The weather had cooperated all spring, allowing the framing to be completed weeks ahead of schedule. While the roofing crew was still finishing the slate roof, the masons completed the front brick facade and continued around the west gable to the rear of the house. Of course, a second masonry crew was busy on the fireplaces where the interior brick chimneys and fireboxes were faced with Prince Edward Island's brown sandstone. Already, the plumbing and heating crews were busy in the basement, first-floor bathrooms, and the kitchen. Everything pointed to a move-in date much earlier than the original December time-line quoted.

Almost every morning, Michael was on site, keeping up with the progress. However, Susan, feeling more expectant every day, found a way to charm him away on a warm day in May.

Michael always had a light breakfast before dawn and returned to the kitchen after finishing the morning livestock and barn chores. When Susan and the boys joined him at the kitchen table, he was just finishing his second breakfast. As always, he had Susan's morning tea waiting.

"Doris just told me that Luc is away with the RCA recruiting team for the day," Susan said.

"I'm glad he took the opportunity to get away from the work on those two houses to go help the recruiting efforts," Michael said. "Now that only a few details remain at Spring Hill, he has been working day and night on some of the finish work he promised to complete for Joseph and Ingrid. He's done an incredibly remarkable job."

"So, Lois tells me," Susan smiled. "With their wedding only four months away now, she's already looking forward to moving in. Joseph and

Ingrid have yet to set a date, but when Joseph returns home from Quebec after his last year at the hospital next spring, there will be another wedding."

"I can't believe all that's happened here since I first arrived in 1937," Michael said. "The Bouchers were Highfield's closest neighbors then, but we were still strangers. I needed help to get things ready for you and your mum to arrive, and they hired on with me the same day. They've been here ever since and are now more family than friends."

"Speaking of Luc's opportunity to get away from working on his house," Susan said as Michael looked up from the ham and eggs on his plate, "I've arranged a morning getaway for *you*."

Michael's fork stopped in mid-air on the way to his waiting mouth.

"And what would that be?" he asked.

"Well, you know how much the boys love to look up and point at the yellow training aircraft that fly overhead every day?" she asked. As Michael nodded, she continued, "With Father's help, I was able to talk with Lt. Mitchell, a friend of Grayson's at the airfield."

"Mitchell?" Michael asked, with a question in his voice. "Yes, I remember meeting an officer named Mitchell, Myron Mitchell, I believe."

"Correct," Susan smiled, "and he has welcomed us to the airfield where we can park the car and let the boys watch the aircraft. The RCAF regularly welcomes visitors to a parking area and an observation station away from the secure parts of the base. I've arranged a meeting with Lt. Mitchell this morning. Case and Reed are excited and ready to go."

Michael had to shake his head and smile as he cleaned up the last of the egg yolk on his plate with his last bite of toast. He looked at the boys in their two highchairs, both utterly unaware of what Susan had just said.

"So, boys," he began, "Mom says you two are all excited about going to the airfield."

By the expression on their faces, it was clear they recognized their father's voice, but they had no idea what he was saying. Michael remained unfazed.

"So," he said, "we'd better get packed up and ready to go, because she promised Lt Mitchell that we'd be there at…" he said, looking up at Susan.

"Nine-thirty," she nodded.

"Did you hear that, boys? Nine-thirty. That gives us about half an hour before we need to be in the car and on our way. Why don't I take care of the dishes? Mom's moving a little slower these days now that she's carrying our newest family member. I'll be up to help her pack your bags as soon as I'm finished here. Does that sound good to you?" he asked as he leaned into the faces of the two toddlers.

Susan had to laugh at her husband, and Michael had to kiss his wife once again that morning. Half an hour later, the family rode in Susan's cabriolet to a civilian airfield that had since become RCAF Station Charlottetown.

As he had promised, Lt Mitchell greeted them at the gate and directed them to a car park where Susan, Michael, and their boys prepared for their tour of the newly renovated and enlarged facilities. A good friend and comrade of Sqn Ldr Grayson Royce, Lt Mitchell was pleased to be able to guide Grayson's friends.

"Sqn Ldr Royce was a superb teacher," Lt Mitchell said. "I try to pass on all I learned from him to those under my tutelage. I hope I honor his legacy."

"Grayson has been a family friend for decades," Susan said. "He and his wife, Michelle, have become as brother and sister to Michael and me. We look forward to the day when their son, Logan, meets our sons here when the war has ended."

"Mr. and Mrs. Moreland," Mitchell continued, "I hope that I am not speaking out of turn. We are aware of your service to King and country, and also that of your father, Mrs. Moreland. All that we have is at your disposal, today and always. Now, how may I assist you?"

Susan and Michael were happy to have an opportunity to watch the take-off and landing drills of the pilots in several training aircraft for the next half hour. Then something, or someone, caught Susan's eye.

"Lt Mitchell," she said, "the pilot who just landed and left the aircraft appears to my eyes to be a woman. Could that be true, or are my eyes playing tricks on me?"

"No tricks, ma'am," Mitchell said. "Your powers of observation have not been in error. That pilot is a woman, one born in Canada but who now makes her home in Maryland, in the United States."

"It was not difficult to observe that her landing was much smoother than that of her peers," Michael said. "Why is that?"

"Her father was Captain E.J. Lussier, a decorated World War I fighter pilot with the Royal Air Force. Though born in the United States, he moved to Canada and earned the British Distinguished Flying Cross for his service. He taught Betty Ann, or 'Bay' as she prefers to be called, to fly years ago."

"Why 'Bay,' Lieutenant?" Michael asked.

"She just shortened her name to her first two initials, making communications faster on the cockpit radio," he answered.

"So, she'll be flying combat missions as her father did?" Susan asked.

"No ma'am, no, she won't," Lt Mitchell explained. "Bay will be traveling to England this fall for indoctrination in the British Air Transport Authority. Her service will be limited to transporting aircraft in and out of war zones. With Bay in those cockpits, more RAF fighter pilots will be free for combat duty."

"That sounds fascinating, Lt Mitchell," she said. "I didn't know such an opportunity existed for women."

"It's new to us as well, ma'am," he answered. "If you'd like, I could arrange for you to speak with her. Her story is quite fascinating."

Susan took one look at Michael, whose nod said, "Whatever pleases you, Susan."

With that, Susan followed Lt Mitchell to the hangar, where several crewmen were still moving some of the aircraft under cover for maintenance. When she returned more than half an hour later, she had quite a story to tell.

"Michael, you probably guessed that Bay is French from her family name," Susan said. "Well, if you did, you are correct, but her family did not immigrate here recently. Her earliest grandfather arrived from Paris in the late 1600s, and her Parisian grandmother three years later. Today, her father is a Squadron Leader in the RCAF. Because Bay has dual US and Canadian citizenship, she can't wait to fly for the RAF. She hopes to fly fighters one day."

"Fascinating," was all Michael could say before Susan continued.

"I told her about Grayson and Michelle and where he is stationed in Kirton in Lindsey. From her training, she knew all about that airfield and virtually every other RAF airfield I could recall in Britain. It's been part of her training for some time. She promised to call on Grayson if ever their paths should cross and to send our regards to both Grayson and Michelle."

Just then, Case registered a feeding schedule violation with a loud cry. Reed joined him a moment later. The boys' bottles were a quarter hour overdue. While Michael dove for the bag of bottles, Susan began the diaper checks.

"I'm happy for Bay and her quest for adventure," Michael said with his hands full of baby powder and fresh diapers. "As for me, my job as a husband and father is all the adventure I need, Darling."

Susan was happy to agree.

Chapter 11

Sir Richard, newly released by Dr. MacMillan to resume his work in his study, leaned back in his chair and took stock of life at Highfield on a warm Saturday morning in late June of 1942. Even though he was sitting at his desk in the center of the house, he could feel all the activity outdoors on the estate. Michael had been busy planting several weeks ago, when the sounds of the tractors plowing, harrowing, and tilling in the fields began early each morning. Now every hour of every day was taken up with watering, weeding, and more tilling.

Susan, who brought her father's morning tea to his study, was already growing rounder each day as Sir Richard's next grandchild bloomed within her. A half mile away on Suffolk Road, Luc Boucher was busy completing the finishing touches on the home for Lois, his bride-to-be, while his brother, Joseph, home on a break from medical school in Quebec, joined to help. At dinner the previous evening, Lady Moncrieff had remarked on the changes she had seen in Joseph over the years as he became a man. This completely unassuming young orphan had become a man of means overnight, and her greatest joy was that his good fortune hadn't altered his tender spirit in the least. The kind-hearted, gentle soul who arrived at Highfield years ago was the same generous and polite young man she knew today.

Ingrid Boucher from PEI and Lois Wilshire from London, though born in different worlds, had grown as close as sisters, and were soon to become sisters-in-law. Despite his wartime service that had almost taken Luc's life, and the injuries at Highfield that had threatened Joseph's life two years ago, these young men would soon have households of their own. Although they would raise their own families someday, they would always be part of the Highfield family.

Sir Richard marveled that amid all the activity at Highfield, the construction of Susan and Michael's new home across Suffolk Road was moving so quickly. According to Michael, the construction was at least a month ahead of schedule. Before too much longer, Michael and Susan, Case and Reed, and their unborn brother or sister wouldn't wake up under Highfield's roof any longer. Sir Richard knew he would miss them, even though he was quite sure he would probably see all of them daily. Such was the joy that Highfield had become. It wasn't the holiday home he had once envisioned. No, now it was a refuge, a place to which anyone who had come would always return. That knowledge continued to bring him warm, enduring comfort.

Sir Richard descended the front staircase to look out the front door toward the driveway. A glance to the east offered views of the barn and paddock, and to the west, he could enjoy sights of the gardens and pastures. His back was to the north, however, where lay the North Path and the tree stands beyond. For all the beauty and comfort the view out his front door brought him, however, he remained ignorant of a danger to the north. While looking forward, he had forgotten the necessity of posting a rear guard. A threat he did not anticipate had become well entrenched in the shade of the trees to the north.

Brenda Kimble had found her way from the back streets of Halifax to PEI three weeks after her escape. She thought back to the three days she had spent in Charlottetown on her last visit. She had arrived from Halifax by train on Steve Verrier's arm, dressed to attend his sister Michelle's wedding. Brenda looked much different now. With her long blonde locks closely cropped and her men's clothing, she was sure no one would recognize her. She bore a hard, almost sinister look that kept people on the street at arm's length. At night, she had business away from Charlottetown, business that she accomplished alone.

It was easy for a girl who had been raised on a farm to find work on PEI in the summer when every farmer needed help, and her job came with a roof as well. A bicycle provided her transportation, and she quickly became familiar with the roads and farms that bordered Highfield on its northern border. The North Path at Highfield didn't end at Highfield's property line. It continued north across a neighboring farm's property until it reached Cove Head Road. Once she found the path there, Brenda had only to follow it over the remains of a stone wall and a few broken fence posts to reach the abandoned path to Highfield. Though overgrown for years, the path was easy to follow. Her battery flashlight provided all Brenda needed to find her way on the darkest night. On a moonlit night, the flashlight was almost unnecessary.

As the summer wore on, Brenda used some early daylight and late afternoon hours to complete her surveillance and record Highfield's habits. Soon she found she could rely on the regularity that every household establishes – the schedules of the day workers, the shopping days for the household staff, and other habitual movements. Without a partner, it took her some time before she was confident that she could predict the comings and goings at Highfield and regularly reach her destination, the fire tower, undetected.

She had been at the tower only once before; it was on the day she was with Steve Verrier at Michelle's wedding reception. As that afternoon wore on, Steve pleaded for a few minutes alone with her, and she let him think it was his idea. As they walked together up the North Path, she didn't have to pump him for information. Like many small-town boys she'd met, he wanted to impress her with everything he knew. They spent half an hour on the fire tower steps that afternoon while he thought he was charming her and stealing kisses. It was some months later that he learned she had planned their rendezvous, duping him while he told her everything she and Ernest Duncan needed to know. Only a flyover of a small plane brought them out of the woods while she hurriedly fixed her lipstick and checked Steve's lips for any she might have shared with him.

Today, almost two years later, she was alone at the base of the tower on a Sunday morning when the regular dayworkers were at their homes and Highfield's denizens were at church in Charlottetown. A morning of discovery awaited her.

Steve had bragged about the radio transmitter and receiver in the cab at the top of the tower, but she could find no power source leading back to the house or to any of Highfield's outbuildings. She had to conclude that the tower was powered by a generator, something most farm girls in Canada had seen before. A thorough look through her field glasses at the underside of the cab at the top of the tower revealed an exhaust pipe, an essential component of a gasoline-powered generator. If she gained access to the radio, she knew she would have to start the generator to power it. That meant she could use the radio only at times when there was no danger that the generator would be heard. With Highfield nearly a half mile away, though, most late nights when all were asleep would probably be safe. Though far from an ideal situation, she had no other options.

When she finally dared to climb the stairs to the cab, she discovered that the trap door was padlocked. After making careful notes listing the manufacturer of the lock and taking a pencil rubbing of its surfaces to indicate the shape of the keyhole, she climbed down and made her exit. Her first foray up the tower was complete.

Three days later, after she had purchased an identical padlock and practiced picking it again and again as Ernest had taught her, she returned with the few small tools she needed to gain entry. Her efforts did not disappoint her, and within a few minutes, the lock was open, and she was inside the cab.

Her goal for the night was to inspect the generator, the transmitter, and the receiver. She wanted to ensure that she could spend as little time as possible transmitting, so the signal could not be traced. She was happy to find the generator was a military field model with a very quiet motor, unlike other generators she had encountered on the farm. She was confident that the next time she climbed the tower, she would be able to start the generator and transmit a signal to her contacts in Quebec.

Brenda locked the trap door and replaced the padlock in the same orientation she had found it. Climbing down the steps as quietly as possible, she reached the ground. Only then was she able to smile as she turned north, entered the underbrush, and disappeared into the night.

Although Brenda left with confidence, there was something she had failed to notice at the base of the tower stairs. When she searched beneath the tower to find an electric cable large enough to deliver power from Highfield, she found only a small, seemingly insignificant cable attached to the bottom step of the steel stairs. It appeared to have two wires; one was attached to the step and the other to the steel base beneath the step. Assuming it must be the usual ground wire that radio equipment always requires, she never gave it a second thought.

The cable she chose to ignore, however, was not a simple ground wire. The cable led underground from the bottom step of the stairs all the way back to Highfield. Michael had installed the bottom step using a simple spring hinge so that any weight on the step greater than fifty pounds brought it into contact with the steel base beneath, closing a circuit. The step was actually a simple low-voltage switch that momentarily sounded a loud, battery-powered buzzer in two locations: one on Michael's bedroom nightstand and a second at Sir Richard's desk in Highfield's study.

Unbeknownst to Brenda Kimble, her trip up and down the tower stairs had sounded the buzzers at Highfield on six occasions that day. With most of the household attending church at St. Peter's, however, she had escaped detection.

Chapter 12

On a sunny June morning at Fletcher Hall in New Mills, Michelle was sitting in bed with Logan in her arms when Grayson finally opened his eyes. She was still giggling at the latest gift Grayson had brought home for their son. Peeking out from beneath Grayson's pillow lay a soft, light-brown mohair bunny rabbit with a button in its ear. Next to Grayson's tousled hair and unshaven face, the two made a very unlikely couple.

"What?" Grayson asked sleepily. "What's so funny?"

"I'm looking at a big bear of a man cuddling with his bunny-wunny," Michelle laughed. "I thought I'd begun to really know you, but I'm seeing a side of my husband I never expected."

"Enjoy your laughter, Darling," Grayson answered, "but remember that yours is nothing to what I've had to endure from the men in my squadron over that toy. The teddy bear I brought home on my last leave had them roaring for weeks before, but this little bunny raised their delight to a new high."

"And why wouldn't it?" Michelle asked. "Those airmen could never have imagined their squadron leader sleeping with a cache of sweet, little stuffed animals like this. You might have done better if you told them the reason before they discovered your fetish."

"I'm sure you are correct," he admitted. "When I explained that I was simply trying to add my scent to them – my wife's idea - before I brought them home to Logan, some of the married men seemed to understand. The smirks on the bachelors' faces were all good-natured, too, so I can't complain."

"I hope you appreciate how much help these soft, furry animals have been for me. When you arrive now, Logan is much less clingy. He's no longer shocked by the big, burly man with the deep voice. The scent you bring

51

through the door is familiar and welcome, and I'm sure it makes him feel more secure."

"I'm all for that, "Grayson said as he sat up and rubbed the sleep out of his eyes. "How about handing that chap over to his father now?" he asked as he reached out for Logan. "You could probably use some time with your tea, I'd wager."

"Yes, I could," Michelle agreed, "but my jealous side also wants to hear all about the latest influx of pilots at the base, especially those of the female persuasion."

"Oh, them," he said, waving her off with his free hand as Logan snuggled into his shoulder. "They're in, out, and gone within hours, leaving as fast as they arrive. As soon as they ferry in one plane, they're taking off in another. A busy bunch, they are, but they're still working to gain the confidence of some of the men."

"Why is that?" Michelle asked.

"Just because the Air Transport Auxiliary is so new, I suppose. Men at war crave the old and familiar. Anything new introduces a challenge they don't welcome. Having women pilots on the airfield is too much of a distraction for some," he said.

"And how about you?" Michelle asked over her shoulder as she stirred her tea.

"As long as they aren't flying fighters into battle, I'll be happy. My men don't need any distractions," he said. "So far, none of the ATA pilots, male or female, are flying anything but transport aircraft and an occasional bomber. I'll be happy if it stays that way. Fighter pilots don't need to be concerned with female pilots or pigeons when they're readying for combat."

"Pigeons?" Michelle said. "Did you say 'pigeons'?" she asked.

"Yes," Grayson answered.

"There are pigeons at the airfield?" she asked.

"Yes," he answered. "On the bombers. Each bomber carries a cage with two pigeons."

"But, why?" Michelle asked.

"All RAF bombers have carried two homing pigeons on every mission since sometime in 1939. Reconnaissance aircraft do, too. If any of the aircraft have to ditch, either over land or water, the pigeons are loosed with the plane's coordinates strapped to one of their legs. When the pigeons fly home, search and rescue missions take over," he answered.

"I had no idea," Michelle said, "but doesn't it take a long time for a pigeon to fly back to base?"

"Not as much as you might think," Grayson laughed. "They tell me a homing pigeon can fly at almost fifty miles per hour and can make flights of up to three hundred miles. Many have returned from as far away as Belgium and France to make it back to their lofts in England," Grayson said as he lowered his feet to the floor and switched his dozing son to his other arm.

"This fellow gets heavy after a bit, doesn't he?" he whispered as he stretched his free arm.

"Yes, he does," Michelle said as she finished her tea and placed her cup on the saucer. Standing to gather Logan from Grayson's arms before returning her son to his crib, she added, "Just so you know, I'm much happier learning about those brave, fearless pigeons at Kirton in Lindsey than I am about those brave women pilots. So, unless you happen to meet Susan and Michael's American ATA pilot friend, Betty Ann, I'll be happier hearing more about pigeons and less about the lady pilots."

Grayson snapped to attention in his blue-striped pajamas and saluted.

"Understood," Wing Commander, ma'am," he said through his smile. "Will there be anything else, Wing Commander?"

"Yes," Michelle said, suppressing her own smile and circling the RAF Squadron Leader before her. "Your son has requested a plush stuffed piglet upon your next arrival, one well-seasoned with your scent. Can he count on such a delivery in the near future?"

Holding back a laugh, Grayson responded, "As the Wing Commander is aware, *plush* stuffed piglets are rare and can be had only at a premium during wartime. I understand there is quite a shortage at present. I can only promise to do my best, Wing Commander."

"Your best has never disappointed us before," Michelle said as she stood on tiptoe to kiss his cheek. "I'll not expect less than your best this time, either, Squadron Leader. Dismissed."

Grayson saluted, made a sharp military turn, and set a course for the bathroom, surprised by the sharp slap Michelle placed on the right cheek of his blue striped flannel pajamas. He watched over his shoulder as Michelle plumped the pillows and climbed back into bed. He decided to make his stop in the bathroom a very brief one. His stay included only the barest of morning necessities and a swift brush of his teeth before he returned to Michelle's waiting arms.

Chapter 13

Lois Wilshire and Ingrid Boucher, soon to become sisters-in-law, had spent every evening for the past several weeks working together at their respective newly renovated homes. With the interior painting and floor finishing completed, their husbands-to-be, Luc and Joseph, were happy to welcome the ladies to take on the remaining details, which were better left to their brides-to-be. The men had no interest in sewing curtains, choosing carpets, and completing the other decorating tasks that would make their houses into homes.

Today, Lois and Ingrid were at Ingrid and Joseph's Tudor cottage, busily painting a stencil of ivy vines just above the chair rail in the dining room. While Ingrid held the stencil firmly against the wall, Lois added several colors to the ivory plaster to bring the vine to life.

"I find it hard to believe that you and Luc will be married in six weeks," Ingrid said, "but what still amazes me is how you and Luc ever came to meet in the first place. Those of us born on Prince Edward Island never expect to marry anyone from as far away as London."

"But the same stands true for you and Joseph, now, doesn't it?" Lois asked. "It took a war to bring us together. Honestly, Ingrid, I can't think of any young man I knew in London who suits me the way your brother does. I can't recall a single bloke who could hold a candle to the gentlemen I've found here in Canada."

"And you've seen the local 'blokes' here, as you call them," Ingrid said with a smile. "In my eighteen years, I've not found one who could turn my head the way that Joseph, an orphan from Suffolk, England, has. And he did it without trying!" she laughed.

"So, you've never been chased down by a fellow you didn't know, who didn't know your name, but who had his eyes all over you, especially in places where he also hoped to add his hands?" Lois asked. "That's what I knew in the East End of London."

Horrified, Ingrid asked, "Is that really what it was like there?"

"Not always," Lois answered. "Sometimes it was worse, but that was when I met them in groups of two or three. That's when they grew really brave. A girl had to plan ahead before taking to the street."

"I guess there's a big difference between living in the city and living here," Ingrid said.

"I'll say," Lois laughed. "Your young men aren't the least bit forward. I had to kiss Luc before he dared to kiss me."

Ingrid's eyes rose in surprise as she said, "I had to set that table for Joseph, too. We practiced kissing one afternoon outside an ice cream store when I visited him in Quebec."

"And now?" Lois asked, smiling.

"Well," Ingrid said, blushing, "you could say that we don't need to practice anymore. But, what about you and Luc?" she asked.

"Let's just say that Luc's appetite, once whetted, has not waned. Luc gets hungrier every day. I'm glad our wedding day is fast approaching! It was easy to hold off those blokes in London, because not a one of them could claim my interest. With Luc, however, I'm afraid I'm beginning to feel as hungry as he is!"

"I think I understand," Ingrid said. "Joseph's studies in Quebec have kept us separate much of the time. However, when he's home and we're together, we've had to be careful about how we plan our time with one another. We, too, find we can hardly wait for our wedding next spring."

"Then we'd best be hurrying our sewing on the curtains for this dining room," Lois laughed, "because you and Joseph may just decide to move your date forward."

Ingrid didn't answer but stepped toward the window and looked out toward Suffolk Road and up the hill toward Highfield. When Lois finished her next few brush strokes, she noticed Ingrid's quiet absence.

"Ingrid? Is something wrong?" she asked.

"No," Ingrid said as she turned back to Lois. "I'm sorry. I was just thinking of how much my life has changed in the last several years."

"How so?" Lois asked.

"It's all since Mr. Moreland came," she began. "My father died two years before that, and our family was in pretty tough straits. Without my father's income, Mother had to find work wherever she could. We lived on a very meagre diet in a cold house with little hope for the future. But then Mr. Moreland came."

As Ingrid hesitated and continued to look out the window, Lois asked, "Came to Highfield?"

"No," Ingrid answered. "He had been there for almost a year, I think, but then he came to our house and parked his flatbed truck in our yard. It was late summer, and Mother had us busy doing the only thing we could do to make our run-down house more presentable – working in the flower gardens. Mr. Moreland, as it turns out, had been admiring our gardens when he drove by, and he stopped to ask if he could hire us to help him with his. We arrived at Highfield that afternoon, and at the end of that day, when we were ready to go home, he stopped to check on our progress. Then he praised our work in glowing terms and paid us in cash. Folding money, it was, not the few coins we expected. A few days later, we all had jobs, Mother included, but that was just the beginning."

"Tell me more," Lois asked.

"He was different from anyone we'd ever known before. He was British, of course, and his speech and some of his expressions were new to us. We'd expected a man like him from England in this huge house to be, well, uppity, you know. We couldn't help wondering if he was just being nice to us because he was better than us, and we were poor."

"You thought he was just patronizing you?" Lois asked.

"Yes, but that wasn't true," Ingrid said. "He respected us and our work and told us so. He taught us so much – how to serve at the table, for instance, but only after *he* served *us*. He always made us feel better about ourselves and proud of our work. Perhaps a better word is *honored* – he honored our work and never made us feel that he - or the Moncrieffs who arrived later – looked down on us."

"And then?" Lois asked quietly.

"Well, then, we learned that Lady Moncrieff and Miss Susan would soon be arriving. It makes me laugh to remember when Patrice saw a family photo of the Moncrieffs with Sir Richard in uniform and wearing his sword. Miss Susan looked like a princess, and Patrice insisted that Mr. Moreland had to marry Miss Susan so that our family could work for them forever."

As Ingrid stopped to smile and wipe her eyes, her voice changed. "Shortly after Lady Moncrieff and Miss Susan arrived, though, our house burned to the ground, and we lost everything. It was a miracle that none of us was harmed, not even our dog, Duchess. Mr. Moreland pulled her out of the fire that day."

"How utterly horrible, Ingrid," Lois said, "I didn't know."

Shaking her head, Ingrid turned to look at Lois to say, "Horrible? Yes, but only for a moment. Our family was safe, and Mr. Moreland had already milled enough lumber to build our new house, and Lady Moncrieff gave it all to us, and so much more. They called us 'family,' Lois. I had never felt more secure."

"You have an amazing story, Ingrid," Lois said as she put her brush down and sat on the floor, inviting Ingrid to join her.

Continuing, Ingrid said, "And then Mr. Moreland hired Jacques, and that's a whole other story, but Mother and Jacques married, and Joseph, who came from England with Miss Susan and Lady Moncrieff, came to live with us. For the longest time, he was just Luc's best friend, but soon he will be my husband."

Ingrid and Lois were quiet for a moment before Ingrid said, "Joseph came from Suffolk for me, and you came from London for Luc, but none of this would have happened were it not for Mr. Moreland and the Moncrieffs. When Miss Susan arrived, she taught us deportment and held high standards at the schoolhouse, the one that Mr. Moreland and Jacques had built, and where I teach now. Then, she guided me to college and to a career as a teacher myself. But more than anything else, she taught me to respect myself and my family."

Ingrid paused for a moment before she began again.

"And I'll never forget," she said, "Mr. Moreland taught Luc and Joseph how to shoot a rifle with a telescopic sight. When Luc went to fight in the war, he immediately entered sniper training. Seven men in Luc's battalion died the first day before Luc ever fired his rifle, but Luc's two well-placed shots ended the list of seven lives lost to the German sniper in those church towers in Crete. If Luc had been just a regular infantryman, he might have been one of the men who were killed that day. I have to believe Mr. Moreland made the difference."

Lois listened closely as Ingrid continued, "There were no coincidences in all these miracles, Lois. Somewhere behind this whole story, we share a faith that there is a God who would have it no other way. And, what a mix we are, Lois! Everyone on this island will marvel at the difference in our dialects. Two couples as unlike in their speech as we will likely confuse everyone. And what about our children? What will their speech sound like?" she laughed.

Lois nodded with a laugh of her own as Ingrid caught her breath long enough to say, "Now, we know that you found Luc and I found Joseph by nothing less than heavenly intervention. But what does heaven have in store for my lonely little sister, Patrice, now that no more young people are coming here from England?"

Just then, as if on cue, they heard Patrice's voice calling from the open front door.

"Ingrid? Lois?" she asked. "Where are you?"

"In the dining room," Ingrid answered. "Come see what we're doing."

Patrice entered the room smiling, and her eyes grew wide when she saw the lines of ivy that circled the room beneath the crown moulding at the ceiling and just above the chair rail where Lois and Ingrid had just finished their work. As Lois stood, wiped her artist brush on a rag, and added it to several others in a can of turpentine, she heard Patrice say, "Wow, that ivy looks almost real."

"It's the highlights and shadow accents that add the life," Lois said, stirring her brush in the can. "Most folks use but one color on stencils, but Ingrid liked my idea to add a bit more life to the single shade of green most painters use."

"But look at you, Sis," Ingrid said, standing. "When I left home this morning, you were on your way to the henhouse and the barn in your braids and your sad old work apron and usual morning frown. Now you're wearing your Highfield service uniform, your hair is tied back in a bun, and there's a sparkle in your eyes. What has changed since then? And what's that basket on your arm?"

"I'm on an errand for Miss Susan," Patrice answered, looking at the floor, "and I need your help. I thought you might be at one of your houses," she added, "so I pedaled down from home and was relieved to see your bikes outside."

"What kind of errand?" Lois asked.

"Well," Patrice answered, an impish grin growing on her face, "Miss Susan gave me a basket of muffins to deliver to the men working at the Morelands' new house."

"All right," Ingrid teased, "but that grin and the sudden color in your cheeks mean something else is up."

"Perhaps," Patrice admitted, biting her lower lip to slow the smile that was arriving there. "She told me she met one of Mr. McLeod's nephews at the worksite yesterday. He arrived from a small town in Scotland called Stirling only two weeks ago. His name is Hugh, Hugh Buchanan."

"And would he be about your age?" Lois asked.

"Just a year older," Patrice smiled, "and Miss Susan said he's very polite, well-spoken, has light brown, almost blond hair, and blue eyes. She asked him if he might enjoy one of her cranberry orange muffins, and he told her he would love to try one. She promised him she'd send some for the workmen today, and, of course, I can't go there alone, so I need one or both of you to be my escort so I can deliver this basket."

"Some of the other workmen have been staying in the cottages at Highfield, haven't they?" Lois asked. "Will Hugh be joining them there?"

"That's what Miss Susan said," Patrice smiled.

"You know," Ingrid said thoughtfully, winking at Lois, "I think it's been over a week since I made the trek up that driveway to see the progress on the new house."

"It's been at least a week for me as well," Lois admitted.

"So," Patrice asked with a plea in her voice, "does that mean you'll go with me?"

"Just try to keep us away!" Lois laughed as she tossed her artist's smock onto the drop cloth beneath their feet. Then, taking Ingrid's hand, she added, "Let's go, Ingrid." Pointing toward the ceiling, she said, "Let's see what's in store for Patrice."

Chapter 14

"It's been so long since Nigel last wrote," Lady Moncrieff said. "I was beginning to worry that something terrible had happened. But this letter arrived yesterday afternoon."

She handed the letter across the tea table to Susan, who had just carried the tea tray into the west sunroom. Susan read the letter while Lady Moncrieff filled their teacups.

"He sounds well, Mother," Susan said when she had finished reading, "but just a bit discouraged."

"I agree," Lady Moncrieff said. "The Japanese fight a different kind of war in the air, it seems, one to which the RAF and the Fleet Air Arm are forced to adjust."

"He's always flown Fairey Swordfish, aircraft which are no match for the Japanese Zeros he mentions," Susan said. "That's why the RAF has the Hurricanes and the Spitfires."

"And now he's bored with reconnaissance missions as the Royal Navy's eyes in the sky, and he's craving the combat missions he misses," Lady Moncrieff said.

"Meanwhile, the Japanese aircraft carriers with all their Zeros have the Allied forces in the Pacific and Indian Ocean fighting defensive battles," Susan said, "wondering where the Japanese will attack next."

"So, it seems, Susan, "Lady Moncrieff said, "so it seems."

"Well, I don't care if he ever gets a Swordfish off the deck again, as long as he comes home," Susan said. "He's hoping for a chance to train on a fighter, but I'm not so sure I like that idea."

"I'll join you there," Lady Moncrieff nodded. "This is no time for a man to go into the air lacking a great deal more experience in a new cockpit. Thankfully, Boyd is in a less exposed position."

"Yes," Susan agreed. "British East Africa seems so much closer to home somehow, and preferable to the middle of an ocean while being hunted by the Japanese."

"And this young lady he mentioned in his last letter seems to have his undivided attention," Lady Moncrieff said. "Kathleen Balfour from Windemere. A war brings young people together in strange ways, doesn't it?"

Just then, the ladies heard laughter and voices approaching from the kitchen. In another moment, Lois, Ingrid, and Patrice, holding an empty basket, appeared. Though a bit breathless, they were alive with energy and bursting with excitement. The trio stopped to compose themselves as Lois knocked at the open door.

"Please excuse us for descending on your teatime, Lady Moncrieff and Mrs. Moreland," she said as all three struggled to contain their energy. "Would you have a moment for us to share some news from the worksite?"

"Of course," Lady Moncrieff said, smiling. "We've just finished a worried conversation concerning our young men at sea. You three seem to have a more positive subject to offer. Please come in and tell us all about it."

In mere seconds, the settee and an armchair were filled. Susan noticed Patrice's empty basket and asked, "Was your mission successful?"

"Completely," Patrice said, wide-eyed. "Mr. McLeod and the rest of the workmen finished every single bite. They especially loved the bit of icing you added."

"I'm afraid I can't take credit for the icing," Susan said. "That was Alida's contribution."

"So, that's the reason for all the excitement we heard all the way from the kitchen?" Lady Moncrieff asked.

"No, Lady Moncrieff, no," Patrice admitted. "There was another reason for that."

With bright eyes and a coy smile, Lady Moncrieff asked, "And his name is?"

"Hugh," Patrice blurted. "Hugh Buchanan. He's from a town called Stirling in Scotland."

"From Stirling?" Susan asked. "Mother, we know Stirling, not far from Edinburgh."

"Of course," Lady Moncrieff said, "and Sir Richard knows several Buchanans from that region. I believe one is with the Royal Army, now engaged on the continent."

"Hugh's father is fighting in the Royal Army in France," Patrice said. "He sent Hugh here for his safety. The McLeods and the Buchanans are cousins."

"You seem to have learned a great deal about this young man after a simple delivery of some cranberry orange muffins, even if they did have icing," Susan teased.

"Well," Patrice began, a bit embarrassed, "Hugh offered to take me on a tour of the site. After being here for only two weeks, he seemed quite familiar with all the details. Of course, I'm not sure I understood everything he was saying. He calls some things by strange names, and I'm not used to the way people from Scotland speak. Does anyone know what a 'joiner' is?"

With her eyes sparkling, Lady Moncrieff said, "A joiner is a skilled carpenter, dear, one qualified to build cabinets and furniture."

"Oh," Patrice said.

"But tell me, Patrice," Lady Moncrieff asked, "You say he gave you a tour? Haven't you seen every bit of progress on the worksite for the last several months? You've visited there every few days right along, haven't you?" Lady Moncrieff asked.

"Well, yes," Patrice admitted, "but Hugh didn't know that. And he seemed very proud to be able to explain everything he'd learned from his uncle, even though I knew he got several things wrong."

"And was he surprised when you set him straight?" Susan asked.

"Oh," Patrice said wide-eyed, "I didn't bother to correct him."

"Very wise of you," Lady Moncrieff nodded. "It's always wise to avoid correcting an interesting young man early in a relationship, unless you're not interested in turning an introduction into a possible friendship."

"I hope I did the right thing," Patrice said, "because I think a friendship could be a good thing."

"Then I can see we have an immediate problem to solve," Susan said as she stood and began pacing in her problem-solving mode behind the settee where Patrice was perched.

"Oh, no," Patrice said. "What kind of problem?"

"It involves a big decision, Patrice," she said seriously, "and you will have to make that decision tonight."

"But what kind of decision?" Patrice asked anxiously.

"You have to decide what you're going to bake for tomorrow morning's delivery!" Susan laughed.

The whole room joined Susan in her laughter. In just moments, Patrice had promises from all the women that their favorite morning pastry recipes for muffins, turnovers, and scones would be available before the day was over.

Chapter 15

It was just before midnight when Michael woke with a start. The wind was roaring outside, and a sideways rain was pelting the east windows. The northeast gale winds that had arrived that afternoon were now gusting at full force. Earlier in the day, the storm had brought lightning and thunder, but now all Michael heard was the wind and rain.

"If it wasn't thunder, then what woke me?" he wondered. With Susan still sleeping soundly beside him, he rubbed his eyes and sat up, letting his bare feet find the cold floor beneath. Just then, he heard the blurt of the buzzer on the nightstand beside him.

He was wide awake in an instant. That buzzer meant only one thing - someone was climbing the steps at the fire tower, no doubt on the way to the transmitter and receiver in the cab at the top.

Within minutes, Michael was dressed and donning his raingear and storm boots at the kitchen door. Hidden under his rain gear was his Walther PPK, two spare magazines, and his battery-powered torch. Although the walk to the tower would be a miserable one, he dared not drive and risk having his truck's engine warn the intruder.

The wind was in his face as Michael pushed through the field to the North Path. The cover of the brush at his flanks provided a welcome windbreak as the wind swirled, which, matched with the fully leafed branches above, made Michael's trek a little easier. Keeping his light low and aimed at the ground directly before him, he found himself within fifty yards of the tower in less than a quarter hour.

He expected to see lights in the cab at the top of the tower and to hear the generator motor running when he arrived, but neither awaited him. As he moved forward, pistol in one hand and torch in the other, he maintained a serpentine path toward the tower steps. There, to his surprise, the enemy who had sounded the alarm at Highfield waited for him.

The wind had shattered the trunk of a fifty-foot-tall pine tree, but the upper portion of the trunk remained attached and hanging mere inches above the bottom step. With the help of his light, Michael watched as the wind bent what remained of the tree trunk, while gravity drew the top down onto the first step of the tower stairway. Then, when the gust abated, the tree trunk stood straighter again, raising the treetop off the step.

Cold, wet, and tired, Michael shook his head. Holstering his pistol, he spent a few minutes breaking off some limbs that threatened to impact the lowest step and sound the alarm beside his bed. The limbs, bare of needles and surprisingly easy to break, told Michael they had been dead for some time.

"Don't worry," Michael said, addressing the pine with its shattered trunk and broken branches, "I'll be back in the morning to take care of this mess."

The winds were already calming as Michael made his way back to Highfield. Leaving his raingear and boots at the kitchen entry, he padded up the back stairs to the nursery to check on Case and Reed before joining Susan in their bedroom. Asleep, just as he had left her an hour or more ago, she didn't stir until his cold, bare toes made a journey under the covers just far enough to encounter her soft, warm left calf.

"Oh, my!" she gasped as her whole body retracted inwards, trying to escape a second frigid assault from without.

"My apologies, Dearest," he said quietly. "I was trying so hard not to disturb you."

"Where have you been?" she asked in her sleepy voice. "You didn't get cold feet like that while lying here in bed."

"No," Michael answered, "I didn't. I needed to go out for a while to check on something at the tower."

"In the middle of the night? In a storm like this? What was so important out there?" she asked.

"The alarm buzzer sounded and woke me. I thought we had an intruder. It turned out to be a tree limb, though. Nothing to worry about," he said as he settled into his pillow.

"Oh," was all Susan said before Michael heard her breathing begin to deepen and sound those soft comfort snores Susan swore only existed in his imagination.

Several hours later, shortly before dawn, the winds picked up again. Michael, already in the barn, didn't hear the buzzer beside his bed sound its warning. Neither did he hear the tower's generator motor start nor see the lights shining in the cab.

Brenda Kimble, taking advantage of the weather, spent a mere fifteen minutes on the radio, long enough to get her orders regarding the arrival of a second Nazi spy, this time one bound for Quebec. Although her presence at the tower had not been discovered in the past, today would be different.

Susan was awake and just coming out of the bathroom when she heard the buzzer next to Michael's alarm clock sound. It surprised her, but remembering what Michael had told her about the tree limbs overnight, she thought no more about it. Moments later, though, Armand Verrier telephoned, and Susan answered.

"I'm sorry to bother you so early, Susan," he said. "I need to speak with Michael if he's available. It's important."

"Of course, Armand. He's in the barn at this hour, I suspect, but I'll have him ring you in just a few minutes. Will that be all right?" she asked.

"Yes, thank you," Armand said. "I'll stay here by the telephone."

Susan was at Michael's side when he returned Armand's call a few minutes later.

"Hello, Armand. It's Michael. Susan said you had something important to discuss?"

"Yes, Michael. Tell me, were you using the tower radio about a half hour ago?"

"No," Michael said. "I did make a trek out to the tower overnight, though, when the alarm sounded on my nightstand. It was a false alarm, though, caused by a pine branch from a wind-shivered tree."

"I'm only suspicious about this morning," Armand said, "because the strength of the signal from the tower is unmistakable. No other transmitter on the island comes close to it. Someone was using that radio this morning."

"I might have already been in the barn and missed the alarm then..." Michael began when Susan interrupted him.

"Michael, the buzzer sounded as I came out of the bathroom this morning, and after what you told me about the tree last night, I didn't think to mention it."

"Did you hear that, Armand?" Michael asked.

"Yes," he said. "We need to make a trip to examine everything at the tower right away. Whoever was there is probably long gone by now, but we need to find out what we can. I'm on my way to Highfield now."

It only took a few minutes inside the cab to confirm Armand's suspicions. In the past, Michael never left the tower without refilling the generator's fuel tank, and this morning the tank was only half full. That told them that the intruder's visit this morning wasn't the first. The intruder had used the generator on several visits to use that much fuel.

Another telling clue involved the rolling office chair in front of the transmitter console. When Michael sat in the chair, his knees hit the counter. Clearly, a much shorter person had adjusted the chair's height while using the radio.

"Amateur mistake," Armand smiled, "not lowering that seat. Might as well have left a calling card."

"So, my instincts tell me we've had a female visitor by the name of Kimble," Michael said.

"She would certainly be my primary suspect," Armand agreed.

"What's our next step, then?" Michael asked.

"I was able to catch part of the code she was using this morning. It's the only one she knows, I believe, the one she and Ernest Duncan used in Halifax. I'll spend some time with it, and perhaps it will tell us when she'll be back. Hopefully, we'll be able to set a trap."

"And I'll spend the day finding her route to and from this tower," Michael said. "That way we'll be able to catch her either coming or going."

"Amen," Armand said, "and amen."

Chapter 16

On a late afternoon in July, more than a mile above the swells in the Indian Ocean below, Sqn Ldr Nigel Moncrieff could see no sign of the aircraft carrier, HMS *Formidable*. Within a few minutes, though, a radio signal from the ship crackled in his ear, calling an end to training for the day. Only a week previously, his flight time had kept him in the familiar open-cockpit Fairey Swordfish, a biplane considered out-of-date by many, though highly respected for its impressive history as a dependable weapon of war. Today, however, Nigel was completing his final day of combat training in a Fairey Fulmar Mk II, a closed-cockpit fighter designed for the Fleet Air Arm as a carrier-based reconnaissance and air-to-air combat fighter.

The Fulmar Mk II, equipped with a supercharged Merlin engine, could reach speeds of 272 miles per hour and had a range of 1,100 miles. Sometimes employed as a dive bomber, the Mk II could deliver 500-pound bombs in 60-degree dives. Like the renowned RAF Hurricanes and Spitfires, the MK II boasted eight machine guns for air-to-air combat, making Nigel's dreams of successfully engaging the enemy in the air a very real possibility.

For all its good points, however, the Mk II was no match for a Japanese Zero in a dogfight. Even the faster, lighter, more maneuverable land-based RAF Hurricanes and Spitfires found themselves outmatched by the much faster and more nimble Japanese fighters. With the MK II's top speed of 272 mph compared to the Zero's 350 mph top speed, the RAF and the Fleet Air Arm had taken a hard look at battle strategies and were able to make some specific recommendations to even the playing field.

In their Fulmar Mk II, Nigel and his navigator had been training all week to achieve and maintain a considerably higher altitude before diving to make initial contact with Japanese fighters. After a quick burst of machine gun fire on the enemy, FAA fighter pilots trained to immediately force their Mk II into a steep climb, avoiding the Zero's machine guns and cannons, while making ready to dive again. Whenever they made contact, their strategy was to take advantage of the Zero's inherent weakness: a Zero's fuel tanks were not self-sealing. Once those tanks were hit by machine gun fire, the aircraft was doomed to explode in a ball of flame.

Today, at the end of three long weeks of combat drills lasting more than eight hours each day, Nigel and his navigator/radio operator, Rodney Capwell, reveled in the relative comfort of the Fulmar Mk II's closed cockpit where the wind, noise, and weather remained, for the most part, outside. Gone was the shouting required in their old Swordfish. In the MK II, Nigel could easily hear the coordinates his navigator provided so that he could pilot them back to the flight deck of the *Formidable.*

Once the Mk II was safely on deck and de-briefing was complete, Nigel looked forward to the luxury of a free hour or so in his cabin when he planned to write a long-overdue letter home. The last one he'd been able to send left the ship a month ago when the *Formidable* was in port in Ceylon, about the same time that the HMS *Revenge*, with Boyd aboard, sailed for East Africa. Now, while Boyd was in port at Killindini Harbor in Mombasa, the *Formidable* continued at sea, hunting the Japanese fleet.

Nigel dug through the small cache of letters he kept in a zippered canvas pouch in his sea bag. Boyd's last letter was on top of the pile, and Nigel shook his head and smiled as he read the first page again.

"The man is in love again," he said to himself, "although this time he sounds more over-the-moon than the last time."

Boyd had found what he called the "Wren's Nest" only a day after the Revenge was safely at port. The Lotus Hotel in Mombasa was their home, and it seemed the whole city had made the Wrens welcome. The city streets, unlike those in London, were well lit and fully alive by day and into the night. For entertainment while on leave, the ladies were welcomed at a local tennis club, and they enjoyed sailing privileges at Port Tudor.

After their initial meeting when Boyd surprised Kathleen at the Lotus Hotel, the two had found it easy to encounter each other regularly on the streets of Mombasa. After her work hours, Boyd made time to arrange dinners and dancing at the Nelson, a local nightclub where Boyd's uniform made them more than welcome.

"Balfour," Nigel mused, "a Scotsman from Windermere? I remember a Prime Minister of that name, Lord of the Admiralty, as well, if my history doesn't betray me. Could that be Kathleen's family?"

Nigel took a second look through his mother's last letter, remembering her description of the construction progress of Susan and Michael's new home, situated across the road from Highfield. Of course, she also mentioned Susan's pregnancy, which led to the need for their new home. Although she never said as much directly, her desire for the eldest to marry and carry on the Moncrieff name was ever present in their discourse, whether spoken or written. Of course, the war had served to diminish that immediacy in her mind, replacing it with her prayers that both her sons would survive the current conflict. Nonetheless, Nigel wished he could give her reasons to hope, but at present, he was still unable to offer his mother the name of a woman who occupied his thoughts the way Kathleen seemed to rule Boyd's.

"I'm sorry, Mother," he said aloud. "I haven't found her yet. Don't worry, though, because I'll maintain an open mind, and when she shows up, you'll be the first to know. For now, however, your name, *Angela*, is the only one that will be painted on the nose of a Fairey Fulmar Mk II. When the fighting is over, I'll see about finding the right daughter-in-law for you and Father."

Chapter 17

After a traditional Friday evening meal of fish and chips at home at Fletcher Hall in New Mills, Michelle dressed Logan for bed but decided to take him for a short walk as far as Hayfield Road. Glancing at the calendar on her bureau, Michelle noticed the date was July 3. June had been unseasonably cool, and now July was following in suit, bringing clouds that hid the sun for most of the morning and afternoon. In the last half hour, though, a break in the clouds had brought the only sunbeams the day offered in Derbyshire.

"It's a bit of a cool evening, my boy," she said to Logan, "so we'll be putting your handsome blue sweater on for our walk. See, Mother is wearing her kerchief, too, because the breeze will be blowing. However, the sun has just appeared to give us his last smile of the day, so let's be gone, my boy."

With Logan safely ensconced in his pram with his diaper bag and favorite plush bunny, the two set out for their walk. Unbeknownst to mother and son, though, hours earlier, two German high-speed bombers, Junkers JU 88s, had taken off from a German airfield in France. Their target was a propeller factory at Lostock, more than thirty miles northeast of New Mills. Their course from Rennes–Saint-Jacques Airport in Brittany brought them across the Channel south of Great Britain and then directly north, flying over the Irish Sea. At Anglesey, their course led them east, flying north of Manchester to their target near Bolton.

The cloud cover being what it was, the pilots and navigators struggled but were unable to locate Lostock, their target. Multiple passes at different altitudes proved fruitless and began to tax their fuel supply. With fuel running low, the JU 88s, still fully laden with the weight of their bombs and ammunition, struck an easterly course north of Manchester and then southeast, directly over New Mills.

At this time of day, traffic was light, making Michelle's walk with Logan a calm and comfortable one. After about twenty minutes, she reached the intersection with Hayfield Road, her turnaround destination. Michelle smiled when she saw the street sign again, remembering that the road was called Hayfield Road here, near New Mills. After all, the road led uphill to Hayfield. However, in the village of Hayfield, the same road was named New Mills Road. And why not? From Hayfield, it led downhill to New Mills.

"Yes, why not?" she said to her son. "Why not, Logan? After all, the street sign will always tell you where you are going. Of course, for us, the road to Hayfield is uphill most of the way, so we'll follow it for only a little while before we turn around and turn downhill toward home."

Michelle pushed the pram up the hill for another few minutes before she stopped. Just as she turned and started down the hill, though, Logan began to whimper. Then his whimper turned into a cry, signaling Michelle that his diaper needed her attention. After she found a level spot off the pavement to steady the pram, she recovered his diaper bag. As she opened the bag, though, she stopped to listen to a sound rarely heard in the skies over New Mills.

"That's an airplane," she said, as she turned to look toward the west, following the sound intently. "And it's not a single-engine plane. I've heard lots of single-engine planes at home for years, always flying over from the training field in Charlottetown."

She listened more closely as the sound grew louder. Though still far away, she said, "And there's more than one, and neither is a single-engine aircraft." Listening once more, she tried to comfort herself by saying, "They're probably ours. At least I hope they are." Turning her attention back to her son, she said, "Logan, this is going to be a quick change."

The fastest route back to safety for the two JU 88s was a straight course over Derbyshire and directly east to the North Sea. However, their fuel supplies were dwindling while their bomb bays remained full, and their load of ammunition remained unspent. When the two JU88 pilots reached New Mills, they decided to lighten their loads to save fuel.

Michelle and Logan were hurrying downhill toward New Mills when both German aircraft broke through the clouds. Michelle watched in horror as the first bomber flew in low and strafed the center of town with machine gun fire. With nowhere to take cover, Michelle pulled Logan from the pram and ran for a drainage ditch at the side of the road. As she covered Logan with her body, the machine gun fire ended, but within seconds, the noise of an explosion shattered the air and shook the ground fiercely. Daring to look up for a split second, Michelle saw smoke and debris falling from the air just as she heard a second, closer explosion that shook the ground more violently than the first. Despite the noise and aftershocks of the bombs, Logan remained strangely quiet while Michelle did her best to comfort him, keeping her voice as calm and reassuring as she could. The sound of the second bomber grew louder, followed by more machine gun fire, and two more explosions that ripped the air and shook the ground.

It was quiet for a moment as the drone of the bombers' engines faded in the distance, but soon they grew louder, this time flying directly overhead toward Hayfield. Michelle heard more machine gun fire, this time coming from the north, followed seconds later by several more explosions. Though the bombs were landing farther away, they continued to shake the ground beneath Michelle and Logan as they huddled in the ditch.

The sound of the aircraft engines faded once again, and everything grew quiet. Then, farther away, perhaps to the south and east, Michelle thought, she heard another explosion and more machine gun fire. When everything remained quiet for several minutes, Michelle dared to raise her head and sit up with Logan in her arms. She smiled as she looked at him. His little eyes were closed, and he was fast asleep.

"Oh, Logan," she said, smiling through her tears, "you *are* your father's son."

Careful not to wake him, she secured him in the pram and picked pieces of straw from his sweater for a minute or two. After taking another moment to rid her own sweater of straw, she turned to walk downhill toward Fletcher Hall.

Had she been farther up the hill toward Hayfield, she might have had a better perspective to see how much damage the German bombs had done in New Mills. From where she stood, however, she could see nothing except smoke rising from two sites. All she could do for the moment was hurry toward Watford Lane, unsure of what she and Logan would find there. Thankfully, they had no sooner turned off Hayfield Road when Grayson's sister, Nancy, appeared, hurrying down High Hill Road toward them. She was still wearing her apron from dinner.

"Oh," she began, nearly breathless, "I wasn't sure you had taken your customary walking route. I was afraid you might have been near Torr Vale, where one of the bombs exploded. I understand another hit the new Swizzels candy factory."

"No, Nancy," Michelle began, "we were just a short way up Hayfield Road. But tell me, is Fletcher Hall untouched?"

"Yes, thank the Lord," Nancy said, still catching her breath, "but we'd both feel so much better, Mother and I, if you were safe at home with us."

"Of course," Michelle said. "Thankfully, Logan slept through the entire attack, but now that I can see the smoke and can hear all the noise where the bombs hit, is there anything we can do to help?" Michelle asked as they hurried toward home.

"Mother has already contacted the Home Guard on that count," Nancy said, and we've offered to take in anyone whose home was hit and needs a place to stay. I'll be joining some of the women at our regular Home Guard Auxiliary meeting tonight to replenish the bandage supply, but your job is to take care of our little treasure here and wait to hear from Grayson. I'm sure he'll find a way to contact you."

Michelle nodded and said no more. She knew Grayson would get a message to her and his family. She needed to be ready to assure him that she and Logan were unharmed. She was also sure that the two German bombers, flying very near to Kirton in Lindsey, would probably be hearing from some RAF Spitfires under Grayson's command very soon. Ordinarily not a betting gal, Michelle would be glad to wager that those Junker 88's weren't going to make it home tonight.

Michelle was right. Minutes after the German bombers wrought their havoc in Derbyshire, two RAF Spitfires were scrambled from RAF Kirton in Lindsey. Their pilots, well-experienced Polish aces from the Battle of Britain, encountered the pair of JU88s over Lincoln, only seventy miles from New Mills. Hit by machine gun and cannon fire, the first bomber crashed, taking its four crew members to their graves. When attacked by the remaining Spitfire, the second bomber, with its starboard engine afire, crashed and burned. Although its crew survived, they were all captured at the crash site.

The telegraph office in New Mills worked late into the night after the attack, and Michelle was able to assure Grayson that the Royce family remained uninjured and their family home unscathed. Choosing her words carefully, she dictated, "All good here. Family and home untouched. Fear nothing. Love, Michelle."

She smiled when she reminded herself that Grayson would be sure to find his way to New Mills to see for himself very shortly.

Chapter 18

It had been a week since Armand Verrier and Michael met to discuss the unknown visitor to the fire tower at Highfield. Since then, Armand had collected several pages of data from recent tower transmissions to share with Michael and Sir Richard. The three men met at the study at Highfield to review Armand's findings.

"I have relied on no one more than you for more than twenty years when it comes to this type of communication, Armand," Sir Richard said. "What have you discovered?"

"Let me give you a bit of background that may prove helpful before I reveal the latest data, if I may," Armand said.

"Of course, Armand. Say on," Sir Richard said as he sat back in his mahogany office chair.

Armand began, "You should know that we've been able to trace all the communications we've followed to known Canadian sympathizers with the Abwehr. By every international standard known in Europe and on this continent, the Abwehr appears to remain far behind SIS in both technology and practice. It appears that the main reason for their dysfunction may rest with their Chief Officer, Wilhelm Canaris. Is that name familiar to you?"

"Yes, I am familiar with Canaris," Sir Richard answered. "I have followed him ever since my early days at SIS after World War I and even more closely since Germany invaded Poland three years ago. Let me tell you what we know of him."

"Of course," Armand said.

"From the early days before and after the start of the war, he appears to have resisted Hitler's goals and methods, even going so far as to leak critical secret intelligence to governments Hitler considers his enemies," Sir Richard said. "Canaris speaks six languages, including English. He won the Iron Cross in Germany as a U-boat commander in 1917 and was later promoted to Rear Admiral. A man with a brilliant mind, he was originally marching in lockstep with Nazi policy, mostly because he feared the alternative of communism and what the threat of another war could do to Germany. When Hitler set his sights on Czechoslovakia in 1935, however, our agents learned that Canaris and others began to favor an overthrow of the Nazi regime. Later, though, after Neville Chamberlain and the French allowed Hitler to take the Sudetenland, Canaris fell back into line, assuming peace would ensue."

"So, his allegiance to Hitler has always been rather shaky, then?" Michael asked.

"Exactly," Sir Richard said, "but when Canaris visited the Polish front in 1939, his disenchantment with Hitler was sealed. He witnessed the burning of a synagogue where several hundred Jews were locked inside and learned of Hitler's express orders for systematic mass murders of Poles in several Polish cities. We believe Canaris, still an honorable man, found he could no longer support Hitler."

"So, the Abwehr has been without a fully devoted leader for some time?" Armand concluded.

"Yes, and as a result, not only here in Canada, but also across Europe, we have been able to foil their agents' best laid plans and stay one step ahead of them," Sir Richard said.

"So, despite the dangers Canaris would face if he were discovered, he has continued to sabotage Hitler's plans?" Michael asked.

"Our sources tell us that he was enraged at the escalation of atrocities ordered by Hitler as the war progressed. After witnessing the aftermath at several sites firsthand, he stopped pursuing collaborators among the populations overrun by the Wehrmacht. Furthermore, he began to leak information that would find its way to the Allies. Still fearing for his life and that of his family, however, he kept his efforts discreet," Sir Richard said. "He has intentionally failed to create the intelligence gathering machine that Hitler needed to succeed in his quest for domination in Europe."

"How does that relate to the situation at hand here, though?" Michael asked.

"There's a direct correlation we have seen with our very eyes," Sir Richard said. "Consider Ernst Hoffman, known to us now as Ernest Duncan, code-named 'E.D.' in Europe. Once an Abwehr agent schooled in linguistics and cartography, he turned to our side in a remarkably short time. His dedication to the Nazi cause was never one that ruled his mind; it simply appealed to a young man with a sad history of childhood psychological trauma. The Abwehr's training was woefully inadequate," Sir Richard said. "Furthermore, we've just learned that E.D. is now in Switzerland, serving with the international resistance movement there. We now have eyes and ears among the Swiss, who, though maintaining armed neutrality, remain among our most loyal allies."

"So, when E.D. met people here like Michael," Armand said, "people who invested enough time and care to get to know him and offer even a meagre hope of a relationship and understanding, he turned on his former 'Employer' as he called the Abwehr," Armand concluded.

"That is correct," Sir Richard nodded, "and then he gave us everything the Abwehr had given him, right down to a small fortune in cash."

"And soon after that, he joined the RCAF and led the RAF to German targets all over Europe," Michael added.

Sir Richard nodded and said, "And all without a whisper of guilt. He cut himself off from every allegiance he once thought he owed to the Nazis who trained him."

"So, then," Armand asked, "how do we deal with the young woman we suspect is trespassing here and using the equipment in the fire tower to contact our enemies?"

"Here are my thoughts," Sir Richard began. "Brenda Kimble, as we know her, is a young Canadian woman of German descent who was treated despicably in her small farming community in Ontario. When she met Ernst Hoffman, another disenchanted German, he used all his charm to take advantage of her native angst to become her hero. Of course, his goal was to recruit her to the Abwehr side. Since they were arrested for leaking sensitive information to the Abwehr and interfering with shipping in Halifax, they haven't seen each other again. So, now that Ernst Hoffman, also known as Ernest Duncan and E.D., has escaped, we believe she will try to find him. Of course, he is more than an ocean away and no longer available."

"How do we know she has been trying to contact him?" Michael asked.

"Because of one more weakness in the Abwehr," Armand smiled. "I told you that the signal we traced from Highfield's tower was the strongest one on the island."

"That's correct," Sir Richard nodded, "and...?" he asked.

"We've kept records of those communications, fully expecting them to be Enigma-based, a code the Allies are still striving to break. We were elated to discover that the Abwehr uses Enigma-based coding in Europe, but not on *this* side of the ocean. None of their sympathizers on this continent, it seems, has an Enigma machine to decode those signals. Brenda Kimble has continued to use the only code she knows, an old one that she learned from E.D. We've broken all those communications," Armand said, holding a stack of paper in his hand, "and the Abwehr loses again!" he smiled.

"So," Michael said as he stood to look at the sheaf of papers in Armand's hand, "do you know when she'll be in the tower again? Does she have a predictable schedule with her contacts? If we know, we can lie in wait for her."

"Not advised just yet," Sir Richard interrupted, looking at Armand, who was nodding. "Since Armand can decode whatever she sends and receives, we can simply use her to our advantage."

"Of course," Michael agreed, as he sat again, "of course. We'll be able to capture her anytime we know she'll be there from now on. The longer we wait, the better."

"You have a great deal of paper there, Armand," Sir Richard said. "What else have you learned?"

"We know a Nazi U-boat landed on our coast in May," Armand began. "Our best intelligence suggests that Brenda Kimble was assigned to meet an Abwehr agent coming ashore and offer him local assistance."

"That is correct," Sir Richard interrupted. "The vessel was U-213 and landed in the Bay of Fundy near St. Andrew. Our man E.D., with the help of the keenly organized resistance in Geneva, was able to send us a full report on U-213 and her passenger several weeks ago," Sir Richard said. "Supposedly, he is a highly trained spy."

Michael and Armand looked at each other and smiled.

"E.D. again," Michael smiled. "Where will he turn up next?"

Turning back to the papers in his hand, Armand said, "We believe Miss Kimble failed to meet him, and since then the agent seems to have disappeared."

"I'm not surprised," Sir Richard said with a wry smile. "Do you recall the value of the cash E.D. buried in canning jars here on the island?"

"Thousands of dollars," Michael said. "A small fortune."

"This most recent Abwehr arrival was probably carrying his own small fortune. He could easily have decided to live a life of leisure here in Canada," Sir Richard added. "I'd wager his wartime endeavors are mere memories by now. Perhaps we'll know when the money runs out. Just the same, Armand, let's keep our ears and eyes open to all the possibilities."

"Of course," Armand agreed with a nod.

"And the future situation?" Sir Richard asked.

"It is similar," Armand answered. "We believe, based on the radio chatter, that another agent may be scheduled to arrive on our shores in the near future. Once again, it appears that Brenda Kimble could be assigned to meet him, shadow him, and teach him enough about Canadian culture so that he raises no suspicions among the local population."

"E.D. has already briefed SIS in London of such a possibility," Sir Richard said while opening a folder at his desk and handing it to Michael and Armand. "I believe I shall have further intelligence to share with you tomorrow at this time. Meanwhile, Armand," he added, "your continued surveillance of local radio transmissions will continue to prove invaluable, I'm sure. I must thank you for your diligence."

The men sat silently for a moment before Michael spoke.

"I wonder," he said.

"Wonder what?" Armand asked.

"After we apprehend Miss Kimble, I wonder if we'll discover a softer side to her, one that might be able to give up the hatred that took her first from a family farm in Ontario, carried her to Ottawa, and then delivered her here. After all, when we first met Ernst Hoffman, he saw us as his enemy. Now he's proven himself to be a loyal and trusted ally."

"Perhaps she could be persuaded," Armand said. "Perhaps."

"And," Michael continued, "we don't have to pursue her to catch her."

"What do you mean?" Armand asked.

"We need only to wait for a time when she's at the tower again," Michael said.

"Of course," Sir Richard agreed. "Call us the next time you recognize the tower radio's signal, Armand, or we'll call you if our alarm sounds at Highfield. While she's busy in the cab on the radio, Michael can take a silent post on the stairs. Once she's closed herself in the cab at the top of the tower, she's already our prisoner."

"Brilliant," Armand smiled, "brilliant."

"Eventually she may learn it's better to partner with us, the same way E.D. did," Michael said. "A number of long conversations in his cell in Halifax and several visits with Fr. Hunt eventually brought him some freedom from the horrors of his past. It's possible he was just the first we've been destined to encounter. Perhaps a second is about to follow."

"Perhaps," Sir Richard said as Armand nodded. "Perhaps."

Chapter 19

It had been three days since Michelle telegraphed Grayson following the bombings in New Mills, but by Monday, she had received no reply. There were any number of reasons why he might not have answered, but her mind always went to the worst. Although New Mills celebrated when they learned that the German bombers had been shot down on Friday evening after dropping their last bombs on New Mills and Hayfield, that news was small comfort for Michelle. She knew that most of Grayson's work at Kirton in Lindsey kept him on the ground, but she also knew that on any given day, he might be called into the air in a Spitfire or a Hurricane, ready to meet whatever aircraft the Luftwaffe sent. Like all the airmen with whom he served, his life was always in peril, whether in the air or on the ground.

By Tuesday, Michelle was nearly frantic. Although some local telephone service had been interrupted by the bombings, the telegraph office assured her that her message had been sent and delivered. Thankfully, a telephone call from the train depot in New Mills later that afternoon settled her fears. Nancy called her to the telephone shortly after noon.

"It's Grayson, Michelle," Nancy called up the stairs. "He's here at the train station. I'm driving to collect him. Quick now. He wants to hear your voice!"

"With Logan in her arms, Michelle hurried down the stairs to the telephone in the front entry. Shifting Logan to her left arm as she sat at the telephone chair, she was finally able to say, "Grayson, Grayson, where have you been? Please tell me that you are well and whole."

"Michelle, love, I'm here, and I'll have you in my arms as fast as Nancy can drive us home," he said.

"You've avoided my question," she said, "and you are worrying me. Could you please tell me? Are you well? Are you injured? I must know."

"They tell me I'll be completely healed and ready to return to service in a week or two," he said. "The surgery was successful, and the doctors want me to rest and heal. Their only concern is avoiding infection."

"Surgery?" Michelle cried. "What kind of surgery?"

"They needed to remove a small piece of shrapnel from my leg. I was very fortunate. The bullets missed me, but I ended up with a small piece of my own plane in my leg. Not to worry, Darling," he said, adding, "Nancy just arrived. I'll see you in minutes."

Michelle, Logan, and Grayson's mother were all waiting at the front entry when Nancy stopped the car at the base of the front steps. When she rushed around the car to open Grayson's door, Michelle started down the steps while fighting away her tears.

Grayson pushed a cane out of the car and slowly extended it to the pavement. His right arm was bandaged, and there was another bandage on the right side of his face. Beyond the bandage, his skin was red and swollen.

"There's the love of my life and my sweet boy!" he said, laughing. "And Mother," he added, "another sight for sore eyes."

Nancy helped Grayson keep his balance, holding his left elbow. As he mounted the first steps, Michelle passed Logan to his grandmother and rushed to take Grayson's arm while Nancy carried his bag from the car. After Michelle settled Grayson in the parlor and collected Logan, Nancy returned the vehicle to the garage, while Mildred went to the kitchen to put the kettle on for tea.

Michelle did her best, but she could not restrain her tears. Clinging to Grayson's left arm with Logan on her lap, she said, "Tell me everything."

Grayson began, "We were on the coast, two of our Polish aces and me, the same boys who brought down those JU 88s on Friday. They're the best, Michelle, gifted and given, and so talented. Anyway, we came upon six Messerschmitts on Saturday, all trying to get home. Each of us got one, but we were getting low on ammunition and facing three more. I dove to lead two of the Jerrys out of formation while our boys took out the other one. By then, though, the last two were on my tail, and I couldn't evade their fire. I went into a vertical spiral, though, just as I had taught those Polish flyboys behind me. The Messerschmitts can't match a Spitfire's speed in a maneuver like that, and as the Jerries tried to follow, our boys blew them both out of the sky."

"But how were you injured?" Michelle asked.

"Oh, sorry," he said. "I was a split-second or so late going into the spiral, and my plane took several hits from their machine guns. We got back to Kirton in Lindsey intact, but I had faced a bit of fire in the cockpit, too."

"Faced?" Michelle asked as she gently pointed at the bandage on his arm and the other on his face.

"Sorry," he said with a wrinkled smile, "not as humorous as I hoped it would be, I suppose."

Michelle couldn't resist his smile, but neither could she help shaking her head and rolling her eyes. She stretched past his bandage to plant a tender kiss on his lips and said, "Please tell me you have a week's leave to be here at home while you heal."

"I'm sorry, my darling, I don't. I asked for a week, but…" he said.

"But, what?" she asked.

"They insisted on two," he said, but the smile that followed turned to a grimace as he reached toward the bandage on his cheek. "Still a bit tender, I'm afraid, but sure to heal, they promise. No worse than a sunburn at the shore."

"Well," Michelle began, "if my kisses or regular applications of your son's soft cheek on yours will help, we'll have you healed in no time."

"As I remember, those were precisely the doctor's orders," Grayson said, while his accompanying smile brought another grimace of pain.

"Let's get you upstairs," Michelle said. "I want to have a look at that leg wound, too."

"I'm all yours," he said with a twinkle in his eye, "but remember, turnabout is fair play. I'll show you mine, if you'll show me…"

With another roll of her eyes, Michelle helped him stand as they headed toward the stairs. Her husband might be wounded, but he certainly wasn't out of the game - at least not yet.

Chapter 20

"We need your help, Susan," Michael said in a tone she rarely heard him use. It was serious, but nothing in it sounded a note of danger in her ears. But the "we" he used had her wondering.

"We?" she asked.

"Yes, your father, Armand, SIS, and I need your help," he said.

"Tell me more," she said, as she relaxed on the settee in the west sunroom.

"I know you'll remember the name, 'Brenda Kimble,' Ernest Duncan's partner in crime," he said, as he joined her on the settee.

"Of course," Susan answered, "As I remember, she remains incarcerated in Halifax."

"That's part of the reason we need your help. You see, she escaped weeks ago," Michael began, "and we've found that during that time she has become a frequent late-night visitor at the fire tower."

"Our fire tower?" Susan asked, surprised.

"Yes," he said, "she's found her way past the padlock on the door and has been using the radio to communicate with German contacts known to her. She must have learned about the radio room in the tower when she was here as a guest at Michelle and Grayson's wedding reception. We believe she's still working with the agents that Duncan abandoned after his escape some time ago."

"But he came over to our side, didn't he?" she asked.

"Yes, and he's become an increasingly valuable asset to the Allies in the last six months or so," Michael answered.

"So, you believe the relationship between the two, whatever it was, has ended?" she asked.

"That's correct," he answered, "and that's where you come in."

"I don't understand," she said, shaking her head. "What can a mother of two who's expecting a third do about a spy in the fire tower?"

"The same thing we did to help turn E.D. – that's what we call Ernest Duncan now – against the Nazi cause and join us," Michael said. "Talk to her, Susan. Just talk to her."

"There must be more," she said. "It can't be as simple as that. Help me to understand what you're thinking."

"E.D. was an injured soul, a survivor of years of abuse in his family home. He found a second home among the Nazis. When I visited him at the jail in Halifax, he told me about Brenda's background, too," Michael said.

"And did she endure the same kind of horrors that E.D. knew as a child?" Susan asked.

"No," he answered. "The abuse didn't come from within her family, but from Canadians who resented her family's German heritage, especially her father's."

"Why her father?" Susan asked.

"Her father commanded a German U-boat in World War I. Your father knew him as an enemy at sea first, but later as a man of honor. He was one of the few U-boat captains who rescued British sailors and civilian passengers at sea. He was able to take some aboard and ferry others to shore. On other occasions, he radioed shore stations and offered rescue coordinates. He was not a heartless, evil enemy like so many others."

"So, Father admired him?" Susan asked, nodding.

"Yes," Michael said, "but he was captured early in the war and remanded to a POW camp in Ottawa. Because his grandparents had emigrated to Canada many years before, he decided to stay here in their community when he was released from detention."

"So, Brenda was born in Canada?" Susan asked.

"Yes. Sadly, however, German populations in Canada, even though they may have emigrated here decades and decades earlier, were treated poorly during the war and for many years after the war ended," he explained.

"Abused?" she asked.

"Too often," Michael answered, "and they weren't victims of only prejudice and discrimination, but also of violence. Many had their bank accounts and property confiscated and were forced to abandon their homes and move to internment camps. There, they faced forced labor and brutal treatment. Young girls like Brenda, separated from their families, were often in the most danger."

"That sounds horrible, Michael," Susan said.

"Yes, and for Brenda's father, a former German naval officer living in a country that had given so many young men to the war, he would always be seen as the enemy," Michael said. "And then came Nazi Germany and 1939."

"And Brenda and her family faced a second wave of mistreatment?" Susan asked.

"Exactly," Michael said, "and that's when she determined to join E.D."

"So, where do I come in?" she asked.

"We plan to confront her soon," Michael said. "We have been monitoring when she arrives at the tower, and Armand can trace exactly when the radio is engaged. Once she is in the cab and busy on the radio, she will not hear us climbing up behind her. With no other exit, she becomes our prisoner. When she completes her radio transmission, I'll announce our presence on the stairs and try to talk her down. We don't believe she will want to listen to any of us men, and we don't want her to consider jumping. That's where a woman's voice might be the answer."

"A very pregnant woman's voice?" Susan asked.

"Even better," Michael said. "Her mother would have been the last person she saw before Brenda fled from Ontario at the age of sixteen. A woman and mother like you will pose less of a threat to her than any man. We need her to give herself up, not to SIS officers or police, but to a woman who can reach her as only a mother can."

After only a minute, Susan said, "I'll need some help getting up all those stairs. I can't remember climbing them since the day you proposed to me. I haven't forgotten that long climb."

"I'll be with you all the way," Michael said, "from your first step up to your final step down."

Chapter 21

It was shortly after nine o'clock on a Saturday evening in the first week of August. The sun had set, and the stars were just coming out when Patrice found Susan in the kitchen at Highfield. She was making a cup of chamomile tea before bed. With two teacups now, the ladies sat together at the kitchen table. Patrice was full of conversation.

"Luc has been spending some time each day with the joiner carpenters who are building the kitchen cabinets at your new house," Patrice said. "They're not the carpenters who built the walls and floors and roof, you know. Now that the double crews have finished and gone home, the cottages are empty once again. The joiners have brought a whole shop of equipment into the house, and they are very particular about the quality of their work," Patrice said. "It's like furniture."

"Yes," Susan agreed. "Michael has been very impressed with their work, too, especially on the staircases."

"Well," Patrice continued excitedly, "while Luc has been working there, he has had a chance to meet Hugh. They seem to have hit it off right from the start. When they finished talking today, Hugh told me that Luc and Lois have plans to see a movie in Charlottetown tomorrow night. Then he told me that Luc had invited Hugh and me to join them. Can you believe it?" Patrice beamed. "My first real date!"

"That is very exciting," Susan agreed, "but what do your mother and Jacques think of the idea?"

"Oh, Luc and Hugh stopped by to meet Mom and Jacques right after they finished work today. Luc introduced Hugh, and he asked permission to invite me to go to the movies with him. Of course, they said, 'Yes,' especially because Luc and Lois would be with us. Oh, I almost forgot to tell you the movie is called 'Song of the Islands' and stars Betty Grable and Victor Mature. Mom *loves* Victor Mature."

"But now comes the big question," Susan said.

"I know," Patrice agreed. "What am I going to wear?"

"Yes," Susan answered, "and I have a couple of ideas."

Before Susan could share her thoughts, though, Michael appeared, thundering hurriedly down the back staircase to the kitchen.

"Susan," he said as he glanced toward Patrice and nodded, "I have a couple of last-minute things to do, and I could use your company if Patrice could listen for the boys for a little while."

"Oh, I'd be glad to stay," Patrice said, "and then you can tell me what you were thinking when you get back, Miss Susan, right?"

"Of course," Susan agreed, "but while I'm gone, think in terms of your favorite colors, the ones you see when you look in your flower beds. Staying seasonal is important. We'll start there, OK? I'm sure I'll have some accessories to offer."

"Super!" Patrice said as she headed for the boys' room upstairs, "Super!"

Once Patrice was out of earshot, Michael said, "She's there now. The buzzer sounded beside my bed. I called Armand, and he was already monitoring the radio signals coming from the tower. He was just about to call me when I rang him. We need to get there as soon as possible. Do you feel up to the challenge?"

"I took a good nap this afternoon, and I woke up refreshed. I'm still a bit nervous, but I'm ready to give it my best," she said.

"Smashing!" Michael said. "Then let's get you a sweater and your most comfortable shoes. We'll need to walk as quickly as is comfortable for you," Michael said. "I'll need a minute to put fresh batteries in our torches, collect a blanket, and find a stout carrot."

"A stout carrot?" Susan asked. "Whatever for?"

"You'll see," Michael said as he hurried away.

The remaining light in the early night sky made their walk through the pasture easy, but once under the cover of the trees that lined the North Path, their torches guided them. Although the distance to the tower seemed longer than usual in the darkness, Michael suddenly pointed and whispered, "We're only about fifty yards away now. Can you see the glow in the cab at the top of the tower?"

Susan followed Michael's finger as he pulled a low-hanging branch from in front of her eyes. There it was – the tower, clearly lit with a warm glow at the top.

"Listen carefully," he said. "Do you hear the sound of the generator motor?"

Taking a moment to attend to the sound, Susan answered, "Yes, I hear it."

"When that sound ceases, and when you see my light signaling you, begin walking toward the tower steps while I come to meet you."

"All right," Susan answered.

"Oh," Michael added, "and keep your torch pointed toward the ground where she won't be able to follow it as easily from the cab, all right?"

"Yes," Susan answered. "And your carrot?"

"More about that when we have you at the top of the stairs," he said as he turned and faded into the darkness.

Though it felt like hours to Susan, in a short time, she heard the low generator roar cease and watched the light in the tower fade away. After another minute, Susan saw Michael's signal, took a deep breath, turned her torch toward the path in front of her, and ventured toward the tower. Michael met her a few steps later and guided her to the bottom of the stairs.

"I've spoken with her briefly," Michael said. "Surprisingly, I felt no belligerence from her in our conversation. She was armed, but she ceded her pistol to me without delay. It's strange, Susan. It wasn't loaded. From what she intimated, she'd never learned to fire a gun. It seems she carried it only to warn potential attackers off."

"I see," Susan nodded.

"She's assured me she has no other weapons," he said. "Now, once we're at the top of the stairs, I'll tell her how to start the generator again so that she's not sitting in darkness. I'll introduce you, but you'll be speaking through a crack in the door. I've tied it nearly closed so you can speak with her, but she won't be able to escape or reach you. Remember, I won't leave you alone, not for a second."

"All right," Susan answered. "I'm ready."

It was nearly a ten-minute climb that Susan had done in less than five minutes in the past. When they reached the last few steps from the top, Michael made a cushion for her from the blanket under his arm. Then he said, "Shine your light over here," pointing to a spot under the cab floor.

Her light landed on a short pipe protruding through the floor. Squinting, she could make out the shape of a carrot stuffed into the end of the pipe. Michael reached over and pulled it out in a single motion.

"That's the gasoline generator's exhaust pipe," he said. "I stuffed the carrot in it so that the engine would stall. When everything grew dark and she heard my voice, I had her full attention. I'll tell her she can restart the generator now, and once she has light again, I'll introduce you, whenever you feel ready."

"All right," Susan said, her tone revealing her nervousness.

"Please don't worry, Darling. You can't do anything wrong. Take one step at a time. Just by being yourself, I'm convinced you'll win her over. I sense she wants to tell her story, and I believe you will be one person she'll be able to trust."

Susan said no more but nodded in agreement.

Michael raised his head to the cab door above and pushed it up, his rope below allowing the door to rise until there was a one-inch crack.

"Miss Kimble," he called, "it's Michael Moreland again."

"Yes," came a tentative voice from within.

"You may restart the generator now so that you will have light. I hold you to your promise not to use the receiver or transmitter any further. May I trust that you will comply with my request?" he asked.

"Yes," she answered.

"Thank you," he said.

When the generator motor roared to life, light poured out through the crack in the door. Michael raised his voice to speak over the engine noise.

"Thank you for cooperating," he said. "My wife, Susan, would like to talk with you now. She has some thoughts for your future, plans for your freedom that we hope you will consider. The cab door will remain secured from this side during your conversation, but we hope to be able to open it fully when your talk is over. Does that sound all right to you?" he asked.

"Yes," came the voice from within.

"Thank you," he said. "The next voice you hear will be Susan's."

Michael retreated far enough to help Susan toward the cab door and arranged his folded blanket for her cushion. Once she was in place, Susan said, "Miss Kimble?"

"Yes, Mrs. Moreland, but please call me Brenda," she answered.

"Of course, Brenda," Susan said, "but only if you will call me Susan."

"Yes, Susan. Thank you," she answered.

Michael moved a few steps down the stairway, giving Susan room to stretch her legs on the narrow passage. Michael could make out only brief parts of Susan's half of the conversation over the generator's drone. What seemed like an hour was only about thirty minutes. When Susan shone her light in his direction, he joined her again at the top of the stairs. In the light of her torch, Michael recognized her weary smile as she dabbed at her wet eyes and wiped her nose with her handkerchief.

"We have an agreement," she said as more tears arrived. "She has accepted our proposal and is ready to come with us. She promised to offer no resistance. As you know, the cottage we have for her at Highfield is ready and waiting."

"Splendid," Michael answered.

"Her story is a sad one," Susan said, her tears appearing again. "I have so, so much to tell you."

Chapter 22

"You're a different one, you are," Kathleen said as she sipped from her tall, icy glass. "So, this drink is called 'Navy Grog,' is it?" she asked.

Sitting across from her at a small round table opposite the bar, Lt Boyd Moncrieff said, "Correct. It's made with three kinds of rum, some sugar, and a bit of citrus. As he tipped his glass, he said, "But what is it that makes me different?"

"For one," she began, "when we were at Gosport, we never enjoyed a club like this." She paused for another sip before continuing, "And none of the other men sailing aboard the HMS *Revenge* has offered to buy me anything but beer. I find beer rather nasty compared to a drink like this."

"I think it's the lime you like," Boyd said, "and here they add something else. I'm guessing some honey and perhaps some grapefruit," he added, taking another sip.

"Whatever it is," she said, "on a hot day like today, it's a wonderful thirst quencher."

"But now you have me wondering, Miss Balfour," Boyd said, glancing around the dining room at the *Nelson*, a night spot popular with British naval officers in Mombasa.

"Wondering what?" she asked.

"Just who are these other officers who have offered a lady like you nothing but beer to drink?" he asked.

"Who said they were officers, Lt Moncrieff?" she asked with a coy smile as she glanced toward the street. "We Wrens seem to attract sailors from every rank, you know."

"Then I'll consider myself well advised to queue up well in advance of the coming weekend, Leading Wren Balfour," he said, "for it would pain me to lose your company to any sailor limited to offering a lady of your quality nought but beer."

"Then perhaps we should coordinate our schedules now," she offered, reaching into her purse for her steno pad.

"Match our schedules so that I won't have to lose moments like this to some beer-swilling sailor?" Boyd asked.

Kathleen's smile widened as Boyd produced an appointment book from his breast pocket.

"Affirmative, Lt Moncrieff," she smiled. "My thoughts exactly."

Her mock 'playing hard-to-get' attitude had them both laughing as they put their pens away to join hands across the table. Truth to tell, they met almost every weekend at the *Nelson* to compare schedules and find every moment they could spend together. Boyd never knew when the *Revenge* would be called to sea or how long he might be away from Mombasa. Everything depended on the enemy, and they were not a dependable entity. Kathleen's orders were less likely to fluctuate, but even though it was unlikely she'd soon be posted away from Mombasa, she didn't want to miss a moment with Boyd while he was here.

Just then, the band began to play "Sleepy Lagoon", a waltz the couple couldn't resist. Once on the floor and in each other's arms, Boyd whispered, "I need something, Kathleen, something only you can give me, no one but you." Then he drew her even closer to him and breathed in the perfume she had dabbed behind her left ear.

Unsure of what Boyd meant, Kathleen's eyes widened. But, knowing him well enough to wait to discover what he intended, she asked, "And what could that possibly be?"

Slowly, he leaned back far enough to whisper in her ear, "A photo, of course. We can stop at the photographer's shop down the street. Actually, I'll need several. There'll be one for me and three others – one for my parents, one for my brother, and one for my sister. I hope that's not too much to ask?"

Melting back into his arms, she asked, "And you don't think it might be too early in our relationship for us to produce something that appears, how shall I say, that *promising*?"

Boyd responded immediately, "No, Kathleen, I don't. My urgency stems from the fear that I might be too early, but I dare not be too late. I can't risk letting another win you and take you away from me. I can't lose you to another, Kathleen, I can't. So, I'll dare to ask even more. Allow me to engage the photographer to take several photos of us as a couple, as well. If I go out to sea, I'll need to remember us together,"

Kathleen didn't know what to think. She knew only that she'd never encountered a man like Boyd. Since they'd met in a classroom in Gosport, she hadn't been able to keep him out of her thoughts. Months had passed before they saw each other a second time, but it seemed to her that they'd never been apart. Often, he knew her thoughts before she spoke, and she was usually able to anticipate his. "Were we made for each other?" she asked herself. Everything in her said, "Yes. Yes, we were made for each other!" But, at that very moment, her next thought offered a contradiction. Shaking her head, she said, "No, we *were not* made for each other. And why not? Because we *are* made for each other. There will never be another like him."

After making Boyd wait for a moment that seemed an eon to him, she offered a response to his appeal.

"In response to your request, Lt Boyd Moncrieff," she said, "I will answer with a request of my own."

Afraid she might have found his appeal out of place and too early in their relationship, Boyd hung his head before looking up to ask, "And what would that be, Leading Wren Balfour?"

"I would request that you ask the photographer to take single photos not only of me, but of you as well, for I will need several to send to *my* family," she said, smiling up at him.

The terror in Boyd's eyes relaxed into joy as he lifted her off her feet to kiss her, a kiss she returned with equal abandon.

Chapter 23

Michael held the Astra 300 pistol in his hand and released the magazine, inserting and releasing it as he spoke.

"This gun was made in Spain, Susan," he said, "I recognize it from my training with SIS. Thousands were sold to both Russia and Germany in the last twenty years or so. I'm sure E.D. must have given it to Brenda."

"And after hearing some of her story, I think your conclusion at the tower was correct. She kept it to warn off potential attackers," Susan said. "She had learned from experience and had good reason to depend on it."

"So, her past is dark?" he asked.

"Painfully so," Susan answered, "and all because her family has German roots. Some of her ancestors emigrated to Canada many decades ago and lived in peace here for generations. During and after World War I, though, thousands of Canadians of German extraction found themselves remanded to internment camps, working in forced labor projects, and separated from their families. Her father came to Canada as a POW during the last two years of World War I. Not wanting to return to Germany, he settled in Ontario upon his release. That's where Brenda was born."

"When she was originally apprehended and jailed in Halifax," Michael said, "your father had SIS complete some research on her family. He discovered that her father had served as a captain of a German U-boat in World War I. Unlike most others, though, he was remembered as an honorable man. He faithfully followed the "prize rules" of the time, first stopping and searching a targeted ship before either taking the ship's crew onto his U-boat or conducting the ship to a safe port. He saw to the rescue of dozens of British sailors and civilians whose ships his torpedoes sank. On more than one occasion, he allowed crews of shipping vessels to lower their lifeboats and abandon their ship. Only then did he fire on the empty vessels."

"Sadly," Susan said, "it seems that noble history never profited him or his family when the current war began. Like many others, Brenda's family had to register as enemy aliens, losing their civil rights and much of their freedom. In their small town, their family and even their church were targeted by hatred. In time, Brenda and her two younger brothers were no longer safe walking to school. Later, their home was vandalized, their windows broken, and their barn set on fire."

"Was that the worst of it?" Michael asked.

"No," she said, "that was only the beginning. Her father was taken to an internment camp in Manitoba, hundreds of miles away. That left the rest of the family an easy target for some of the locals."

"How bad was it?" Michael asked.

"Without their father, the family was reduced to utter poverty. While fishing in a nearby pond to help feed the family, her two younger brothers were attacked by a gang of six young men. They were lucky to survive the beating they received," Susan said. "But after that, two from the gang came for Brenda."

"And?" Michael asked.

Susan looked away for a moment before turning back with tears in her eyes.

"The worst, Michael. The worst," she whispered, hanging her head.

Michael waited a quiet moment until Susan could speak again.

"She was fifteen years old, Michael. Her brothers were twelve and thirteen. Who knows how much more they endured? I learned all this after only twenty minutes with her tonight," she said. "I'm sure she has so much more to tell."

Michael wrapped his arms around his wife as she leaned into his chest, her cheek against his heart.

"You've done so much for her tonight, Susan," he said. "She needed someone to listen, someone with nothing to gain, with no ulterior motive. She found someone she could trust, she let down her guard, and let her walls of protection collapse."

"You're confident she won't run away as soon as she feels we're not looking?" she asked.

"She could," Michael said, a hint of doubt in his voice, "but where would she go? Her radio contacts here have no names, no addresses, and nothing to offer her. I have a feeling that she craves the safety and comfort of family. By listening to her story, you offered her that tonight."

"And now she's in a cozy cottage with a warm bed, a wardrobe of clean clothes, and all she could want to eat. Still, I'm sure her head is spinning with doubts about her future," Susan said.

"Perhaps," Michael answered, "but we also left her with an unlocked door. That alone will be a miraculous change for her. She's been a prisoner of sorts ever since her family was labelled as enemy aliens in Ontario. Her brothers were beaten, she was abused, and her family was split up and sent away. Here, however, she doesn't have to remain a prisoner any longer."

"Interesting," Susan said, still in Michael's arms. "E.D., another injured soul, found her in Ottawa. He used her to help him maintain his cover, I assume, but then it seems he abandoned her."

"It seems," Michael said, "but he had few options to help her when he escaped. Remember, too, relationships come hard to people with injuries like his, and she needs healing of her own. Hopefully, she'll find reasons to respect herself so that she won't need to give herself away like that again."

"Perhaps," Susan said, looking up at Michael, "so we can't let her down. She needs every reason to keep trusting us. I set a nine o'clock breakfast date with her in her cottage. I'll be there spot on time. I'll pray she'll still be there when I arrive."

"Until then," Michael said as he turned her around in his arms, bringing her back to rest against his chest, and placed one hand softly on her bulging abdomen, "you and ours, she or he, need rest now. I'm on my way to the kitchen for your chamomile tea. I'll deliver it to your nightstand in a jiffy."

And he did, but he was too late. When he placed the cup and saucer on her nightstand, her head was already snuggled deep into her pillow, and every breath she took told him she was enjoying the soothing sleep of the just.

Chapter 24

Lois was nearly beside herself. Patrice had chosen to wear her lacy peach frock for her date with Hugh, but an instant later she exchanged it for her light blue embroidered dress. Another moment passed when she left both behind for her red jumper and her lacy white blouse. Then, just as quickly, she returned to the peach frock. As she held it up against herself in front of the mirror again, Lois shook her head and said with a smile, "Patrice, Patrice, it's just an evening at the films, not a proposal of marriage. Please relax. You'll wear yourself out with worry."

"I know," Patrice admitted, "but it's my very first date, and I don't want to disappoint Hugh."

Lois, upon hearing Patrice pronounce "Hugh", felt her eyebrows rise involuntarily. She knew she couldn't let the pronunciation stand.

"Patrice, my dear, if you don't want to disappoint the young man, you will need to pronounce his name correctly," she said.

"What do you mean?" Patrice asked. "It's a simple, one-syllable name. *Hugh*," she repeated.

Wincing, Lois responded, "Ouch!"

"What's wrong?" Patrice asked.

"You're naming a letter of the alphabet, my dear girl. His name is not the letter U that is found between T and V. His name begins with the consonant 'H,' which must be respected. Listen carefully as I say his name."

Patrice scowled as she leaned in to hear Lois pronounce, "Hugh".

Shaking her head, Patrice said, "I don't understand. What's the difference between 'Hugh' the way you say it and 'Hugh' the way I say it?"

"It's the H," Lois said. "It's part of the word. Try starting with a gentle 'huh' and then adding 'you.'"

Patrice gave it a try, saying, "huh-you," "huh-you," "huh-you."

"You're getting there, Patrice, but now shorten your 'huh' until it almost disappears. 'Hugh,'" Lois said.

After a few more tries, Patrice began to make some progress and eventually made her two syllables into one smooth word, "Hugh."

Relaxing her shoulders from their nervous posture close to her ears, Patrice was able to offer her gratitude.

"Lois, I couldn't even hear the difference at first! Thank you! I can't imagine mispronouncing his name for an entire evening. You've saved my life!" she said as she hugged Lois around the neck.

Lois had to laugh. "Well, now that you can pronounce his name, maybe I can tell you a few other things that will help you win a man," she grinned.

With wide eyes, Patrice looked directly at Lois, intertwined her fingers, and drew her clasped hands close to her heart. In her most serious tone, she said, "You must tell me everything, Lois. *Everything*."

Again, Lois had to laugh. "All in good time, Patrice. For tonight, here's one piece of advice. Laugh at his jokes. A man loves a woman who finds his sense of humor amusing. However, be careful not to overdo it."

"I've got it, Lois," Patrice said seriously. "Laugh, but don't overdo it."

Elsewhere, while the ladies were busy preparing for the evening, Luc had just picked Hugh up for the drive to the Boucher home. Hugh was carrying two white roses in his hand.

"So, this is the new automobile you told me about yesterday?" Hugh asked as he got into the front seat.

"That's right," Luc said, "new to me, at least. It's six years old now, but it was new in 1936. It's a Ford Model 48 slant-back coupe."

"We don't have Fords like this in Scotland. They're a different breed there, much smaller, you know," Hugh said.

"So I understand," Luc said. "What make does your family drive?"

"Father favors a Bentley, but they are so large that most drivers have difficulty negotiating our narrow roads in them. Your roads, especially your highways, are much wider than ours in Scotland. The Bentley would do better here, but it does have one advantage lacking in every Canadian car I've seen, though."

"What's that?" Luc asked.

"The Bentleys are equipped with lovely small bud vases at the front and rear seats where a man can place roses like these in a swallow of water to preserve them. I'm afraid mine may be wilted before I can present them."

"Then I shall have to accelerate to get us there as soon as possible," Luc said as he downshifted the Ford. "We can't let a gentleman arrive with wilted roses!"

Minutes later, the two were parked at the Boucher house, where the ladies waited within. After Doris and Jacques greeted Luc and Hugh at the door, Hugh presented his first rose to Doris and, bowing to her nod, presented the second to Patrice, who received his offering and managed an unpracticed curtsy. Her smile, however, could hardly have beamed brighter.

As the first to approach Luc's car, Hugh opened the door on the passenger side and, offering his hand, helped Patrice into the back seat. Following her immediately, he sat close beside her and again offered his hand, clasping hers warmly within. For Hugh, it was customary for a gentleman to help a lady feel secure by holding her hand when riding in an automobile. For Patrice, however, having her hand in his grip raised a modest blush to her cheeks and served to increase her heart rate.

The newsreels that preceded the feature film, "Song of the Islands," reported weeks-old news of the air and sea war in the Pacific. Thankfully for Luke, there were no scenes of ground fighting that might have retrieved difficult memories for him. The movie, though entertaining, remained far from the realities of life on Prince Edward Island in 1942, perhaps just what two young couples needed for entertainment on a summer night.

When they left the theater, Hugh insisted on buying ice cream cones for both couples at a nearby shop on Grafton Street.

"You've provided the transportation, my good man," Hugh said to Luc. "The very least that I can do is to provide the sweets, although, by some divine favor, we seem to have arranged for the sweetest of the sweets to accompany us tonight!"

With that, Patrice found her opportunity to laugh and caught Lois's eye as she added a wink of approval.

During the drive home, Hugh held Patrice's hand once again, but a few minutes into the drive, she managed to loosen her fingers from his grasp to intertwine them with his. Though a bit confused at first, when his eyes met hers, Hugh seemed to understand, and he squeezed her hand just enough to tell her so. Though uncharacteristic for her, Patrice kept her smile quietly within.

Luc took a long route home, driving toward the northern extreme of the island before turning south on Suffolk Road. As they drove, Hugh talked about the things he missed in Scotland.

"What I miss most is my dog, Angus. We were constant companions, you know," he said.

"Is he a hunting breed?" Luc asked.

"Oh, my, yes," Hugh replied. "He's a Gordon Setter, with an admirable nose. He leads me to the birds every time we hunt. We've never come home empty."

"Our dog, Duchess, is a red setter," Patrice offered, "but right now she's too busy raising a litter of pups to hunt."

"But Simon, a Springer Spaniel and the pups' sire," Luc began, "is trained to the gun. Mr. Moreland is usually too busy to hunt him these days. Though we're not in bird season right now, he might welcome someone with the time to get Simon out for a run, now and again."

"Ah, yes," Hugh said, "but I'd surely need a guide, I would."

"Patrice knows the fields, the trails, and the ponds as well as anyone," Luc offered.

Hugh turned to Patrice to say, "Do you have ponds for fishing here as well?"

"Of course," Patrice answered. "I can guarantee that you will catch two good-sized bass after a short paddle across Out and Back Pond."

"Paddle, did you say?" Hugh asked.

"Yes," Patrice answered, "in the canoe."

There was a moment of silence in the car before Hugh said, "We canoed and fished regularly at home, and, in season, we hunted just as often. I don't mean to be forward, but if I weren't taking advantage of your hospitality, would there be a convenient time when I might be able to stretch my limbs, follow a dog on scent, and get my feet wet in one of your ponds while fishing sometime soon?" Hugh asked.

"I think we could arrange that," Luc smiled as he caught Patrice's eyes smiling back at him in the rearview mirror. "I'm tied up for most of the weekend, but I'll wager that Lois and Patrice could find an hour or two to orient you to the estate, show you some of the trails, and introduce you to the pond. Would tomorrow afternoon be available, ladies? What do you think?"

Lois nodded and turned to Hugh to say, "I'm free tomorrow afternoon after one o'clock. That would give us several hours until our evening meal. How about you, Patrice?"

Trying to contain her smile, Patrice answered coyly, "I wouldn't be free until about one thirty or so, but after that, I'm game."

"Then, let the games begin," Hugh smiled as he squeezed Patrice's hand. "I'll do nothing all night but anticipate the afternoon tomorrow."

Chapter 25

The late-summer sun rose early, and it was already high in the sky on a Tuesday morning in August when Susan greeted Lois in the east sun-room at Highfield. Lois, quiet by nature, rarely asked to talk with Susan, but when she did, Susan was happy to find time to listen. As one would expect, Susan had a fresh pot of tea and a plate of scones waiting on the tea table.

"Thank you, Mrs. Moreland, for making the time to talk with me this morning," Lois began, "because I have some excellent news to report from London."

"I'm always happy to hear good news," Susan began, "and if it's from London, I hope it concerns your family."

"It does," Lois said, smiling, "it does. The last time we talked, I had very little hopeful news concerning my sister, Biddy, and my brother, Wilfred."

"Yes, I remember," Susan said. "You were very concerned and quite understandably overwrought. Tuberculosis, especially when it concerns children, is, after all, one of the most impossible burdens a family can bear."

"And that's where the good news comes in," Lois said as she retrieved a letter from her shoulder bag. "I received this letter from my mother just yesterday morning. It seems a most unexpected and wonderful gift arrived at her flat by post some weeks ago. You know how long it takes for letters to cross the ocean these days."

"I understand," Susan said, "but tell me what you have there. I can't bear to wait another moment."

"It's a letter from a solicitor's office in London. In short," Lois began, "an anonymous benefactor has provided funds for Biddy and Wilfred's care at Stannington Sanatorium in Northumberland. They specialize in caring for children with tuberculosis at Stannington, and what's more, the funds also provide for housing and all my mother's needs at a privately-owned flat nearby."

As Lois handed Susan the letter, Susan was overcome. "Lois," she said, "Stannington is the first sanatorium in England to be built specifically to treat children. There is no better treatment facility anywhere in the world."

"So I understand, Mrs. Moreland," Lois said, "and the second remarkable benefit of this gift is that my family will no longer be forced to live in fear of the bombing in London. I can hardly believe our good fortune."

Susan took a moment to look at the papers in her hand as Lois said, "The solicitor evidently knew that I was away from home, and he provided a second copy of all the details for my mother to send me. Isn't it remarkable?" she asked.

Thankfully, the solicitor had also provided a clear and concise explanation of the conditions of the bequest, summarized in layman's terms. As Susan and Lois read every word and celebrated over their tea, Susan mused for a moment and tucked something away in her memory. Something she saw in the solicitor's letter waited for her consideration at another time. Their conversation turned to more local matters.

"So," Susan said, "I haven't heard from Patrice yet about her date with Hugh. As her chaperone of choice, what can you tell me?"

"I'll never be able to describe the evening in the wide-eyed way that Patrice would," Lois laughed, "so I will let her fill you in on the details. However, what I can tell you is that Luc and I have no concerns about Hugh. He is a fine young gentleman, not only polite, but also caring, and very kind."

That afternoon, Susan and Michael shared a few quiet moments before dinner, a rare occasion for them. The boys were with Sir Richard in the west sunroom, playing while the shadows of the day began to grow longer. While Michael and Susan enjoyed the quiet of the east sunroom, Susan filled Michael in on her conversation with Lois.

"I can only guess at her mother's relief and joy," Michael said. "How helpless a parent is when a child is ill, and to have two children in such dire need is a burden I cannot fathom. Now, no longer helpless, she must be elated."

"Lois certainly is," Susan began. "She has suffered with a certain degree of guilt at being the only family member to escape the London bombings and to retain her good health. Remember, tuberculosis took her father some time ago."

"Yes, I remember that now," Michael said. "But..."

"But?" Susan asked.

"I see that something else is floating about in your mind, Mrs. Moreland," he smiled. "Care to share it?"

"It's probably just a coincidence," she said.

"What kind of coincidence?" he asked.

"Well, I recognized the solicitor's letterhead," she said.

"And?" Michael asked.

"It's the same firm that is handling Joseph's inheritance," she said quietly.

"And you wonder if Joseph could be responsible for…" he said without finishing his thought.

"Yes, I do," she answered.

The two were quiet for a moment before Michael spoke.

"I would not be surprised," he smiled. "After all, when Luc marries Lois in the fall, she will become a true family member in Joseph's mind and heart. Imagine the blessing for an orphan who has never known parents or siblings, to inherit not only a family, but also an extended family. Then, imagine being penniless one day, and the next to inherit the means to care for your new family's most dire needs. Lois's mother, Biddy, and Wilfred will be precious members of his extended family, treasures for whom he will feel responsible, souls he cannot lose. As financially blessed as he has become during this last year, a heart as big as his will continue to beat, if only to care for every family member in need. He can't help himself. After all, his name is *Joseph*. He will always be a provider and caretaker for his family. He's a remarkably generous young man!"

It took a moment for Susan to respond as she lowered her head and thought back to the day she first met Joseph at the orphanage in Ipswich.

"Who could have known, when he came here as an orphan with only a change of clothes and a family prayerbook, that he would become the wealthy, selfless benefactor that he is today," she said, tears filling her eyes.

"Then let us vow to keep his secret – if it is his secret," Michael said. "Lois may awaken to a suspicion, too. But we can leave that to them. These two couples are building new families that join two continents on the firmest foundation they will ever need. They love each other, and what one has, none of the others will ever lack."

Dabbing her eyes with her handkerchief, Susan said, "Well said, Michael, well said."

Chapter 26

After supper that same night, Michael and Susan took some time in the west sunroom to watch the sun find the horizon. Together they melted into their cushions on the wicker settee and leaned their heads back to relax for the first time all day.

"Thank you for introducing Armand and me to Brenda this morning, Susan," Michael said. "I'm sure it wasn't easy for her to face two relative strangers for an interrogation. She told us you had brought breakfast for the two of you and spent some time in conversation. You did a great deal to ease her fears. It helped our work immensely."

"I could only imagine what she might be thinking and feeling after we discovered her in the tower and brought her home. I wanted her to feel safe and secure. She's spent too much time running and hiding," Susan said.

"And you spoke with her again, after we finished, didn't you?" he asked.

"Yes. I wanted to leave her some more clothes and other necessities and asked if we could have lunch together," she said.

"And after the hour Armand and I spent with her, did she seem fearful or uncomfortable? It's interesting. We didn't have to ask many questions. She seemed free to volunteer more information than we had expected," Michael said.

"I was surprised at how open she was with me, too," Susan answered. "After our lunch, we toured the dairy barn, the henhouse, and the paddock where she met Abe and Billie. After she'd seen the rest of the livestock, we walked through some of the gardens. She's been away from her family farm for so long, she seemed eager to fill her senses with all that feels familiar to her."

"And after that?" Michael asked.

We sorted through the basket of clothes I brought. I wanted to see what might fit her well and what she might like. At the bottom of the basket,

I had included a pair of my riding boots. I thought she might need to wear them for some of her work in the barn. Her eyes lit up when she saw them," Susan said.

"Did her family keep horses?" Michael asked.

"Only one," she answered, "for a short time in Ontario. Of course, I'm not up to riding right now, but tomorrow after breakfast, I'm hoping she and Ingrid can give Abe and Billie some exercise so that she can see the rest of the grounds."

The two sat in silence for a long moment before Susan said, "I know what it is."

Turning his head just slightly toward hers so that he could see her face, Michael asked, "What 'what' is?"

"What I sense Brenda is feeling," she answered.

"Which is?" Michael asked.

"Well, when we surprised her at the tower in the dark of night, she must have felt *captured*," Susan said.

"And now?" he asked.

"Now, I think she's beginning to feel *rescued*," she said thoughtfully.

"Ah," Michael said, and after a brief pause, he continued, "*rescued*. Perhaps she does."

"They sat together in silence for a long moment before Michael spoke.

"Rescued," he repeated. "That reminds me…"

"Reminds you of what?" Susan asked.

"Reminds me that you've had a long day, Mother, and right now I have an opportunity to rescue *you*. I'm going upstairs to get the boys ready for bed so that you can sit here, relax for another few minutes, and enjoy the sunset," he said.

"Oh, you are my hero, Michael Moreland," she smiled.

One kiss later, which, as usual, he stretched into two, and he was gone, leaving Susan to her thoughts. As she leaned farther back into the cushions on the settee, some other parts of her conversation with Brenda came to mind.

"I took the name Kimble when I ran away to Ottawa, because the German name 'Kimmel' could make me a target wherever I went," Brenda said. "But Kimmel wasn't my father's family name. He took it after he was released from the POW camp at the end of the war."

"But why would he exchange one German name for another?" Susan asked.

"He never told me until he was about to be taken away to the internment camp. He wasn't sure he would ever come back, and he wanted me to know about his life before he came to Canada," she said, "especially about his time at sea in the Great War. He made me promise not to tell anyone that he served in that war because of what might happen to us."

"I see," Susan said.

"He was a captain of a U-boat and one of the youngest officers to serve in that capacity. He told me how horrible it was to be at sea for months at a time with fifty other men, only two toilets, no showers, near darkness much of the time, and with the air full of fumes from fuel and exhaust."

"It sounds unbearable, Brenda," Susan said.

"Because a U-boat could travel thousands of miles without refueling, they could be at sea for weeks, even months before making landfall, and much of that time they were submerged in what he described as 'a dimly lit tomb,'" she said.

"Where did he sail?" Susan asked.

"He said his orders kept him following shipping lanes in the Atlantic, from the British Isles to as far away as the Caribbean Sea near the coast of South America," she said. "His targets were almost always cargo ships. He told me that before the end of the war, his was only one of more than three hundred U-boats that Germany launched, with some sailing as far away as the Indian Ocean and the Pacific."

With that, Brenda paused, looked at Susan, and said with tear-filled eyes, "But none of those things mattered. It wasn't where he sailed or how many ships he sank. That didn't matter to him."

"What *did* matter to him?" Susan asked.

"The people on the ships," Brenda answered.

It was a moment before Brenda could go on. When she began again, her voice was softer, and her words carefully chosen.

"He told me that early in the war his orders allowed him to fire a warning round at targeted ships and permit the crew and passengers to lower their lifeboats and escape before he ordered torpedo fire to sink the ship. However," she continued, "those orders soon changed. Warning shots were no longer permitted. He had to send the torpedoes without warning, and those who perished, merchant sailors and civilians alike, were left to the sea."

Both women sat in silence for a long moment before Brenda continued.

"He wept and wept, remembering every order he gave that killed the innocent, all those he watched flailing in the waters that became their grave," she said. "His relief came only when his vessel was finally captured, and he was sent to a POW camp here."

When Brenda fell silent, the women sat for several minutes before Susan spoke.

"And the family name your father exchanged for 'Kimmel'?" Susan asked.

Shaking her head as she looked at the floor, Brenda said, "He never told me." Looking up at Susan, she continued, "He realized that he'd told me more than he intended. His story had simply fallen out of his mouth. I'm not sure he ever told my mother any of it, but for some reason, he shared it all with me."

It was another long moment before Susan spoke.

"Your father knew your heart, Brenda. He knew you cared for people just as he did. He told you his story because he knew you would respect him and treasure his trust."

Brenda paused before nodding and saying, "Perhaps you're right."

After another pause, Brenda shook her head and raised a wry smile.

"You know," she said, "my father's capture from life in a German U-boat in the last war was more like a rescue. He was saved from a life that was killing his soul."

"And your capture, Brenda, in a small, dark cab filled with generator fumes at the top of a tower. Could there be any similarity?" Susan asked.

Chapter 27

It was nearing five o'clock on a warm September afternoon, three days after Michael and Susan retrieved Brenda Kimble from Highfield's fire tower. Michael and Armand had just arrived at Sir Richard's study.

"We spoke with Brenda for a good part of the morning today," Michael said as he and Armand took seats in front of Sir Richard's desk. "She confirmed the intelligence received from SIS two weeks ago. The Abwehr has scheduled the landing of one of their agents sometime in the first two weeks of November, probably not far from Quebec."

"Since we last met to discuss that agent, we've also been able to learn his identity," Sir Richard said. "His name is Werner von Janowski." The Abwehr uses the code name 'Bobbi' for him. To SIS, he's known as 'Watchdog.'"

"Interesting," Armand nodded. "She told us her German contacts have asked her to intercept him upon his arrival and spend several days acquainting him with Canadian manners, customs, and idioms so that he doesn't give himself away."

"Did she also tell you of the other spy who arrived aboard a U-boat in the Bay of Fundy some weeks ago?" asked Sir Richard.

"Yes," Michael said. "She said she was delayed in arriving at the port, and she was not able to meet him. Her assignment was to escort him to Halifax. She hasn't been able to contact him since his arrival."

"We have had further intelligence," Sir Richard said.

"Please, tell us more," Armand asked.

"His name is Alfred Langbein, an Abwehr lieutenant." Sir Richard said. "After sailing from Germany aboard U-213 on April 25, he was expected to arrive during the second week of May. Unaware of how strong and high the tides in the Bay of Fundy were – the highest in the world - U-213's captain had difficulty getting his passenger to shore. He also had to contend with a thick fog and couldn't land until May 12.'

"And after his landing?" Armand asked.

"Langbein found his way to a general store in St. Martin, calling himself Alfred Haskins from Toronto. It appears he was welcomed by some of the locals, who were even kind enough to drive him to his destination in St. John," Sir Richard said.

"And then?" Michael asked.

"Contrary to his orders to travel on to Halifax, it seems he headed for Montreal and hasn't been in contact with the Abwehr since," Sir Richard said. A wry smile appeared on Sir Richard's face as he added, "I have a theory about his disappearance."

Leaning forward, Armand said, "Tell us, please."

"Do you remember, gentlemen, how much money E.D. buried in several locations on our island?" Sir Richard asked.

"The exact value escapes me," Michael answered, "but it was a small fortune."

"Exactly," Sir Richard answered, "and I would wager that Langbein was supplied with a similar amount of cash. His assignment was to infiltrate the docks in Halifax and take up E.D.'s work. I believe Langbein realized the risk that his assignment would pose for him and is now living off the treasure with which he arrived. We'll keep searching for him, of course, but, in the meantime, I believe his danger to us is minimal."

Armand asked, "And what do we know about the next Abwehr agent we expect to land here?"

"We expect him to arrive on U-518 in much the same way as his predecessor," Sir Richard began. "U-518 is scheduled to launch an inflatable raft off the coast near New Carlisle, a village they trust will have a small and unsuspecting population, where he won't raise suspicions. They'll deliver him to shore under the cover of darkness, as they did Langbein. In time, they hope he'll make his way north to Quebec."

"I'm amazed," Michael said. "Brenda has been in contact with German sympathizers here for some time, and yet the detail of SIS intelligence far outweighs hers. How can this be?" he asked.

Sir Richard smiled and leaned back in his chair. "I'm pleased to tell you, Michael, that a good deal of the credit for this intelligence goes to you."

Surprised, Michael asked, "To me? How?"

"Because of our friend, E.D.," Sir Richard answered. "He's found a niche in Switzerland now, you know. The Swiss have eyes and ears in every resistance corner in Europe and beyond, and E.D. has become a trusted friend in each of those corners. Everything I've detailed to you originated in either Bern, Zurich, or Geneva through him."

"Fascinating," Michael said. "So, all we have to do is keep our intelligence up to date and find a way to capture the spies on arrival."

"It's not quite that simple," Sir Richard said, "but that's where we will start. Meanwhile," he said as he opened the bottom drawer of his desk and lifted out a bottle of Dewars, "We owe a long-overdue toast to our partner in the field."

Michael retrieved a tray and three waiting glasses from the side table and delivered them to Sir Richard. A moment later, each man raised his glass as Sir Richard offered a toast.

"To E.D., a man once our enemy, but now a welcome comrade-in-arms. Long may he prosper in our common quest to defeat our foes."

Chapter 28

"So, Hugh," Luc asked, "Even though she's my youngest sister, tell me, what impressions of Patrice remain with you now that you've spent an afternoon with her?"

Luc was surprised at how readily Hugh responded. While his words still hung in the air, Hugh answered, "I think she may have been misnamed."

The two men were working at Hillside, where Luc was busy installing a turntable in the center of the round table in a room labeled "Breakfast Room" on the plans. At the same time, Hugh was happy to check one more job off the list of final joinery tasks yet to be completed.

"Misnamed?" Luc asked. "How so?"

"Well, as you said, we spent the best part of the afternoon together, and we got on quite well, I must say. Of course, we're still new to each other, but although we've spent only an evening at the films and a few hours exploring Highfield, that was enough time to come to the obvious conclusion that your sister was misnamed," Hugh said once more.

"If not 'Patrice,' then what should her name be?" Luc asked.

"I rather think she should have been named Rosalind," Hugh said.

"Rosalind?" Luc asked. "I've never heard the name 'Rosalind' except when I was studying Shakespeare with Mrs. Moreland some years ago. Wasn't that the name of a young woman in one of Shakespeare's plays?"

"Exactly," Hugh said, nodding. "She appeared in 'As You Like It,' a Shakespeare comedy. In the third act, Rosalind says to her friend, Celia, 'Do you not know I am a woman? When I think, I must speak.'"

"Oh-h-h," Luc answered with a smile, "I think I know what you mean now."

"It's not a criticism," Hugh said. "I hope you understand that it's more of, how should I say, an *observation*, a refreshing one, at that. I suppose I'm more acquainted with young ladies in Scotland who rarely express their thoughts on the spot. They tend to rehearse conversations, draw conclusions, and announce them later, usually when one cannot recall the previous conversation, which is sometimes days old. At home, men regularly pain themselves, trying to discover what a young lady is thinking, wearing themselves out playing detective, searching for clues. Not so with Patrice. If one wants to know what that young lady is thinking, one needs only ask."

Luc had to laugh. "Of course, she's my sister, Hugh," Luc said, "so I know her only too well. I can't say I've ever needed to ask what she's thinking, though. She usually spares me that need by announcing it from the start."

Hugh smiled broadly as he nodded in agreement. "Yes, she is very forthright, almost outspoken. However, along with the refreshing open book she presents a fellow, there's also that extra sparkle she carries in her eye that makes a bloke like me wonder what *else* she's thinking."

"Can't help you there, I'm afraid, Hugh," Luc laughed, "because I'm always trying to catch up with a similar sparkle that my Lois carries in *her* eye."

"So, we take our chances, then?" Hugh asked. "We'll never be sure what's going on inside the heads of the fairer sex?"

"Every man since Adam has faced that challenge, my friend. It's easier if you simply get used to waiting until she chooses to announce what's on her mind," Luc laughed. "Just remember, it will generally be more than you anticipated."

With a smile and a nod, Hugh changed the subject. "As I understand it," he began, "you've been with the Moncrieffs here for several years."

"Yes, that's correct, Hugh. My family lived close by for years before Mr. Moreland first arrived. It was almost two years later that Lady Moncrieff and Susan arrived from England," Luc said.

"Then Mr. and Mrs. Moreland weren't yet married?" Hugh asked.

"No, they weren't," Luc laughed, "but it was Patrice who spoke her mind when Mrs. Moreland was still 'Miss Susan' to all of us. Patrice chided Mr. Moreland, insisting that he and Miss Susan were destined to marry. It was embarrassing then, but we still admire her outspoken tenacity now."

"Quite a young lady, that sister of yours, Luc," Hugh mused, "quite a young lady."

"And your tour of Highfield's grounds," Luc asked, "did you see anything that piqued your interest?"

"Numbers and numbers of things," Hugh answered. "Simon was our constant companion, and though we weren't on a hunt, a Springer Spaniel always is."

"Always," Luc laughed.

"And then Patrice showed us the fields where the geese arrive to feed on the corn later in the season," Hugh said. "She spoke of decoys and a rifle with a scope that you use to harvest geese."

"That's right," Luc said. "We never lack for goose on the table in season."

"And then we went to the pond you call Out and Back. Patrice promised me at least two fish before we paddled to the other side of the pond and back, and she was spot on," Hugh said. "You know, Luc, your sister is very competent with a paddle. She insisted that I man the bow so that I could cast accurately while she minded the stern. I've never met a woman so highly skilled with a paddle."

"She's been at it for some time," Luc said, "and she's not one to leave a task unlearned, even if it's a skill a man might expect only of another man."

"You have no fast-moving streams hereby, I understand?" Hugh asked, "No white water?"

"Sadly, no," Luc answered.

"Perhaps if she came to Scotland, I could introduce her to them. There are whole new levels of paddling skills Patrice might master there," Hugh said.

"Uh-huh," Luc said, not lifting his head from his work. He had to smile at this young Scotsman who, after only two outings with Patrice, was already picturing her in a canoe with him in Scotland.

"Of course, we've a war to win, yet," Hugh said, "and prayers to say for those on the battlefield. My father is there, you know, and I understand you've been there as well, Luc."

"Yes, I was," Luc said, "but only briefly. Some early wounds ended my ability to serve and brought me home. I trained and fought beside some noble men who are always in my prayers. I will be happy to add your father to my list tonight."

"Thank you," Hugh said. "Would that I were able to serve myself. A case of asthma since early childhood prevents me from meeting the physical requirements for active service. Father hopes the sea air here will help to heal my lungs. That is another of my prayers. I pray to fulfill my duty to serve our King and country and to disappoint my father no longer."

Luc's heart stung at Hugh's last words, "…disappoint my father no longer." He wondered how long Hugh had borne such a burden. Pursuing the subject with him didn't seem right at the moment, though. "Perhaps Mr. Moreland will have some wisdom for me," he thought. For now, however, he finished with the task at hand, gave the new turntable a gentle spin, and said, "There. What do you think, Hugh?"

Hugh abandoned the sheaf of papers in his hands to spin the turntable himself, adding, "Spot on, Luc. I can already see the tea, sugar, cream, jams, and marmalade, each in its place and only a gentle spin away from every person at the table. Spot on!"

Chapter 29

E.D. awoke to the sunlight creeping past the blackout curtains in the basement windows of the sparse quarters he shared with other resistance operatives on a nondescript alley in Geneva. The blackout curtains hadn't been hung to keep the interior lights from attracting enemy night bombers, as they were used in cities like London. These were designed to discourage the prying eyes of local street and alley denizens from looking *in*. E.D. had arrived in Geneva only last night, having traveled by rail from Zurich after spending the two previous weeks sowing confusion among German occupation forces in France.

The Swiss resistance operated internationally, with people in various locations, including London, The Hague, Brussels, and even Paris. On any given morning in Geneva, E.D. might awake amongst five or six other resistance fighters, all itinerant brothers and sisters-in-arms from resistance cells in France, the Low Countries, Germany, and Spain. Today, however, he awoke alone. He was accustomed to being alone, but for some reason, today, he realized he was more than alone. He was lonely.

Traveling to Zurich from western France was always dangerous and never easy. When it grew particularly risky, E.D. found it helpful to don his Nazi officer's uniform. Once he approached the Swiss border, where his escape route intersected with a network of other resistance operatives, he could abandon his uniform and become a civilian once more, at home with the German language that many Swiss still spoke.

When E.D. arrived at Genève-Cornavin station the previous night, no one was waiting for him in the shadows near the platform. That was a good sign, meaning his compatriots saw no need to warn him of any immediate danger. Although Switzerland had maintained armed neutrality during the war, many German Swiss, although not active supporters of the Nazi political ideology, considered the Allied nations that sent armies to attack

Germany their enemies. With so many German Swiss maintaining a loyalty to Germany, resistance agents like E.D. were never without Swiss enemies.

The Swiss who supported the Allied cause, and especially those active among the Swiss resistance, were well-known among other active underground resistance groups across Europe. The help they offered both Jews, Allied soldiers, and other refugees who had escaped to Switzerland from behind enemy lines was invaluable. For many desperate refugees fleeing for their lives, Switzerland was a safe temporary home on their way to Spain or another safe haven.

Looking back on his last two weeks in France, E.D. had to smile. As he did, he sat up, stretched, and shook his head. "He has made it so easy," he said aloud, "so easy."

Recruited by the Nazis in his teens, E.D. had been taught to idolize the Führer. Now, after witnessing a trail of atrocities that Hitler ordered in a growing number of German-occupied cities, he realized that behind the fierce dictator persona that Hitler broadcast to the world, there lived a desperately fearful man, one who craved power so that he could feel invincible. Having promoted himself to the position of Germany's Führer in 1935, he began his absolute rule on a foundation of fear.

Those the Führer had gathered as his military advisors soon discovered that Hitler considered himself a superior military strategist to any he had chosen. As a result, anyone offering an opinion contrary to Hitler's could face swift and terrifying consequences. Highly ranked officers often faced dismissal, forced retirement, or demotion in rank, while others suffered imprisonment and even death. Furthermore, one's immediate family was rarely spared a similar fate. The Führer's Gestapo and SS regularly employed tactics steeped in threats until virtually all of Germany's military leadership was infected by the same culture of fear. E.D., recognizing this inherent weakness, began to employ it as a tool a resistance fighter could use regularly to his advantage.

Before leaving Le Chambon-sur-Lignon, a French city well-known as a haven for Jewish refugees on their way to Switzerland, E.D. dressed in his Nazi captain's uniform and carried forged orders identifying him as Hauptman Hans Wagner. At a checkpoint near the Swiss border, he encountered a German patrol led by one Leutnant Karl Klein. When E.D. arrived at the checkpoint, Klein asked to examine his orders. Unfazed, E.D. used a simple tactic that had never failed.

"Leutnant Klein," E.D. began in his most impatient and condescending tone, "you do recognize the uniform of an officer who outranks you, do you not?"

"Certainly, Hauptmann Wagner," Klein said, looking at the ground before looking back toward E.D., but never daring to look him in the eye. "Begging your pardon, sir," he continued nervously, "I am not permitted to make any exceptions. My superior officer, Oberleutnant Schmidt, who reports directly to Major Bauer, who reports to…"

"Ah-h-h, Major Bauer, you say?" E.D. interrupted, throwing his head back in delight, "Yes, an old brother-in-arms and a close friend of mine who I am sure would not be pleased to learn that I have been detained unnecessarily. Of course, you will allow me to contact him via your field radio," he said as he reached past Klein toward the checkpoint radio. Continuing, E.D. said, "I must tell him that a certain Leutnant…" he said impatiently, waving his hand to instruct Klein to offer his name again.

"Klein," the nervous officer said, quickly adding, "but I'm sure there is no reason to delay you any longer, Hauptmann Wagner." Retreating helplessly and handing E.D.'s orders back to him, Klein continued. "I'm sure your paperwork is in order, sir. Please accept my apologies for the delay."

As Klein saluted E.D., the remaining soldiers at the checkpoint saluted in like manner. With a look of disgust, E.D. retrieved his papers from the young officer's hand and answered with a half-hearted salute of his own, adding, "Heil Hitler!" before going on his way.

E.D. carried an inward smile, knowing that the Third Reich's defeat was sure. "Hitler will ignore the best military minds Germany has to offer and demand they enforce whatever serves his ego. When his plans fail, heads may roll, but his egotistic goals will remain unchanged. As the Third Reich's military goals fail to be realized, morale will falter among men in every rank. It's only a matter of time," E.D. said to himself. "Every day, the culture of fear he created weakens the resolve of the men who have followed him. Only time will tell, but time is on the Allies' side. For today, though, Hitler's innocent victims seeking asylum beyond the war zones that he controls are the ones who most need our help."

E.D. left his thoughts and returned to the present in Geneva as he dared to lift the blackout curtain just enough to peek out toward the street. There, morning foot traffic was beginning to appear. Looking out the window to the left, he noticed a young woman stop near the entrance to the alley, waiting to cross the street. She was wearing a long gray raincoat and carrying an umbrella. When she turned her head, he noticed her blonde hair peeking out from under her kerchief. He leaned closer to the window, desperately wiping away the dust and cobwebs that obscured his view. He watched for a long moment until the young woman crossed the street and was out of sight. Then, the tears came.

His tears were no surprise to him. They arrived at odd moments these days, always triggered by a present circumstance that dared to reach into his past. There was a time when he would have eschewed them, banishing them as shameful signs of weakness, but that time had passed. This morning, he let them turn to quiet sobs and reached for his handkerchief.

It was more than a year and a half ago in Halifax that he and Brenda awoke to the sound of RCN shore police breaking the lock on the door of the room they shared. Taken entirely by surprise, E.D. could do nothing but surrender. He remembered the look of sheer terror in Brenda's eyes as she looked into the sailors' gun barrels and felt the handcuffs tightening on her wrists. He knew she was reliving the day in Ottawa two years earlier, the day when RCA soldiers came to take her father away.

Her mother had heard rumors that more soldiers were scheduled to return within two weeks to move the rest of the local German population to an internment camp. The rumor proved accurate, and soon many of their neighbors, harmless people who'd done nothing wrong except to be born with German surnames, were condemned to forced labor and imprisonment at the camps. With no father to protect them, the camps were no place for a young woman like Brenda. Her mother stayed with Brenda's younger brothers, but, after leaving her mother's tearful embrace, Brenda ran and never looked back.

After E.D. fled PEI at about the same time, he traveled west, eventually making his way to Ottawa. There, he discovered Brenda only a few days after she had arrived in the city. A lost soul, too young and too innocent to be left alone on the streets, he befriended her. The desperate look in her eyes was one that he recognized. As a German agent on Canadian soil, he needed cover, and the wary young blonde he met on the train platform in Ottawa might be just what he needed to remain undiscovered. She was wearing a long gray raincoat, and all the worldly goods she owned were hidden beneath it. A few well-chosen words spoken quietly in German turned her head, and when their eyes met, two lonely, injured souls became, in that moment, one, but for purposes no more intimate than survival.

Her heart's injuries were new, and because his injuries were older, the years had freed him from some of the harsher effects of the long-suffered angst that once left him hard and cold. He offered her a sort of simple kindness and understanding that she desperately needed. The couple didn't need to share many details concerning their past lives. His apparent lack of bitterness gave her a reason to hope for some freedom for herself.

"Yes," E.D. had to admit, "she is a beautiful young woman," but what knitted her to him was the almost immediate trust she placed in him. For several months, she became his constant companion, ready to do whatever he suggested, but not only because he was a Nazi agent and she was a victim of her German roots. No, something deeper united them, something that told them they needed each other. He felt it, too. Both knew what it meant to be victimized, but he made her feel safe and protected, and she made him feel wanted and worthy. When they were imprisoned in Halifax, however, he knew he had failed her, and that's what brought his tears tonight.

"I abandoned her," he whispered to himself. "When I saw my chance to escape that mildewed concrete pit where they kept me, I didn't give her a second thought. I know I could have done nothing to help her while I was escaping, but I'm still the one who brought her to Halifax and trained her in coding and radio communications. I'm the one who was supposed to protect her, but instead, I am the one responsible for her imprisonment. I never suspected they'd be coming for us, and now I can do nothing to help her."

Outside his window, the sun was higher now, and the young blonde woman had long since disappeared into the Geneva foot traffic that E.D. watched as he peeked beneath the blackout curtains again.

Just then, he heard furtive steps coming down the inside hall and approaching the door to his room. As the steps grew louder, E.D. leapt from his bed and reached for his pistol. Waiting behind the door in the gray morning light with bullets chambered and ready, he heard a voice outside his door, a voice he recognized.

"E.D.," the voice said. "It's Hugo. A message for you, different than any we've seen before. Open up, if you will."

Hugo and E.D. were no strangers, but rather long-trusted brothers-in-arms. Hugo was on the same bomber with E.D. when their plane crashed in France many months earlier.

When E.D. opened the door, the two men kept their reunion greetings brief as E.D. rushed his friend in and closed the door. In the semi-darkness, their smiles testified to the bond between them.

"A message for you, mate," Hugo began, "but not from any of our usual sources. High level it is, this one. They had to get a British prayer book to decode it. From what I can gather, it was relayed here from across the ocean."

Printed on a small piece of flash paper - paper made to erupt in flames and turn into ashes at the touch of a match - E.D. struggled to read the note in the semi-darkness. He opened the door a crack to let the hallway light fall over his shoulder and read,

> BK, free as a bird.
> Flew the coop for higher fields.

E.D. couldn't believe his eyes, but before he could say anything, Hugo spoke.

"I don't know what that means to you," he said, pointing to the flash paper, "but it didn't mean a thing to any of us at the radio. Listen, I'm on the rails for Zurich in less than an hour. Running now, mate."

Once more, the men embraced, hearts as one until E.D. was left alone again, shaking his head and re-reading the message.

"They found a way to get a message to me from across the Atlantic, with news that Brenda is free. I can only believe that she escaped, too," he said. "It says she 'Flew the coop for higher fields,' but what does 'higher fields' mean?"

It took another moment of pacing and mumbling to himself before he spoke aloud.

"Higher fields? Highfield? Do I dare believe she's found refuge there?"

Chapter 30

Susan smiled as she remembered hearing, "You can take a girl out of the country, but you can't take the country out of the girl." Those words were so evident in Brenda's life now that she woke up each morning at Highfield. She was born on a family farm, and every member of her family learned early what it took to make a farm successful. After all, their livelihood depended on their ability to grow their own food and care for their livestock.

When Brenda arrived at Highfield, Lois and Luc's wedding was still more than two months away. After only three weeks of introduction to all of Highfield's regular daily tasks, especially those required to keep the livestock, gardens, pastures, and the farm stand running smoothly, Brenda was ready to take on most of the daily management, allowing others to pour their energies into the wedding particulars.

Luc and Lois had thought through detail after detail together. The wedding service would be at St. Peter's, of course, with Fr. Hunt presiding. To no one's surprise, the bride and groom chose Ingrid and Joseph as their Maid of Honor and Best Man. Ingrid and Joseph were also happy to host the reception at Luc and Lois's newly finished home on Suffolk Road. Luc and Lois had only recently chosen the name "Spring Hill" for their home, named for the hill where the house stood and the spring that fed the pond in their backyard. They had asked Fr. Hunt to offer a blessing on the house and announce its new name on their wedding day.

Amid all those preparations, Brenda proved herself a tireless worker, up with the chickens before dawn and only ready to rest when the last of the livestock had been fed and tended at the end of the day. Susan found her one night, long after dinner, in the front room of the henhouse, candling eggs and boxing them in cartons. Seeing a dim light, Susan walked through the henhouse door to find Brenda sitting on a stool at the worktable. As

Susan entered, Brenda was about to finish candling the last of the eggs she had collected that day.

"There you are," Susan said as Brenda put the few remaining eggs in a carton. "I wondered what took you away from dinner so quickly."

"There's always something to do when livestock need care," Brenda smiled. "I had to collect the eggs because the farm stand ran out today. I think I have enough here to fill their shelves in the morning."

"When I arrived at Highfield," Susan said, "I didn't know what egg candling was. We didn't keep chickens at Clifton Manor in England."

"I grew up with chickens and eggs," Brenda said, "and no one wants to break an egg into a frying pan at breakfast to find a baby chick growing inside! Holding an egg up in front of the light like this," she said, "is the only way to see what's going on in there."

"So, I understand," Susan laughed as she joined Brenda at the table.

As Brenda put the egg candler away, Susan asked, "Could I ask you a question, Brenda?"

"Certainly," she answered.

"You've been with us for several weeks now," Susan said, "and adjusting to the pace of life here at Highfield must be overwhelming."

Brenda nodded as Susan continued, "I couldn't help but wonder tonight why you left the kitchen table so hurriedly when you heard Ingrid and Joseph arriving to talk about the upcoming wedding."

Brenda lowered her head before saying, "It's not the wedding that concerns me. I feel bad about what we did two winters ago. Joseph is the one, isn't he? I saw his limp."

"The one?" Susan asked.

"The one Ernest and I injured so badly. Ernest never told me everything. He said it was best if I didn't know everything he knew. Really, I'm not sure he trusted me not to give away his secrets," Brenda said.

Susan saw the tears welling up in Brenda's eyes before she answered, "Yes, Brenda, it was Joseph."

"I only knew that Ernest had two men in mind, and they were older. He never mentioned anyone else," Brenda said, "especially not a young man Joseph's age."

"Then, Ernest knows something about my father and Michael that made them his targets?" Susan asked.

"Yes. He said King George and the Prime Minister in London sent them here. He told me that your father and Michael oversaw all of England's spies," Brenda answered.

"And now that you've seen life at Highfield for two weeks, met my father and Michael, and observed what they do all day, do you think you should believe everything Ernest said?" Susan asked.

"I've seen Michael up with the sun every day and working constantly to keep the livestock happy and all the trucks and tractors running, and all the while working to complete your new home. It's hard for me to believe he's a spy," Brenda said, "and your father, as far as I can see, is just an old gentleman with grandsons to entertain."

Susan laughed and said, "Yes, Michael stays busy most of the time, and people still remember that my father served the Royal Navy in the First World War with the rank of Rear Admiral. Following the war, he went to work in London at the request of the Prime Minister. I'm sure he has enjoyed conversations with the King and the Prime Minister about matters of state during the current conflict, and he always keeps Michael informed for the sake of security here at Highfield. We know some people will target those associated with the British government for various reasons. Father and Michael are men of service to the Crown, but one could hardly call them spies when they are always here at Highfield."

"So, Ernest didn't know everything he thought he knew?" Brenda asked.

"I would have to say he didn't," Susan laughed, "and I could tell you some things about Ernest that *you* don't know. But, first, let me tell you about Joseph."

"About Joseph?" Brenda asked.

"Yes," Susan answered. "Because of the injuries to his leg, he spent a good deal of time under care at the hospital and later at home. However, it was not an unfruitful time for an amazing young man. His time spent among doctors and nurses instilled in him a desire to become a healer himself. After he was released from hospital care, he studied long and hard and became a nurse, but that's not all."

"What else, then?" Brenda asked.

"He has since gone on to medical school to become a doctor. Before another year is over, he will reach that goal," Susan answered. "What Ernest intended to be harmful turned out to be good."

"But does Joseph know who I am and what I did?" Brenda asked.

"Do you mean the things you helped Ernest do?" Susan answered. "No, Brenda. Only my family and Armand Verrier know anything about you. Yes, you were here as a guest at Michelle and Grayson's wedding, but your appearance has changed enough that no one, especially those among the younger people, appears to remember you. You're simply a young woman who grew up on a farm in Ontario and decided to move east. You came to this island in need of work, and Highfield is pleased to have found you. As far as Joseph is concerned, I don't think anything you did in the past would matter to him. He knows that his injury led him to a lifetime career as a doctor, an honorable and higher calling than any he could have imagined for himself. Without his injury, he would never have considered it."

After a moment, Brenda said, "I still think I owe him an apology."

"If you'd like, I will arrange a time when you can talk with him," Susan said, but I can't tell you when. Everyone has so much to do these days."

"Of course," Brenda said, "Thank you. I would like that."

The women were quiet for a moment before Brenda spoke again.

"You probably think that Ernest and I were lovers."

"You weren't?" Susan asked.

"No," Brenda said. "After what happened to me, you know, what those two did when they attacked me in Ontario..." She stopped and looked away as if looking at something far in the distance. "I couldn't imagine ever being with a man. It's not that I didn't like Ernest. I did. I still do. He was a gentleman. He cared for me in small ways, like remembering that I liked dark chocolate, the kind he would buy for me. But then there were times when he was suddenly cold, and distant, and dark," she said as she turned her face to look at the floor. "Those times were scary."

A moment passed before she brightened and looked at Susan again.

"Ernest could be funny sometimes, you know, and he was handsome enough. He thought I was pretty, so pretty that he taught me how to gain other men's attention. I could flirt to help open doors for us. I guess you could say he used me, but I think he also had a kind of quiet respect for me, maybe for all women. He taught me how to fight, you know, how to defend myself. But, when we were alone, he never touched me, never suggested anything, never made me uncomfortable like that, ever."

"And you liked him?" Susan asked.

"More than I liked any other man, I suppose," she said. "He looked out for me and protected me. I never lacked for anything when we were together." Brenda blushed as she said, "He called me *'meine kleine taube'* sometimes."

"*Meine kleine taube*?" Susan asked.

"Yes. He told me his mother used to call him *'meine kleine taube'* when he was young. It means 'my little dove'. Oh, and then there was the little dove he fed out the window," Brenda said.

"Out the window?" Susan asked.

"It was when his father would lock him in the basement," she said. "He told me a corner of one basement window was broken, and a small piece of glass was missing. Every day, Ernest would feed a little dove with scraps of bread he saved. He said it must have been a runt or one that fell out of a nest. He felt sorry for it."

Brenda was quiet for a moment before she added, "When I heard that he had escaped, I thought he would probably take the emergency stash we had hidden away. We had hidden money, clothes, a radio, ID cards, and a gun. I thought it would be gone, but he left it all for me."

"Brenda, there is something more I think you should know," Susan said.

"About Ernest?" Brenda asked. "Do you know where he is? Is he all right?"

"Let's go to the library in the house," Susan said. "There's a lot to tell."

Before they finished talking that night, Brenda learned about the changes Michael had seen in Ernest after their many conversations in his cell in Halifax. Susan also mentioned the times Ernest spent talking with Fr. Hunt. Then she described the details of his eventual escape, about the messages he sent Michael not long afterward, and the treasure Ernest left for Joseph. Finally, she told Brenda about his enlistment in the RCAF, his service with the RAF in Europe, and his current service with the resistance in Switzerland.

"He's not the same man I knew, Susan. It sounds like he's made a complete change," Brenda marveled.

"He's certainly not the man you last saw the night you were both arrested, Brenda," Susan said. "Michael is the one who first witnessed the changes. You might want to talk to Michael sometime."

"I'd like that," Brenda said.

After a long moment of silence, Brenda looked up to say, "If there were ever a way I could write him a letter, I would appreciate your help."

Making no promises, Susan said, "Let me see what we can do, Brenda. Let me see what we can do."

The two sat in silence for another moment before Susan said, "There's one other thing I think you should know."

"Yes?" Brenda replied.

"It's about my father," Susan began. "There's a reason you weren't remanded to the authorities in Halifax when you came down the stairs from the fire tower. My father has taken responsibility for you with the authorities. As far as the Canadian government and the RCN are concerned, you are under his care and custody. It's a very unusual responsibility, somewhat risky for him, and something he has never done before. He didn't want to see you return to jail. He believes that you can find a better home here. You are welcome to stay as long as you like."

As tears welled up in her eyes, Brenda raised her hand to her mouth to stifle her cry. After a minute, her sobs abated, and she said, "I can't believe anyone could care for me like this. How can I ever repay him?"

"There's only one way, Brenda," Susan said.

"Yes?" Brenda asked.

"Never give him a reason to regret his decision."

Chapter 31

Following dinner, Lady Moncrieff and Sir Richard sat together on the settee in the west sunroom, sipping their after-dinner drinks. While Lady Moncrieff enjoyed a snifter of sherry, Sir Richard enjoyed two fingers of Jameson, the Irish whiskey he favored most.

"The newspapers don't help me comprehend where we stand in the war, Richard. Of course, they publish the latest facts as they receive them, but I'm hoping you can paint a picture with a broader brush for me. After two and a half years of German domination in Europe, can you give me any hope that the tide will turn soon?" she asked.

Turning his eyes from the horizon to look at his wife, Sir Richard began, "I wish it were as simple as the two of us watching the sunset tonight. We know the gorgeous colors we see in this sunset, that is, the fire God has set in the sky this evening," he said, pointing to the horizon, "will soon give way to darkness. For the next eight hours or so, we will have only the stars and the moon to comfort us until dawn. This war is like a very long night with no dawn yet in sight. However desperate that may sound, I can offer you a few rays of hope from the latest discussions I've enjoyed from London SIS reports."

"Say on, please, Richard," Lady Moncrieff pleaded. "You have my full attention."

"I can bore you with the facts of recent battles won and lost and where I believe the Allied forces and our Axis enemies will strike next," he began, "but I prefer to share my studied historical convictions on warfare rather than comment on the daily reports of battles that offer no true perspective."

"Please, Richard," she said, "my heart is hungry for a reason to believe that the madman whose armies rule most of Europe will someday know a sound defeat."

"That, my dear, I can guarantee," he said.

"But on what basis?" she asked. "Elaborate, please, Richard."

"For several reasons, my dear, but primarily for the reason you have already named. A madman rules Germany, a madman who refuses to learn from history and ignores those minds schooled in warfare who serve him. A mere glance at recent history would remind any loyal German that fighting a war on two fronts will lead to defeat. World War I proved that. With the Russian Empire on one front and most of Europe on the other, Kaiser Wilhelm was doomed."

As Lady Moncrieff nodded, Sir Richard continued, "Hitler is sleeping with some strange bedfellows he calls his allies. However, all of them have watched him turn on his former Soviet ally, invading Russia without warning. Since then, Hitler's Wehrmacht has indeed made some remarkable advances toward Moscow, but Hitler doesn't understand the concept of attrition. Both sides will lose thousands of men in battle, but the Soviets can send more than twice the total population of Germany to war. Hitler doesn't know it yet, but I believe we will see the Soviets push his Wehrmacht back to his front door."

Lady Moncrieff had to smile as she reached for his bottle and topped off her husband's glass.

Sir Richard took a sip before continuing. "Mussolini, another madman, would like to think that Hitler won't turn on him or abandon him to the Allies, and the Japanese can only rely on distance as their protection from a German attack. However, one fact remains: Hitler will never share his rule with anyone. He'll endure Mussolini's bravado as long as it helps the Nazi cause, but Hitler knows Italy has no real military prowess. I predict Hitler will abandon the Italian upstart in the end."

"So, Hitler and the Nazi party will defeat themselves," Lady Moncrieff began, "and we have only to keep them fighting on both fronts until they run out of men and machines?"

"In effect, yes," Sir Richard said. "Of course, we also have the war in the Pacific to fight, and the Japanese are a formidable enemy. While Japanese surprise tactics gave their Emperor, Hirohito, some early victories, our American allies have already begun to level the playing field. Most recently, the Japanese navy attacked the United States on its west coast, in California and the state of Washington, but the damage they inflicted proved inconsequential."

"But the Japanese have also made many air attacks on Australia in February and March," Lady Moncrieff said.

"Yes," he answered, "but they've lost the advantage of surprise, and their physical distance from their targets remains our ally. The Battle of the Coral Sea halted their advance toward Port Moresby, and they lost four aircraft carriers to the US fleet in the Battle of Midway. The Japanese are forced to rely on their navy to deliver supplies, equipment, and ground troops to all their Pacific targets. However, the Royal Navy and the US Navy have a larger number of ships available at sea, and the United States' shipyards are building hundreds more. The Japanese have, I believe, bitten off more than they will be able to chew."

"When I look at the globe in your study, it amazes me to find how small an island Japan is, and how much the people of that small island have done to wreak havoc on the world," Lady Moncrieff said.

"Yes, it would seem impossible, but again, I believe they, too, will find that attrition is their enemy. They will lose men, aircraft, and ships, and all the other weapons of war, faster than they can replace them. Their enemies, the Allies, and especially the US, will out-manufacture any country in the world when it comes to producing the weapons needed to defeat the Axis powers. Time is on our side," he concluded.

"Richard," she said, "I believe you when you say that time is on our side, but every day our sons are at sea or in the air in harm's way. I want it to be over. I want them home with us."

Topping off her snifter and offering his glass in a toast, he said, "To the day we are together again. To the grandsons and granddaughters our sons will sire. To peace," he said, "perfect and lasting peace."

With a clink of their glasses and a long sip, the couple leaned back into the settee, watching the last rays of the autumn sun disappear into the treetops.

Chapter 32

Ordinarily, a bride and groom who had recently celebrated their twentieth birthdays might seem too young to be marrying, but this was wartime, and both Lois and Luc had seen enough of war to know that one mustn't let war put off living. Lois had survived the Blitz in London and was fortunate to find her way to Prince Edward Island to escape the constant threat of Luftwaffe bombs. Luc had enlisted, trained, and gone to war. He returned, bearing the scars he suffered while saving the lives of his comrades. No, they weren't too young to marry, and, though they were born worlds apart, they were ready to vow themselves to each other, forever.

St. Peter's Cathedral once again welcomed some warm friends through Fr. Hunt, who had a way of taking all the tension out of wedding rehearsals. Ingrid was happy to be Lois's Maid of Honor, while Joseph was ready to serve as his brother's Best Man. Lois had asked Michael to give her away, and he couldn't have been more proud to do so. Patrice was ready to embrace her role as a bridesmaid, especially because Luc had invited Hugh Buchanan to be her escort. Although none of Lois's family would be able to attend, Jacques and Doris Boucher and the Highfield family, from Sir Richard and Lady Moncrieff to Case and Reed Moreland, were ready to fill in all the voids.

Doris and Susan had taken time to create a beautiful wedding gown hand-fashioned from a dress they found in Charlottetown at St. Onge's. To the simple but elegant white dress, the ladies added lace that they accented with several rows of silver and gold embroidery, pointing, they said, toward anniversaries twenty-five and fifty years away.

With Michael's help, Luc and Lois had turned an aging farmhouse into what had become a new home. Spring Hill was ready to welcome the newly married couple when they returned from their honeymoon, but tonight

Joseph and Ingrid had planned a rehearsal dinner at Spring Hill, where they would also host the wedding reception the next day.

Following dinner, when the house was nearly empty again, Joseph found Susan to ask her a question.

"Miss Susan," he began, "as you know, Ingrid and I have been helping Luc and Lois with all their wedding preparations, and all of Highfield has been invited to the wedding and the reception."

"Of course, Joseph," she replied. "Is there a problem?"

"Well, yes," he said. "Ingrid left an invitation at Miss Kimble's cottage, but we haven't had a reply. We are both hoping that she will attend the wedding and the reception. We were wondering if she hasn't responded to our invitation because she may not have a proper dress to wear. A young woman coming from a farm so far away might feel uncomfortable attending a wedding if she couldn't be properly dressed."

"Oh," Susan said. "Joseph, I don't think her failure to respond to your invitation has anything to do with a dress. I think it's for another reason."

"Another reason?" he asked. "But what could that be?"

Susan thought for a moment before saying, "Perhaps we should find out. Could you meet me in the kitchen at Highfield in half an hour?"

"Of course, Miss Susan," he said, "but why?"

"I'll try to bring Brenda there to tell you herself, all right?" Susan asked.

When Michael and Susan arrived at Highfield a short time later, Michael escorted his wife to Brenda's cottage door and left the two alone. Later, when Joseph arrived at Highfield's kitchen, he found Susan and Brenda waiting for him there.

As he sat down with the two women, Susan nodded to Brenda, who began, "I know you don't remember me."

"Have we met before?" Joseph asked.

"Not formally," Brenda said, looking more at the table than at Joseph. "I was a guest here for a wedding several summers ago."

"Miss Michelle's wedding?" Joseph asked.

"Yes," Brenda answered quietly.

"No, I don't remember," he said. "I think we spent most of our time serving that day. I really don't recall any of the guests, only the family."

"I was with Steve, Michelle's brother, but really, I was here for another reason," Brenda said.

"Another reason?" Joseph asked.

"Yes," Brenda began. "I was here to see Highfield and gather information for a man I knew. He worked for some people in Germany."

"Some people in Germany? Nazis?" Joseph asked.

"Yes," she said. "They wanted him to hurt people here who were important to Great Britain."

"Like Sir Richard?" Joseph asked.

"And Mr. Moreland," Brenda added. "While I was here for that one day, I took a walk with Steve up the path to the fire tower."

A knowing look came over Joseph's face as he said, "Then you also passed the sawmill."

"Yes," Brenda said, looking down at the table.

"And later you told the man what you saw there?" he said.

"Yes, I did," she said.

"You knew what he was planning?" Joseph asked.

"No," she answered. "He never told me. All he wanted from me were my eyes and ears. I told him there was a tower and a sawmill, a sawmill like the one we had at my family's farm in Ontario."

"Did you help him do anything else there?" Joseph asked.

"No," Brenda answered. "Months later, in the winter, he left with a saw, and when he had finished his work, he told me what he'd done to the trees. It was several weeks after that that he told me what happened to you and how badly you were hurt. I'm so very sorry," she said as she began to sob into her handkerchief.

Joseph was quiet for a moment before he said, "You know you're not to blame, don't you?"

"What do you mean?" Brenda asked. "You were terribly hurt."

"But you didn't plan the attack or help him execute his plan," Joseph said. "That man thought he was doing something good, and I know he didn't intend to hurt me. In the end, the tree limb that broke where he cut it and those logs that began rolling onto me were among the best things that ever happened to me."

"Susan has explained that to me," Brenda began, "but, still, you could have been killed."

"That makes no difference between you and me," Joseph said. "All that matters is that you didn't set the trap or intend the injuries. That man used you, and I just happened to be in the wrong place at the wrong time. I hold you faultless," Joseph said as he reached to grasp her hand.

When Joseph's hand closed on hers, Brenda's sobs erupted into painful cries full of woe. Her body shook for a full minute until she was finally able to speak again.

"Thank you," she said. "I never thought I would ever be free of the guilt I've felt."

"I'm glad you can have some peace," Joseph said. "I came to my own peace when my doctors and nurses became my friends, and I eventually found a calling. Perhaps you don't know that the man you were with found his peace by providing me with the means to study and begin a career of service to others. I have forgiven him, and I hold you faultless. I have only one question for you."

"Yes?" Brenda asked.

"Can you forgive yourself?" he asked. "Can you set yourself free, raise your head, and go on with your life, no longer carrying a burden that is not yours to bear?"

Standing, he said, "If you can, then come here and accept my embrace so that you will never need to bear that burden again."

Brenda stood and rushed into his arms, where Joseph received her silent sobs. Susan was not without her own tears, and when their tears subsided, the secrets that brought three souls together that night would never be mentioned again.

Chapter 33

Lois and Luc's wedding wasn't the largest nuptial gathering St. Peter's had seen, but it might have been the warmest and most comfortable wedding that Fr. Hunt had ever blessed. Both the bride and groom had walked through some lonely and difficult times, times far from home and family. War brought Lois to Prince Edward Island, separating her from her family in London. War took Luc to a battlefield in Europe that nearly cost him his life. But war had also brought this couple together, two young people whose pain had earned them a maturity belying their age. War had separated them for a time, but now, the union of their hearts was a gift that war could never take away.

Since Lois arrived at Highfield from London, she had never left Prince Edward Island. Except for his time away at war, Luc had only rarely been away from the island himself. For their honeymoon, Luc and Lois decided to tour New Brunswick and Nova Scotia, exploring some of the most beautiful places the Maritimes had to offer. After two weeks away, their new home would be waiting for their return.

After breakfast on the Monday morning following the wedding, Susan and Lady Moncrieff were reminiscing about their weddings and honeymoons when Susan abruptly changed the subject.

"I've had a thought, Mother," Susan said.

"Yes?" Lady Moncrieff said with raised eyebrows. "Something interesting?"

"Actually, Mother, it may be the answer to several concerns I've had about Highfield recently. With the work at our new home..." Susan began.

"Hillside?" Lady Moncrieff interrupted. "That's the name you chose, as I remember."

"Correct, Mother," Susan began again. "With the work at Hillside nearing completion, I believe we need to look at the changes our family's move will mean for you and Father."

"Are there particulars you have in mind?" Lady Moncrieff asked.

"Several, but they are also related to some personnel changes soon to befall Highfield," she said. "As you may remember, Alida and Phillipe have been invited to move to their daughter's home in St. John. The Henaults have been with us since Michael first arrived years ago."

"Yes, so I understand. I'm sure Doris and Jacques will miss them, for they joined us only shortly thereafter," Lady Moncrieff said. "Those two couples have seen years of work and change here."

"I'm sure you're right, Mother, but there are other changes in the family we also need to consider," Susan said.

"Such as?" Lady Moncrieff asked.

"Well, now that Luc and Lois have married and will be setting up their own household, they will not be as available to attend to the needs here at Highfield. Then, when Joseph and Ingrid marry, we may lose Ingrid's help as well. Granted, Brenda Kimble has been an excellent recent addition to the staff, but she can't do the work of two or three others.

Lady Moncrieff nodded as Susan continued, "Without Michael and the boys and me, Mother, Highfield will be a very quiet place. The way Father keeps to his study most of the day, you'll be without company a good deal of the time. Patrice loves being with you, but we'll need her in the kitchen more often when Alida goes, and I'm afraid Jacques will not be able to cope well without Phillipe's help."

Lady Moncrieff sat back in her chair for a moment before saying, "I think I need another cup of tea, a strong one."

Susan smiled as she reached for the teapot. After she filled her mother's cup, she said, "I haven't come to you with a list of concerns without a plan for their solution, Mother. Give me a moment to explain. If you agree with my plan, we'll have to convince Father and Michael."

"Convince Richard and Michael?" Lady Moncrieff asked.

"Yes, Mother," Susan answered. "Convince them it's *their* idea."

"Oh," Lady Moncrieff smiled. "We're quite practiced at that now, aren't we? All we need to do is announce we have an overwhelming problem, impossible to solve. Men being men, those two will be happy to jump into the breach to help us find a solution."

Susan had to smile. Of course, her mother was correct. Nonetheless, over the next few minutes, she laid out a plan, clearly describing each problem and her suggested solution. When she finished, Lady Moncrieff was delighted.

"It's a smashing plan, Susan, good for all involved. How shall we proceed?" she asked.

"You take care of Father, and I'll take care of Michael," Susan smiled. "We need to gain their ears before supper tonight. By tomorrow, I'm sure they'll get together to add their own thoughts, to make the plan *theirs*. By the next day, they'll be trying to sell *our* plan to *us*."

Lady Moncrieff said, "Done, Susan. Now let me get my daybook so I can note some of the details."

That night, after Case and Reed were snug in bed, Susan and Michael went to the kitchen, where the air was cooler. After breakfast that morning, Michael had refrigerated a pitcher of leftover coffee. Tonight, he poured two glasses of coffee over ice, added sugar and milk, and stirred each glass with an iced tea spoon. He served Susan a glass as he sipped on his own.

"I think you'll find it refreshing," he said as he enjoyed another swallow.

After her first tentative sip, Susan remarked, "Oh, it is good, just what I need to cool off after a long day. I need to relax. I'm tired of worrying about problems with no solutions."

"Problems? What problems?" Michael asked, taking Susan's bait.

"Well," she began, "it's complicated, Michael, and it affects so many people who could use our help, and Father won't want to get involved in Canadian wartime politics, and..."

"Whoa!" Michael said, raising his hand as if he were stopping traffic. "Let's start at the beginning, one issue at a time."

"All right," Susan said, surrendering. As she let her shoulders drop, Michael leaned in to listen.

At the same time, Sir Richard and Lady Moncrieff were sitting on a settee in the east sunroom, enjoying the cool evening breeze. While Susan filled Michael in, Lady Moncrieff began her conversation with Sir Richard.

"I'm sure you are aware that two of Highfield's family who have been here since Michael arrived will be leaving soon," she said.

"Yes," Sir Richard answered, "I understand that Philippe and Alida are moving to New Brunswick."

"Yes, St. John to be exact," Lady Moncrieff said, "but their exit will leave a gaping hole in the morning chores at the barn and henhouse, not to mention Alida's work with Doris in the kitchen and the laundry."

"I see," he said. "I must talk to Michael about a solution."

"I'm afraid you'll find that Michael is quite busy attending to the last construction details at Hillside. Also, when he and Susan and our grandsons move to their new home, we two will be the only ones rattling around here," she said. "I hope neither one of us suddenly needs their help overnight. That will require a telephone call and a long wait for them to arrive."

"I hadn't considered that," Sir Richard said.

"Of course, we also need to consider that some of our young people are setting up their own households," she said. "Now that Luc and Lois have married, Joseph and Ingrid won't be far behind. Those young people have helped us with everything from farming to hunting, including planting, harvesting, and caring for the livestock for some time. I've always admired your goal of self-sufficiency here, but before long, we won't have the family labor force required to meet your goal."

After a moment, Sir Richard said, "I've been so busy on the radio to London that I've left all these details and worries to Michael."

"Well," Lady Moncrieff continued, "I've spoken with Susan, and she has informed me that Michael has turned over every stone available to find help for Highfield, but most of the young men on this island have gone to war. Other men are needed at their family homes. However, there may be a solution," she said.

"Which is?" he asked.

"It begins with someone like Brenda Kimble," she said. "Her background on a farm has already made her an immediate and welcome employee, skilled and ready."

"That's right," he said. "We're fortunate that she comes from a farming family."

"You are aware of her family's sad situation in Ontario?" Lady Moncrieff asked.

"Yes," he answered. "Because of his former military service, Brenda's father has been remanded to a camp in Manitoba, while the rest of her family remains at an internment camp in Ontario."

"And her father's occupation?" she asked.

"He once served honorably as a U-boat captain in World War I. I have great respect for the way he saved the lives of many captured civilian and military personnel," he said.

"And his occupation before he was sent to Manitoba?" she asked.

"He and his wife, along with Brenda and two teenage sons, kept a small farm."

"And we're losing two young men at Highfield before long," she said.

"Yes," he nodded.

"But that's in addition to the older couple we're losing, the ones who live next door to Highfield," she added.

"Correct," he said as an idea formed in his head. "Philippe and Alida are selling their house and ten acres, a home where they've lived for many years."

Lady Moncrieff sat quietly as he leaned back in his chair and formed his next thought.

"Their property is contiguous with Highfield, and that property will need both a new owner and a new tenant," he said.

Lady Moncrieff continued to listen as her husband thought out loud.

"Now, if the responsibility for Brenda's family's internment could be transferred to someone appropriate *here*, that family could move in *there*. The entire family could be together again and securely employed at Highfield," he said.

"Do you think that's possible, Richard?" she asked. "That's a very ambitious plan, full of politics and paperwork. Are you sure that's something you should be taking on?"

Sir Richard thought for a moment before saying, "I believe the indecent treatment that many fine people of German extraction have endured in this country will someday be seen as a blot on Canadian history. I've had several talks with Miss Kimble. Though she is a wounded soul, her heart is soft. She and her family have been victimized and separated for too long. I believe they deserve a fresh start far from Ontario. There will certainly be a few obstacles to overcome, but I also have a few favors I can call in."

Sir Richard sat quietly for a few moments before he said, "So many injured families will find it hard to forgive those who wronged them. If we can help even a few on that road, we will have done well."

"Of course," Lady Moncrieff said.

After another quiet moment, he said, "I'll need to speak with Michael before we begin this process, Angela. As Highfield's superintendent, we will need his full support before we undertake a venture like this."

"I certainly hope that you two will be of one mind," Lady Moncrieff said, "because your plan is an ambitious and honorable one."

"When I explain our thoughts," Sir Richard said, "I'm confident that he and I will come to a gentleman's agreement."

"*Our* thoughts?" Lady Moncrieff asked.

Smiling and shaking his head, Sir Richard stood and took her hand as she stood to join him. As they embraced, he said. "I've followed you down similar paths for too many years, my darling, to believe that my best thoughts in situations like this have ever been anything but *our* best thoughts.

Chapter 34

It was just before six that morning, and Susan's eyes were still closed when Michael returned from the barn, full of excitement.

"Susan," he said, as she opened one eye, "it was just this morning after Brenda finished collecting the eggs and mucking out the cowbarn before Philippe arrived that I had this thought."

It was an hour before breakfast, and the boys were still fast asleep. Susan was barely awake when Michael sat down in her dressing chair and leaned forward to talk with her where she lay in bed.

"What thought did you have, Michael?" Susan yawned.

"It's about Brenda's family," he said, "but it also has to do with Alida and Philippe."

"What do you mean?" Susan asked as she struggled to sit up. "What about Alida and Philippe?"

"Well," he said, "as we discussed last night, they're about to retire, leave Highfield, and go to live with their daughter in St. John."

"Yes," Susan said, "you told me."

"But that leaves their house empty," he said, "and there's no market for a house on Prince Edward Island these days, not with a war going on."

"All right," she answered.

"And we've all but lost Luc's help with all the daily chores, and Joseph is in Quebec most of the time. Brenda has been a great help to fill in some of the gaps, but with so many people leaving Highfield, we need even more help," he said.

"All right," she said again, "but do you have a solution?"

"Well," he began, "I know this is a stretch, but, like you said last night, we've all seen how capable Brenda is. After all, she was raised on a farm, a family farm. She has two brothers who were also raised on that farm, and her father and mother are about the same age that Philippe and Alida were when I first arrived here."

"So, what are you saying, Michael?" Susan asked as she sat up in bed.

"It came to me when you mentioned her family last night that there might be a way we can rescue Brenda's family from the internment camps. They're separated and living under miserable conditions, and they need to be together again. That family is a perfect fit for Philippe and Alida's house. Since the Henault property borders Highfield, and because there's no good real estate market during wartime, Highfield could help them by buying their property."

"And then what?" Susan asked.

"Then, if your father can get Brenda's family released from the internment camps, they could come here and begin a new life, far away from all the grief they faced in Ontario," he said. "Your father is very impressed with Brenda's father's World War I record as a U-boat captain, you know."

"All right," Susan said once more.

"Then Brenda's family would be free, Susan. They could live in their own home, enjoy regular work they know, and Highfield would be able to fill all the vacancies in our workforce. Most important of all, though, Brenda's family would be together again and living far away from all the anger, danger, and threats of the internment camps."

Fully awake now, Susan hid her smile as she said, "It would be best if you talked with Father first, don't you think, Michael? I wouldn't mention anything to Brenda until you've spoken with him, all right? Your plan sounds like a big step," she said, "one that he would need time to consider."

"Absolutely," Michael said, "and that's why I already left a note for him under his door. I hope to speak with him right after breakfast this morning."

"I certainly hope Father can help," Susan said, "especially for Brenda's sake."

"I couldn't agree more heartily, Susan," he said, "and that's why I'm planning on visiting with your mother when your father and I have finished talking."

"Mother?" Susan asked. "But why?"

"Don't you remember?" he asked. "Your mother worked a miracle with your father for us many years ago," he said, "and that's why we have our family here today. I'm betting she can work another miracle with him, one that will bless another family. If I can't convince him," Michael said, "I'll wager she can."

Susan reached out two hands to Michael's face, drawing his lips to hers for their first morning kiss.

"You never cease to amaze me, Mr. Moreland," she said.

"And I hope I never will," he laughed.

Chapter 35

It was an unseasonably warm October day at Hillside, with the temperature reaching nearly 80 degrees at noon. For the first time in many months, Hillside was quiet, almost eerily quiet for Michael's ears. The only workman for the day had just driven away, and Michael was left to his own devices.

"It's finished," Michael said as he stood in the pantry between the garage and the kitchen.

"It's finished," he said again, as if he was trying to convince himself. Although completed by the McLeods in record time, Michael had to say one more time, "It's finished," trying to believe that their new home was really ready for his family to move in.

Michael had one last task inside the house before he left for lunch at Highfield, but he couldn't help making a final tour of inspection. Oh, he'd supervised almost every installation at Hillside for the last nine months, and was confident he would find nothing amiss, but he couldn't help making a full wander through the house before he went home for lunch.

"Home," he mused. "Highfield will only be home until tomorrow at this time when we move the last crate across Suffolk Road and up the drive to the garage at Hillside."

Taking his time, Michael walked from the pantry to the kitchen, enjoying its white tile floors, soapstone countertops, and walnut cabinets with glass doors that displayed the fine china and glassware within. Then he moved on to the dining room with its mahogany table and its twelve matching chairs, all with blue velour cushions. When fully extended, the mahogany table would seat fourteen, large enough for most gatherings the Moreland family might anticipate.

The fireplace in the parlor was the largest one in the house and Michael's favorite. The McLeod's had found a cache of pink New Hampshire granite for the mantle and hearth in a shade that Susan loved. Though not his first choice, Michael had to admit that it complemented the color of the red mahogany floors and paneling perfectly.

The first-floor study was well-appointed, with three walls lined with bookshelves, complete with a generous counter and cabinets beneath. Under the window on the east wall, a wide cushioned bench with bolsters on each end offered a perfect nook for reading or enjoying an afternoon nap.

The front entry floors were finished with polished bluestone, durable and pleasing to the eye. As Michael passed the front door, he saw Susan drive up in her cabriolet and turn toward the garage. He ran past the kitchen and pantry to the breezeway connector to greet Susan as she pulled up to the garage door.

"What is this?" Susan asked, pointing to a finely finished mahogany post that reached eye level next to her car door.

"It's a surprise," Michael said as he poked his head into her car to get his afternoon kiss."

"But what kind of surprise?" Susan asked with a little giggle in her voice.

"See the two buttons on the post?" he said. "Just push that top button and see what happens," Michael answered.

As she did, the garage door in front of her opened.

"Do you mean I'll never have to get out of the car to open the door?" she said.

"That's right," he answered. "Now push the lower button."

Susan pushed the lower button and watched as the door closed.

"You'll find two buttons on the wall inside that work the same way," he said.

"Oh, Michael, when I think of groceries, two boys and a third baby in the car," she said, looking down toward the child she was carrying, "I rejoice at this kind of convenience."

"The manufacturer couldn't offer anything like this, so I met with our electrician to work out the details. Glad you like it, Darling," he said, stealing another kiss.

Once indoors, the boys were glad to settle in the playpen for their nap, while Michael and Susan made their final moving plans.

"We've nothing at Highfield but a change of clothes," she said. "It's hard to believe we'll be sleeping here tomorrow night."

"I agree," he said, "but that's because there may be a few things missing, things we need before we can make Hillside our home."

Puzzled, Susan asked, "What do you mean?"

"Let me show you," he said as he took her arm and led her back to the dumbwaiter in the pantry.

Susan wore a knowing smile as she said, "I should have known, Michael Moreland. This dumbwaiter is your favorite toy."

"But," he answered, "not a toy today. Just push the button labelled '1,'" he said. "The car is in the basement now, staying nice and cool. Bring it up to the kitchen, if you please."

Susan pushed the button, and when Michael opened the door, her eyes grew wide. Inside, she saw vase after vase of fresh flowers.

"There are arrangements for every room in the house," he said, "and this is just the first installment. Come on. Let's deliver them."

And so, they did. Michael had to disappear to the basement two more times, but, in the end, no room lacked a fresh arrangement. What's more, though, Michael and Susan visited each room together, leaving no room unadorned.

"It seems a shame to decorate all six bedrooms with such sweet arrangements," Susan said, "when we will be occupying only two."

"But remember, Darling," he answered, "Fr. Hunt will be here to offer his blessing on Hillside, and that will include a blessing for every room. Every room needs to be prepared and ready to receive a guest at any time."

"I couldn't agree more," Susan said.

Just then, Case or Reed, or both, woke up, and their familiar call brought Michael and Susan downstairs. As Susan dug into their diaper bag, she came across an envelope her father had given her an hour before.

"Oh," she said. "I almost forgot. Father asked me to give you this," she said. "He seemed a bit puzzled and said he hoped you would know what it's about."

Later, when Susan left Hillside and drove with the boys to Highfield, Michael sat at the kitchen table looking at the envelope. The addressee's name and address had been obliterated. Neither was there a return address to be found, but the envelope bore the remnants of two postmarks, one Swiss and the other Spanish. The Spanish postmark was the most recent of the two.

"So," Michael said, "this letter has seen some international travel."

Inside the envelope, he found a photo that had then been microfilmed by British V-Mail somewhere on its journey and later enlarged on this side of the Atlantic. Everything about this piece of mail puzzled him. Michael found himself looking at a blurry photograph of what appeared to be one half of a Canadian $100 bill. There was no letter or note to accompany the photo. As he looked closer, he saw what appeared to be a pair of initials written on the face of the bill. It read, "B.K." He could see nothing else of interest in the photo.

"Interesting," Michael thought. "I'll have to ask Brenda about this."

Chapter 36

"I can't believe it," Brenda said as she looked at the photo Michael had given her. "I can't believe it," she repeated as she sat down to take a closer look.

Michael and Susan had stopped at Brenda's cottage just before noon to ask her about the picture that Sir Richard had received through SIS channels.

"So, you recognize those initials and that half of a Canadian bank note?" Michael asked.

"Yes, I do," Brenda said, "but please wait here for just one minute. I need to get my bag." As she turned to go to the bunkroom, she stopped to add, "I'm sorry. Please sit down, if you'd like. I'll be right back."

Susan and Michael sat down in the two remaining chairs in the cottage entry. When Brenda returned, she was holding something in her hand.

"Here," she said as she handed Michael a piece of paper. "Here's the other half."

Michael immediately recognized the left half of a $100 Canadian bank note. Something was different about this one, though. The initials were not B.K. The initials on this note read, "E.D."

"There must be a story behind this," Michael said. "It's not just a coincidence."

"No, it's not," Brenda said. "It's something Ernest suggested after we'd been together for six months or so. You see, he knew that we could be discovered, arrested, or separated at any time. He was concerned about losing touch with each other. It was as if he wanted to be sure that our relationship, however one might describe it, wouldn't be lost. He'd already lost his family. I was without mine, too. I think he wanted whatever we had to last. So, one day, he produced a $100 bill and a pen. I was overwhelmed. I'd never seen anything larger than a $10 bill before. After we initialed it, I watched as he cut it in half. He gave me the side with his initials, and he kept the side with mine. Then we promised that if ever we were separated, we would find a way to meet again and put the bill back together. There would be enough money to celebrate our reunion, and plenty left over to make another start, if that seemed right."

"Well, it makes sense now, Miss Kimble," Michael said.

"Please," she said, "please call me Brenda."

"Of course, Brenda," he said. "Now, so that you know," he continued, "we sent Ernest a cryptic encoded message a short time ago, a message only he would be able to understand. Once deciphered, it read '*BK, free as a bird. Flew the coop for higher fields.*'"

Brenda thought for a moment before saying, "So, that means he knows I escaped, '*flew the coop*,' right? And, if he sent this message to Sir Richard," she said, holding up the picture Michael gave her, "he must suspect that '*higher fields*' meant that I could be found at Highfield?" she asked. "That's why he sent the picture?"

"That's what we believe," Susan said. "Now," she continued, "speaking for myself, I must presume that he kept his half of the $100 bill for a very good reason. It must be very valuable to him. And," she continued, "I also believe he sent a picture of his half to let *you* know he's still looking toward the future."

Leaning forward, Brenda asked, "Do you really think so?"

"Uh-huh," Susan said, nodding her head. "Yes, I do."

Michael, being Michael, said only, "I can't draw conclusions like that from this evidence, but I can't rule them out either."

"I understand," Brenda said, and then, turning knowingly toward Susan, she repeated, "I understand."

"There is one other matter we want to mention to you," Michael said.

"Yes?" Brenda answered.

"It concerns your father, your mother, and your brothers," he said.

Leaning forward but looking puzzled, she answered, "Yes?"

Sir Richard has written to several Canadian authorities to ask for your family to be released from the internment camps where they are now being held. He is requesting that they be remanded to his oversight here on Prince Edward Island. He is offering to take responsibility for them as he already has for you."

Michael stopped for a moment while Brenda sat wide-eyed and silent, nodding in disbelief.

"Now," he continued, "there are many details to work out, and the Canadian authorities can be very slow to respond. One of their biggest complaints against Mennonites is their stand as pacifists. The authorities resent anyone not willing to go to war."

"But we're not Mennonites, Mr. Moreland," Brenda said. "My family left Germany as Lutherans, and we've never worshipped anywhere but at a Lutheran church."

"That is a great factor in our favor, then," he said. "Now, there are also a myriad of details to pursue here at home. We know of a farmhouse and ten acres available, as well as jobs waiting for all your family. If your parents are ready to leave internment and their home in Ontario, a new home will be waiting for them here on Prince Edward Island. We are a praying people, Brenda, and we know that you and your family are, too. We don't want your family to stay one day longer than necessary in the camps, so we are praying for a miracle."

Before Michael could finish, Brenda was already in tears and rushing into his arms. Michael stood, her arms tight around his neck.

"Mr. Moreland," she said, "how can people like me deserve people like you, people to care for me and for my family as you do? I can't believe your kindness."

"Brenda," Michael said quietly, "it's only because all of us at Highfield, at one time or another, have been blessed in the same way. We're just paying our dues for everything that's been given to us. You don't have to deserve anything, Brenda. You only need to give back when you see someone you can help, that's all."

"Now," Susan said, "we need some information like full names and ages, birthdates, and your family's last address. We'll also need the names of anyone who lived nearby your home in Ontario, people willing to vouch for your family's character. So, here are some papers Sir Richard needs you to fill out. Please get them back to Michael or me, and the sooner the better."

"I'll have it done by supper," Brenda smiled, and with one last hug for the Morelands, she sat down to review the papers in her hand.

Chapter 37

Following worship at St. Peter's on Sunday morning, the last tasks required for Michael and Susan's move from Highfield to Hillside took less than an hour. Tantamount to packing one's bag when leaving a hotel, except for the necessities that accompany two eighteen-month-old boys, the Morelands were packed and settled at Hillside and ready for Fr. Hunt's arrival for the house blessing at three o'clock that afternoon. All of Highfield joined the Morelands, along with representatives from the architect and the builder. The guests had opportunities to tour the house and grounds, which clearly boasted the latest in technology and comfort, while retaining the old-world charm of quality in wood and stone. Later that evening, however, both the Moncrieffs and the Morelands found themselves at a loss.

"I feel so foolish, Richard," Lady Moncrieff said. "Susan warned me that the change might prove disconcerting, but I didn't listen. I've never known the house this quiet. I've never known the house without them," Lady Moncrieff said. "I thought I was ready for this day, but suddenly I'm worried, knowing there's no one nearby to answer a need at night or to sit at tea with me in the morning."

"I never thought I'd say such a thing," Sir Richard began, "but I already miss those two boys. We've gotten to know each other, and I miss the way they always smile and laugh at my antics. I agree, Angela, it's become very quiet here without them, now."

"We'll need to think about some help, Richard," Lady Moncrieff said, "perhaps someone overnight and even through the day. With Alida retiring, Doris won't be able to fill in all the gaps. What do you think about that new girl, Brenda?"

"Well, I'd prefer Lois, but she's a married woman now, and Ingrid is readying a house for her marriage to Joseph. Patrice is my favorite, but she's still young in my mind. Now, Michael and Susan tell me Brenda has a good heart, but she's a farm girl. I'm afraid she might not be at home here."

"And if Patrice was her teacher? Her coach?" Lady Moncrieff asked. "Perhaps she's a fast learner."

"I suppose," Sir Richard said, "but I'd favor seeing if the two would be willing to share the position. Then when one isn't available, the other could be."

"That sounds like a splendid possibility," she said. "Shall I call on them tomorrow to ascertain their willingness to consider the position?"

"I'll leave it to you," he said. "Keep me posted on the progress, won't you?"

"Of course, my dear, of course," she said.

At Hillside, after Case and Reed were asleep, Susan and Michael had the house to themselves. However, on the first night in their new home, they weren't entirely comfortable. Everything felt a bit foreign. As both lay in their bed looking at the ceiling, Michael broke the silence.

"There are no house noises here," he said, "nothing familiar or usual, the kinds of sounds one anticipates after years under the same roof."

"I agree," Susan said, "it will take some time for us to recover an aural sense of home to comfort our ears at night."

"I'm thinking of Highfield all the time," Michael said. "I grew to depend on the usual and customary there, a place where the stairs under my feet felt natural. Here, there's an extra step to the second floor. I'll get used to it, but for now, it simply feels odd."

After a moment of silence, Susan spoke.

"I worry about Mother and Father without help in the house at night. "Nothing I said could convince them they might need help."

"I was thinking about Brenda," Michael said, "but she's so new to Highfield and she's more of a farm girl than the sort of young woman in service that your mother and father might expect."

"But the position they need to fill covers a good part of the day and all night as well. I've wondered if Patrice could share the hours with Brenda and help her with anything she doesn't know. I'm sure the job will take both of them," Susan said.

"A capital idea, and I'd wager a quiet night alone in the house, like tonight, might convince your parents to begin thinking along the same lines," he said.

"Then I'll make a visit with the boys in the morning to check in and offer the thought. Perhaps they'll be ready to listen by then," Susan said.

Just then, the telephone on Susan's nightstand rang. With a quizzical look on her face, she looked at Michael before picking up the receiver.

"Hello?" she answered. "Mother? Yes. It's very different for us as well." Looking at Michael, she added, "We already miss Highfield's ambiance, the sounds and scents that made it home. Oh?" Susan said. "You were thinking about adding some help?" Susan nodded as Michael sat up to listen. "Oh, Brenda?" she paused. "And Patrice? I think that's a wonderful idea, Mother. And Father? He agrees? Well, then, why don't I stop over in the morning, and we'll discuss particulars. Then, perhaps we could invite the young ladies to discuss your thoughts over tea? How about nine? Oh, nine-thirty would be better? Lovely, Mother. All right. See you then."

"Remarkable," Michael said, shaking his head and smiling as Susan replaced the receiver. "Perhaps everything will work out smoothly enough to set both our minds at ease."

"I hope so," Susan said, "but remember this. The hours those two young women will be spending day and night with Mother and Father are hours they won't be spending outdoors in the barns and gardens. You'll be driving back and forth between two houses all day, coming and going constantly. I think your days are going to be a lot busier from now on, Mr. Moreland."

"Oh, I wouldn't worry about that," he said. "I'm confident something will work out that could be better than either of us could imagine."

"Now you sound like my parents before the reality of their situation finally struck them," Susan answered.

"Still," Michael said, "I wouldn't lose any sleep over it. I don't plan to."

"Pardon me, then, if you please," she said, yawning. "I'm going to close my eyes and fall asleep in our new bed in our new bedroom in our new home. There will only be one night like this in my life, and I'm not going to miss a minute of it. Sleep tight, Darling."

With that, Susan rolled toward her nightstand, plumped her pillow, turned off the light, and snuggled into the fresh, sweet-smelling linens.

On the other side of the bed, Michael lay with his eyes open. It was only another minute or so before he heard the first few notes of Susan's cute little snore. A short time later, Michael yielded to his exhaustion, and Hillside's master bedroom welcomed a second snoring occupant.

Chapter 38

After their first breakfast at Hillside, Michael headed for Charlottetown on his usual morning errands. A short time later, Susan made her way to the garage with the boys and secured them and all their necessities in the back seat of her cabriolet. Then, a little tentatively, she pushed a button on the wall and watched as the garage door opened. A broad smile of delight met the sunshine of the new day as she backed her car out of the garage and stopped to reach for the lower button on the post outside. A push of that button lowered the door, just as Michael assured her it would.

"I think I could get used to this," she said with a smile. She turned down the drive toward Suffolk Road and crossed to Highfield's driveway just beyond.

Lady Moncrieff was waiting for her at the front door when she arrived. With the boys settled in their playpen in the study, Susan sat with her mother and father. Sir Richard spoke first.

"Your mother and I have a thought we'd like to share with you, Susan. It involves some changes here at Highfield since your move to Hillside. May we explain?" he asked.

"Mother telephoned and mentioned a few thoughts last night," Susan answered, "I'd love to hear the details, Father."

For the next twenty minutes, Sir Richard and Lady Moncrieff outlined their thoughts on a transition among the staff at Highfield, which was almost identical to the solution Susan and Michael had discussed the night before at Hillside.

Swallowing her relief, Susan offered, "What a well-thought-out plan! I hope the young ladies will be as excited about it as you are. Are you still planning tea at nine thirty?"

"Yes," Lady Moncrieff answered. "Of course, your father rose early this morning and has all their expected responsibilities and a potential schedule charted and graphed for them," Lady Moncrieff said with a smile. "He's still 'the Admiral,' you know."

"It's just my way of helping them map a few things out," he said, searching for a way to excuse his habit. "There are a good number of moving parts to a machine like Highfield, you know."

A voice coming through the door agreed, "Yes, there are," Michael said. "Excuse me, if you will. I hope I'm not interrupting."

"Of course not," Lady Moncrieff said. "We've just divulged a plan for some changes in Highfield's staff with Susan. Why don't you tell him about it, Susan? I'm going to check in at the kitchen for a moment."

Looking into Michael's knowing eyes, Susan summarized her parents' thoughts as if they were a brand-new idea.

"I see no reason why that won't work," Michael began, "I think it's brilliant."

"I know it takes those two young ladies away from your staff for several hours each day, Michael," Sir Richard said, "but I hope their absence won't cause a problem."

"Not at all," Michael said, "not at all. But, let me tell you why."

Everyone leaned in to hear what Michael had to say.

"Several weeks before we were ready to move to Hillside," he began, "I realized how often I would be occupied there during regular working hours. I knew I couldn't let the burden of my absence threaten the efficiency of a well-oiled machine that has taken years to develop. I felt Highfield deserved regular, uninterrupted full-time supervision, the kind I will no longer be able to provide."

Sir Richard nodded, and Lady Moncrieff and Susan leaned in to listen.

"So, two weeks ago," he began, "I prayed for an inspiration concerning an essential addition to Highfield's full-time staff. I had an answer very shortly and immediately arranged a conversation with a highly skilled and very apt young man. I've been waiting anxiously to hear his decision about taking on the bulk of my daily responsibilities. I got my answer by telephone earlier this morning."

Surprised, Susan asked, "Two weeks ago?"

"Yes," Michael said. "I knew we would need someone qualified to take over many of my regular daily duties, and someone who could eventually become proficient in the administrative tasks and paperwork required to keep Highfield running smoothly."

"Splendid," Sir Richard said. "So, you believe your candidate is qualified?"

"Absolutely. I have every confidence that before the year is out, this young man could prove himself ready to assume the position in its entirety," Michael said.

"When is he prepared to begin?" asked Sir Richard.

"Well," Michael began, "having returned from his honeymoon just yesterday, Luc will be arriving here in an hour or so."

"You cad!" Susan said as she issued a mock slap. "You had this planned all along, and you never said a word."

"Not so, Susan," he laughed as he raised his hands to protect himself. "I was not at liberty to say anything. I talked with Luc before he and Lois left for their honeymoon. The decision was his - well, theirs," he said, correcting himself, "and, he smiled, "another bit of good news is that Lois is pleased to join her husband at Highfield as another half-time staff member. Doris may be losing Alida, but she will be gaining Lois."

Susan sat with her mouth open, unable to speak as Lady Moncrieff said, "A capital idea, Michael. How good it will be for Highfield to have a sterling young couple on board to greet the future here."

"Yes," Sir Richard agreed. "Luc and Lois will make an excellent team, full of youth and vitality."

"There's just one thing more," Michael said with one eye still on Susan. "Hugh Buchanan has applied to finish the rest of the season here as Luc's assistant. Those young men have built a solid working relationship at Hillside, and, with your approval, Hugh is happy to write his parents for permission to stay on. He also wants to tell them how much his asthma has improved in our ocean climate. Having an extra hand through the fall harvest will be a welcome bonus for Luc."

"Done!" Sir Richard smiled.

Just then, Brenda and Patrice arrived for their first staff meeting with the Moncrieffs, and Susan and Michael took their leave. On their way out the door with their hands full of boys, Susan said, "Luc and Lois are the obvious answer to the conundrum we discussed last night, but I will confess, I never thought of them."

"With Spring Hill finished, and all the final details at Joseph and Ingrid's new home complete, this opportunity at Highfield is an answer to prayer for both our families," Michael said. "Work is scarce on the island, even for a man as skilled as Luc. But now, a settled young man with a devoted wife has found more than a secure job. They'll be able to make a career here at a time when Highfield needs them. They will be family more than ever. I can take no credit. God is good."

"But you can, Michael," she said, "you asked for a solution to a problem, and you listened for an answer."

"Yes, I did," Michael agreed. "I've spent too many hours wearing myself out searching for answers, when simply asking for a solution and sitting still long enough to hear the answer works so much better. I must say, I recommend it."

"And I," Susan said, "will take your recommendation."

Chapter 39

E.D.'s mission to Munich in the fall of 1942 brought him into contact with several students who were leaders of a resistance movement known as "White Rose." One young man named Willi Graf had served in the Wehrmacht as a highly commended medic. His service eventually brought him to France, Belgium, Serbia, and Russia. In Poland, he saw the horror of the Warsaw ghetto and was a first-hand witness to atrocities that left him traumatized. After winning the Iron Cross for his service, he earned leave from his duties with the Wehrmacht to return to his studies in Munich in the spring of 1942.

The members of White Rose wrote and distributed anti-Nazi leaflets aimed at audiences of the German intelligentsia. E.D.'s contact with the students was necessarily brief and dedicated solely to delivering messages of support from like-minded members of the resistance in Geneva and Zurich. Although E.D. hadn't returned to Munich since he was a student there some eight years earlier, this trip was his third in the last several months.

Munich was the city where his father had abandoned E.D. and his mother before leaving to fight in World War I, and the last home E.D. knew. After he finished his cartography studies at Ludwig Maximilian University in 1934, the Abwehr sent E.D. to the United States. When he left Germany, he lost regular contact with his mother. Now, some years later, each time he found himself in Munich, he spent every available moment searching, trying to locate her. Heavy Allied bombing attacks had destroyed much of the city, a prime target known as the birthplace of the Nazi party. The neighborhood he remembered from his childhood was decimated. He knew there was a good chance his mother hadn't survived.

Melting into the student population, E.D. walked what remained of the streets, trying to find the apartment building where his mother might yet be living. Their home had been only a few blocks away from the university, which had also suffered from the Allied bombing raids. He inquired of the people he found there, but no one remembered a woman named Elke Hoffman.

"She could have abandoned the city years ago," he said to himself. "If she had stayed in our old flat, she probably would have died there."

E.D. was passing a group of students sitting on the steps of one of the university libraries that he remembered well. From the middle of the group, he heard a voice that turned his head, a voice he had never forgotten. There was no mistaking the guttural sounds emitted from a larynx wounded by a British bayonet during World War I. Professor Hans Gerber, a professor of geography and one of E.D.'s most admired teachers, held his students' undivided attention, even on a warm, sunny day outdoors on the steps of a library scarred by war.

E.D. took a place at the rear of the group, looking past and through the students, his eyes locked on Professor Gerber. He couldn't help but smile. Professor Gerber had not only been E.D.'s professor and academic advisor, but also a family friend. He was well-known for reaching beyond the classroom for students who needed more than just a classroom teacher.

As the professor dismissed his students and turned toward what was left of the sidewalk, E.D. raised his voice and called, "Herr Professor Gerber, I have only one question."

Professor Gerber stopped in place and, without turning his head, asked, "Herr Hoffman?"

As he turned to look at E.D., he held back a smile while saying, "You never had only one question. The first always led to a second, and that to a third," he said as he raised one finger in the air and smiled, "but each, a worthy inquiry."

As the two shook hands, the professor said, "So, let me guess. I'm to retire, and you are here to take my place?"

Laughing, E.D. said, "No, Herr Gerber, I've known no other man worthy of that place. I am in Munich for only another hour."

"I wish it could be longer," Gerber said. "In days gone by, on a day like today, I would enjoy some of your mother's apple strudel. After you finished your studies and went out into the world to find your fortune, she and I saw each other in the streets quite regularly. She told me always how proud she was. When your father didn't return, she relied on the gifts you sent her. "Every month," she would say, "every month like clockwork, my Ernst remembers me."

160

"I'm afraid I've lost touch with her of late, Professor," E.D. said. "I made it my habit to wire her the means to care for herself, but a year ago, the bank here in Munich was unable to reach her. The letters I wrote were returned and labelled 'Undeliverable'. With all the bombing in Munich, I've feared the worst and have come to find her. Thus far, however, I've learned nothing."

"And you won't," Professor Gerber said, "not here. To preserve her life, she left Munich very suddenly more than a year ago."

"To preserve her life?" E.D. asked, "Oh, from the bombings, of course."

"No," Gerber said. "She faced a much more sinister threat."

Seeing the puzzled look on E.D.'s face, Gerber said, "You don't know, do you? About your mother's family?"

"What about her family?" E.D. asked.

Looking to the left, then the right, the professor said, "Not here. Come with me to what is left of my office. We can talk there."

The professor's office had suffered damage from the bombings. The windows were boarded up, and there was evidence of a fire on the wood paneling. In the remaining untouched corner of the room, the two men sat in leather armchairs.

Professor Gerber began in a quiet voice, "Your maternal grandfather, a merchant who traveled widely, met the woman he would marry in Vienna. They lived in Vienna for two years before moving to Munich. They told no one she came from a Jewish family."

E.D.'s face blanched. "My grandmother was Jewish? I had no idea, Herr Gerber, and now Hitler is purging the population of Jews and those descended from Jews, people like my mother, and now me," he added, shaking his head.

"Sadly, yes," Gerber said. "I understand the SS and the Gestapo are searching through census records and many other sources of public and private records, even records of marriages and baptisms. Their searches are exhaustive, and innocent people like you and your mother have faced significant danger when discovered."

The room was quiet for a moment as E.D. took in the situation. Then he said, "Herr Gerber, my work has taken me to places where I have witnessed the horror of this inhuman plague. I can understand my mother's need to escape. But tell me, please, did she say anything to indicate where she planned to go?"

The professor thought for a moment before saying, "Only one time can I remember her mentioning that some of the Hoffman family emigrated overseas, two, perhaps three generations ago. She mentioned a town called Newstadt, as I recall."

"In the United States?" E.D. asked.

"No," the professor said. "I believe it was in Canada."

E.D.'s head was reeling. "I can't imagine how she proposed to travel that far away," he said.

"The last time we spoke, she told me of some resistance fighters who were helping refugees get to Spain and from Spain across the ocean," Gerber said.

E.D. knew some of those resistance fighters and the dangers involved in their life-saving work. However, his mother was not a young woman, and she might not have been able to endure the rigors required to make the dangerous journey that almost always led over the Pyrenees. The paths over the mountains were littered with the corpses of thousands of refugees.

Though overwhelmed with surprise coupled with grave concern for his mother's welfare, E.D. managed to say, "Herr Professor Gerber, I cannot thank you enough. When I am in Munich next, I hope we will meet again."

"And I will look forward to seeing you then, Ernst," he said. "Until then, my friend, auf wiedersehen."

E.D. walked away, his head spinning with question after question. "Could my mother have found her way to Canada? Where is Newstadt? Would it be a large enough city to be identified in an atlas or on a map? I can take comfort in knowing she didn't die here in Munich, but how will I find her now?"

E.D. had no answers, only more questions. His immediate goal was to make his way back to Geneva. With his bag already on his shoulder, he turned his face toward Munich's East Station and began the first leg of his journey back to Switzerland.

At Highfield, less than a week after Sir Richard began his inquiries with Canadian authorities concerning the Kimmel family, he shared his initial findings with Lady Moncrieff, Michael, and Susan.

"We've been able to locate Brenda's mother and brothers. They are being held at Petawawa Camp 33 in Ontario. Although they were born in Canada and have never lived in Germany, they are considered enemy aliens," Sir Richard said. "From what I understand, the population in the camp is growing each day. The most recent additions include several hundred civilians of Italian descent."

"And the living conditions?" Lady Moncrieff asked.

"Many are housed in tents and temporary buildings, which offer minimal protection against the winter cold. The present summer conditions, though less harsh, are still painful. Often, families who wish to stay together have been sent to sugar beet farms, some as far away as Alberta and Manitoba. Thankfully, the Kimmels are still in Ontario."

"And Brenda's father?" Susan asked.

"He is being held at Camp 132 in Medicine Hat, Alberta," Sir Richard said.

"But that's across the whole country," Susan said.

"Correct," Sir Richard said. "Because of his previous military service in World War I, he is considered a more serious threat. Medicine Hat is a more secure location."

"And the two years he spent as a prisoner-of-war mean nothing now that we are at war with Germany again?" Michael asked.

"Correct," Sir Richard agreed, "illogical, but correct. But, despite all these ignoble details, there is some hopeful news to report."

"Please tell us," Lady Moncrieff said.

"Camp 33 at Petawawa is facing serious overcrowding. From my initial contact with the commandant, I sensed a willingness to decrease the population by releasing three detainees to our custody. I believe his final determination could be less than a week away," he answered.

"And how do things stand with Brenda's father's case?" Susan asked.

"That case may be a little more difficult, Sir Richard began. "Those in charge consider former German military officers a much more serious threat than that which a mother with children might offer. One factor on our side involves my service to the Crown during World War I, when Brenda's father also served in the German navy at sea. I believe today's decision makers will consider our former status as wartime enemies a guarantee that I will keep a close watch on him if he is placed in our custody."

"Is there anything we can do in the meantime?" Lady Moncrieff asked.

"First, we must agree on an assumption I believe we've all made," he said. "Shall we assume that the Kimmel family will accept our proposal and make their new home with us on Prince Edward Island?"

"I, for one," Michael began, "find it hard to believe they would choose imprisonment over the freedom and opportunities they could enjoy here."

Looking to Lady Moncrieff and Susan, Sir Richard asked, "Agreed?"

As Lady Moncrieff and Susan nodded, he continued, "Then we must secure a home for them. I've spoken with Alida and Philippe concerning Highfield's interest in purchasing their home. With the wartime housing market so depressed, we offered a pre-war price for the house and acreage, provided they left the house furnished, including all the kitchen utensils. They were overjoyed, as was their lawyer. He advised them he could have the necessary papers prepared within a few days."

"I understand their daughter, Louise, has had their new quarters prepared for months now," Lady Moncrieff said. "According to Alida, Louise told them they needed to bring nothing but their suitcases and their family photos."

"Luc and I can make a tour with Philippe to see what we might need to do to freshen things up for the Kimmels," Michael said. "With Hugh Buchanan as his right-hand man, Luc will be able to train him in making minor repairs and painting. A new coat of paint will work wonders on an old farmhouse."

"And I'll make an appointment with Alida," Susan began, "so that Brenda can make a visit and see everything. I'm sure she'll have some ideas about how to make the house into a home where her family will feel comfortable."

Just then, Patrice knocked at the study door.

"Excuse me," she asked. "I'm sorry to bother you, but a telegram just arrived for Sir Richard."

She handed him the telegram and turned to leave. When she was out of earshot, Sir Richard said, "It's from the commandant at Petawawa. He writes, "Transfer of detainees Kimmel, one Greta (female), one Friedrich (male), and one Carl (male), from Camp 33 Petawawa, Ontario, to the custody of Rear Admiral Sir Richard Moncrieff, *approved*. Surface transport of detainees by rail, *approved*. Itinerary to follow."

Susan was on her feet in an instant.

"I must find Brenda immediately to share this news. She'll be overjoyed!" she said as she hurried toward the door.

At the same time, Michael stood to say, "I think I need to collect Luc and Hugh so that we can make that visit with Philippe. It sounds like we could be meeting three more Kimmels soon."

Lady Moncrieff watched Michael disappear before asking, "And what shall we do with ourselves now that this meeting has been adjourned?"

"Let me see," he said as he checked the daybook on his desk. "Ah, yes," he said. "It's just as I remembered. Two young men should be waiting for me in the kitchen presently. We have a fishing outing on our schedule. Of course, I'll do the fishing from the shore, but both boys will have their first opportunity to handle the wet, slippery bass, making sure the fresh scent of fish settles on them and on their clothing. Then I'll deliver them to their mother, who will undoubtedly thank me for helping the boys follow another one of the well-trodden paths their father and grandfather have so thoroughly enjoyed."

"And what will their laundress have to say about the residual scent of fish on their clothing, Richard?" she asked.

"Very little, I suppose," he said. "As I understand it, her name is 'Miss Maytag,' and she resides in Hillside's new laundry room, next to the pantry, you know."

Rolling her eyes, she went on to ask, "And following that escapade with our grandsons? What else have you on your schedule today?"

Consulting his daybook once more, Sir Richard said, "Oh, here it is. It appears I've made a reservation for lunch in the dining room of the Charlottetown Hotel. Did you know that they have some of the best seafood dishes on the island and a delicious lobster stew? Perhaps you'd care to join me, my dear?"

"I'd love to, Richard," she replied, "but I'd rather avoid the odor of fish until we arrive in Charlottetown. Will you be able to cleanse *your* residual fish odors after your outing with our grandsons?"

"Of course," he answered. "I'm sure she'll take care of everything."

"Who will take care of everything?" she asked.

"Why, Miss Maytag's elder sister," he said. "She lives in *Highfield's* laundry room."

Rolling her eyes once again as she rose from her chair, she said to herself, "I don't know why I ask these questions, except that it appears to amuse him."

Chapter 40

"It's happened only once before, and that was years ago, before the war," Nigel said as he raised his glass. "Having leave together in the same port? Unheard of!"

Raising his glass to meet his brother's, Boyd answered. "Who could forget it? We were anchored in Portsmouth then, but now we're halfway around the world in Mombasa."

"We happened upon Grayson that day, didn't we? We, the Royal Navy, surrounded Grayson, the RAF, at the bar, as I remember," Nigel laughed.

"We had him worried for a moment, but only for a moment," Boyd said, "I'm sure we won't be seeing him here today."

"True enough," Nigel answered. Changing the subject, he said, "I'll be needing your assistance for the next few days, if you will. I'm new to Kilindini Harbor. You must point me to your favorite haunts. We're not sure how long the *Formidable* will be at anchor here, so I want to use my shore leave to the greatest advantage while I can."

"Then, I'm your man," Boyd answered as he stood and raised his glass. For a starter, you'll need to follow me to the Wren's Nest. I'm meeting Kathleen there in an hour. You might find a young lady there who could be persuaded to grace your arm at dinner with us tonight."

"The Wren's Nest?" Nigel smiled. "Then I'm glad I took the time to polish my brass this morning. Lead on, my brother!"

The Royal Navy had sent the HMS *Revenge* to Mombasa, where she was serving primarily as an escort for ships sailing south from the Suez Canal. Her age was showing, for she lacked the speed, the armament, and the weaponry required to face the Japanese fleet. The *Formidable* had arrived in port from Colombo in Ceylon, though it was rumored she might soon be ordered home for refitting to meet the requirements of faster and better-equipped aircraft.

Boyd took the next half hour to orient Nigel to downtown Mombasa before leading him to the Lotus Hotel, known to many British servicemen as the Wren's Nest. Just as Boyd and Nigel approached the front entry, Kathleen stepped out of the elevator with another Wren.

"Kathleen," Boyd called across the room as he and Nigel headed her way. "I want you to meet someone."

When Kathleen and her fellow Wren were still a few steps away, Boyd said, "Please meet my brother, Nigel. He's a Squadron Leader with the Fleet Air Arm sailing aboard the *Formidable*."

Kathleen smiled and offered her hand.

"We watched the *Formidable* arrive in port," nodding to her friend, "didn't we, Cheryl?"

Cheryl, a striking brunette with dark brown eyes, smiled and said, "They didn't name her '*Formidable*' for nothing, did they? She casts an impressive shadow, that one."

Cheryl had Nigel's immediate attention. While Boyd and Kathleen shared their greeting kiss, Nigel drew Cheryl's outstretched hand to his lips to offer his.

"Nigel Moncrieff," he said, "at your service."

"Cheryl Beatty," she said, "a friend of Kathleen's since childhood. I must chide her, however, for she never mentioned that Boyd had a brother."

"I never expected to meet Boyd's brother," Kathleen said, looking at Nigel, whose eyes were still locked with Cheryl's, "but now that you are here…"

"Perhaps you and Cheryl could join us for dinner at the Nelson," Boyd interrupted, "if you are free, of course, Miss Beatty?"

"I, for one," Nigel managed, "would be honored if you would join us, Miss Beatty."

"Then, how could I refuse?" she laughed. "I have a Royal Navy airman at my service, and my best friend with her beau. Who knows what else the evening has in store?"

"Then let's find out!" Boyd laughed. "Kathleen and I will lead the way. We'll leave it to you two to follow."

The dance band at the Nelson was in perfect form that evening, and with the addition of several officers from the *Formidable*, the dance floor was packed. Nigel's dinner conversation with Cheryl continued as they danced.

"Your family name is familiar to me," he said, "but I can't recall why."

"Perhaps my father's history of service with the Royal Navy has something to do with it," Cheryl said.

"In the Great War?" Nigel asked.

"Yes," she answered, "In World War I. He was best known for his service in the Battle of Jutland."

"Of course," Nigel answered, "my father has mentioned him numerous times while schooling Boyd and me. Father has always been very proud of his service at Jutland."

"So, our fathers served together?" she smiled. "Who knows what else we may have in common?"

"Thus far, we've found we both favor Navy Grog, enjoy dancing, and we've discovered that our fathers served as Royal Navy officers during wartime, as we are serving the Royal Navy today. That seems to be a sound enough foundation for the first night," he said.

"The *first* night?" she questioned. "*First* presumes there will be others, does it not?"

"Then, I must beg forgiveness for my presumption," he began, "however, Miss Beatty, I will acknowledge my sincere hope that there will be others. Many others."

"In that case, let us make a small step forward tonight, shall we?" she asked.

"Such as?" he questioned.

"When this dance ends, you will leave Miss Beatty on the dance floor," she said.

"But…" he said as she interrupted.

"And," she smiled, "you will escort *Cheryl* back to the table."

Finally able to exhale, Nigel answered, "That will be my pleasure, as long as I leave the floor as *Nigel*."

"Done," she said, smiling, "on one final condition."

"Which is?" he asked.

"We plan our second night together before our 'good night,' tonight," she said, looking up at him.

"Nothing will please me more, Miss Beatty," he laughed.

"Likewise, Mr. Moncrieff, likewise," she agreed.

In his quarters aboard the *Formidable* later that night, Nigel wrote a long-overdue letter home. He began by telling his parents that he and Boyd were in port together in Mombasa. He concluded with news that he had met a striking young Wren named Cheryl Beatty. In conversation over dinner, he'd learned that her father was a man that Sir Richard knew well. Nigel was also careful to add that before their first evening ended, they had already planned their second evening together.

Chapter 41

Seven days after rail travel from Camp 33, Pettawama, Ontario, to Charlottetown, PEI, for Greta, Friedrich, and Carl Kimmel was approved, Brenda's mother and brothers boarded their first train. There would be many trains, for their destination was more than 1,500 miles away. On a Tuesday morning in October, the steam locomotive, belching coal smoke and cinders from its stack, finally left the station, the same station where the Kimmel family had arrived two years before.

Once aboard the train, Greta Kimmel succumbed to a bout of silent sobs. Some were sobs of relief, for their imprisonment had come to an end. Some were sobs of grief, for her husband was still held captive, somewhere. She sobbed for her sons, thin, emaciated, and dressed like paupers. When she saw her reflection in the train window, she cried for herself, a thin-faced, gaunt woman who looked old for her years, dressed in little more than rags.

For four long days and nights, they occupied the same seats, ate whatever their ration tickets would buy, and cringed at the looks of pity and disgust other passengers sent their way. Finally, the train they boarded in western Ontario reached the ferry to Charlottetown.

For Brenda, the wait on Prince Edward Island had been nearly intolerable. To help her, Susan retrieved an atlas from Highfield's library and traced the rail trip from Ontario to Charlottetown, following the train routes as closely as she could. Together, Susan and Brenda followed her family's progress toward their new home every day.

At the same time, the Highfield family stayed busy at Alida and Philippe's farmhouse. The interior boasted a fresh coat of paint, several new carpets from Highfield's attic, and some others from Hillside. After they finished weeding and tilling the kitchen vegetable garden, Patrice and Ingrid led a team that weeded and refreshed the flower beds that surrounded the house. Once the interior painting was done, Michael, Luc, and Hugh organized the contents of the barn, everything from hand tools to plows, harrows, and tillers. Finally, Michael's crew checked the electrical and plumbing systems in the house. They repaired several failed outlets and light switches while fixing all the leaky faucets and slow-draining sinks. When they were finished, every door and window opened and closed as they should, every electrical appliance operated correctly, and all the plumbing lines functioned as expected. Guessing at sizes based on Brenda's memory, her brothers' closets and bedroom bureaus were filled with clothing suitable for the fall season. Susan and Lady Moncrieff also filled Brenda's mother's wardrobe. Finally, with the refrigerator and pantry stocked and all else complete, Michael mowed a fresh path through the east pasture that led straight to Highfield.

With the house ready for the Kimmel family's arrival, there was nothing to do but wait. Brenda was content to stay at the guest cottage until her family arrived. She wanted to move in together with her family.

When the afternoon train pulled into the station in Charlottetown, Michael and Brenda were waiting with Lady Moncrieff's sedan. Late summer trains were often close to full, and it took several minutes for the passengers to disembark and collect their luggage. Michael and Brenda ignored the First-Class cars at the front of the train and searched for the Kimmels toward the rear. Finally, Brenda saw Friedrich poke his head out of the window in the last passenger car and peer toward the landing. When Brenda saw him, she left Michael and ran toward her brother, shouting, "Friedrich, Friedrich, we're here, we're here!"

Friedrich gave a quick wave before disappearing into the train again. Seconds later, when Brenda arrived, he was there once more, helping his mother down the steps. Carl followed with the single suitcase that held all their worldly goods.

Brenda's tears were a mix of joy and grief. Though she was overjoyed to see her mother and brothers, all three looked so thin and gray and ragged. Her mother looked so much older, and her every movement revealed pain and exhaustion. Carl and Friedrich had lost weight, too, but their exhaustion was not as evident.

After she introduced Michael, Brenda got her mother settled in the back seat of the car. While Michael stowed their suitcase in the trunk, Friedrich and Carl joined their mother. Brenda sat in front, leaning over the back seat toward her family.

Michael drove more slowly than usual, while Brenda told her family what lay ahead for them.

"The people here are good people, Mother," she began, "more kind and more generous than you can imagine. We have a house to live in, larger and more comfortable than we have ever known before. We have an electric pump and hot water in the house. There is no outhouse, because we have a bathroom with a bathtub. There are electric lights in every room, an electric refrigerator in the kitchen, and a kitchen stove that uses gas – no more wood to split every day. There is a barn and ten acres of land for us to farm. Next door is an estate called Highfield where all of us are welcome to work for good wages, if we'd like, more than we could ever earn at home."

"This is for us?" Greta asked. "But why? Who would do this for us?"

"They are people who cared for me when I didn't deserve their care," Brenda said. "It's a long story, Mama, more than I can tell you right now, but Michael, here, is one of them. You'll meet more in just a few minutes."

"But, your father, Brenda," her mother said. "We don't know where he is or when he will return to our farm looking for us."

"Oh, but we do, Mama," Brenda said, "Father is coming here, too, Mama, coming in about a week, all the way from Alberta."

"From Alberta? They sent my husband to Alberta? I've heard only horrible things about Alberta," she said as she began to sob.

"But, Mama, he's well, well enough to travel and join us here soon. But here we are," she said as Michael turned the car into the driveway and stopped in front of the barn.

Everyone was silent for a moment as the Kimmels looked out the open car windows at the house, a tall, white, two-story farmhouse, surrounded by blooming flower beds. Behind the house, they saw the kitchen garden with corn ready for harvest and tomato plants full of red fruit. As they got out of the car, Friedrich saw a freshly painted sign at the kitchen door. It read, "Willkommen."

After Michael opened the trunk and handed the Kimmels' suitcase to Friedrich, he nodded to Brenda and took his leave. The Kimmels had endured a long journey and had much more to take in before the day ended. Already overwhelmed, they needed no one but Brenda to welcome them to their home today. There would be many days ahead that would be better suited for other introductions.

Chapter 42

It was after dinner and near sunset on a Saturday night when Sir Richard and Lady Moncrieff were enjoying after-dinner drinks in the west sunroom and waiting for the sunset.

"I find it so comforting that our sons are together in Mombasa, away from the immediate danger of the Japanese who appear to have their hands full farther east. However, parts of our letter from Nigel seem somewhat out of character for him, wouldn't you agree?" Lady Moncrieff asked.

"Out-of-character?" asked Sir Richard. "Oh, you mean the part about the young lady?"

"Yes," she answered, "He's never written to us about a young lady before. He's only just met her, but he sounds hopelessly smitten."

"Perhaps," Sir Richard said, "but isn't it about time he allowed someone near his heart? Besides, her family is well-known to us. It may be an entirely appropriate match."

"Her family?" she asked.

"Yes. You know, the Beattys of Cheshire. Her father and I were together at Jutland in the Great War," he said.

"Of course," she said. "I had forgotten. But you do mean to say World War I, don't you?"

"Nothing but semantics, Angela," he said.

"I know, but those who continue to say, 'Great War' are labelled as old people. Let's remain as young as we can as long as we can, Richard," she said with a smile.

"Aye, aye, Captain," he said, adding a mock salute. "But know this," he said, lowering his voice, "tomorrow I shall share the company of another officer of World War I, but one who captained a German U-boat."

"How is that, Richard?" she asked.

"Michael and I are driving to Moncton to retrieve Brenda's father," he said. "One of the internment camp officials refused to transport him further. We'll have ample time to de-brief him during the drive home."

"He was a U-boat captain in World War I?" she asked.

"Yes, but a man of principle and honor. I'm looking forward to learning more tomorrow," he said.

The next day, while Sir Richard and Michael were driving to Moncton, Lady Moncrieff was hosting tea for the Highfield ladies who were eager to meet Greta Kimmel. After a week in her family's new home, Brenda felt her mother was rested enough to meet the Highfield household.

"We are so pleased to see that you are feeling well enough to join us for tea," Lady Moncrieff said. "Thank you for coming."

That simple greeting was enough to bring Greta to tears. "I cannot thank you enough for the miracle of our rescue, beginning, as I understand it, with my daughter," she began. "And even now, your husbands are on a mission to rescue my husband, Gerhardt. We will ever be in your debt."

"Mrs. Kimmel..." Susan began.

"Greta, if you please," she smiled. "Mrs. Kimmel makes me feel old."

"Of course, Greta," Susan said, "we find ourselves living in such times that human life is no longer respected as God's gift. It was your daughter's heart that moved us to help you and your family. We consider you and yours a gift to us."

"How kind of you to say such things," Greta said. "The people in the town where my grandparents were born, the townspeople who sent us away, did not offer such kindness." As she dried her eyes, she added, "We still pray for them."

"Someday," Lady Moncrieff said, "when they come to themselves, they will look back in shame at how they hurt the innocent among them. Until then, we will join you in your prayers."

The ladies sipped and talked for another hour before Susan said, "We understand your husband will arrive in time for your evening meal. Have you something special in store for him?"

"Oh, yes," she said with a sparkle in her eyes. "My Brenda, here, *meine kleine taube*, my little dove, taught me how to use the wonderful oven in our new home. I am preparing *Schweinebraten* – a roast pork – with red cabbage and dumplings, and a Black Forest cake for dessert."

"Then we shan't keep you any longer, Greta," Lady Moncrieff said, "and we shall all look forward to the day when your husband has sufficiently rested and our families can dine together."

Brenda and Greta took their leave and followed Michael's new mown path across the east pasture toward the schoolhouse and the Kimmels' home. Greta, still overflowing with gratitude, said, "I can never be more thankful than I am tonight, Brenda. I had lost hope that we would ever see your father again. Already, Friedrich and Carl are gaining back the weight they lost in the camps, and their cheeks have taken on their natural color once more. I had begun to believe we were doomed to die in the camps, but look now at the miracle of our rescue! How can we not celebrate our freedom every moment?"

"I will not disagree, Mama," Brenda said, "and seeing Papa's face again and hearing his laugh will make our family whole once more."

"Yes," Greta said, nodding. "Yes, it will."

Brenda grew thoughtful for a moment before saying, "Mama, at the tea you called me, '*meine kleine taube*'. I've never heard you use that expression before."

"That's because I never heard it before we were sent to the camps. I learned it from another woman there. She was older than me, and very kind," she said.

"Do you recall her name, Mama?" Brenda asked.

"Of course. I could never forget the name of a woman as kind as Elke."

"Elke?" Brenda asked. "And her family name?"

"Hoffman, I believe," Greta said. "Yes, that's it. Elke Hoffman."

Chapter 43

When Michael telephoned Highfield from the ferry landing in Charlottetown, Susan was happy to send Patrice to tell the Kimmels that Mr. Kimmel would be arriving shortly. Patrice had just arrived at the house and left her message with Brenda when Michael drove the Ford sedan into the Kimmels' yard. Respecting the family's need to keep their long-awaited reunion and celebration among themselves, Michael and Sir Richard made a quiet exit and returned to the car. The Kimmels needed to be together with Gerhardt Kimmel once again in the arms of his wife and children.

As Michael and Sir Richard were just about to drive away, though, Brenda ran to Michael and pressed a folded note into his hand. He could tell by the look in her eyes that there was something important within. After he dropped Sir Richard at Highfield's front door and parked the car in the garage, he opened her note and read it on his way to the kitchen door. She had written:

"I believe Ernest's mother is at the Petawawa internment camp. A woman named 'Elke Hoffman' befriended my mother there and spoke of a son named Ernst. If possible, could I meet you after breakfast tomorrow to share more of what I've learned? Thank you, Brenda."

Guessing that Sir Richard would be catching up on SIS communications after driving to and from Moncton all day, Michael checked his office in the study and found him sitting at the radio console. When Sir Richard removed his headphones, Michael said, "I think you should see this," and handed him Brenda's note.

After reading the note and adding it to the stack of papers on his desk, Sir Richard sat back in his chair, shaking his head.

"When will this fellow cease to amaze me?" he said. "He's spent time in Canada, his father died in Canada, and now his mother may have found her way here, too? I can't wait to see what Brenda has for us in the morning."

It was only a few minutes after breakfast when Brenda tapped at the study door. As Michael opened the door, Sir Richard called, "Come in, Brenda," and motioned toward a chair opposite his desk. She seemed a bit nervous, but as she sat down, she was able to smile when Sir Richard spoke.

"Thank you for your kind note, Brenda. Michael and I would be delighted to hear everything you can tell us. Please don't leave out a single detail."

A quarter hour later, after Brenda had reviewed her conversation with her mother and after Sir Richard and Michael had asked every question that came to their minds, the men thanked her again, and she took her leave.

"There's little doubt in my mind that Elke Hoffman is E.D.'s mother," Michael said. "She's from Munich, where we know he was raised and attended university. She told Greta Kimmel about the abuse she and her son endured, and how her husband never returned after the war. And the *meine kleine taube* phrase puts a bow on the package."

"And she didn't spare Mrs. Kimmel the reason why she fled Munich," Sir Richard began. "I find it interesting to pair her reason for fleeing Germany with our knowledge that E.D. has been working in the center of international resistance efforts devoted to rescuing Jews and other persecuted populations from Nazi hands. SIS has been following his travels and assignments since he began his work out of uniform, and he has now been commissioned as an SIS agent. The persecution and atrocities he witnessed, if shared with the US Office of Strategic Services, might bring the Americans farther into the fray in Europe, a place where they are sorely needed."

"Farther into the fray?" Michael asked.

"Yes," Sir Richard said. "Our troops have witnessed atrocities firsthand, things the American troops have not seen. We need a way to share our first-hand experiences with our American cohorts to help spur their efforts forward."

"Are you suggesting that SIS should bring E.D., a man technically missing-in-action from RAF service and active in the resistance in several countries across the ocean, here, to testify before OSS?" Michael asked.

"That I am, Michael," Sir Richard said. "That I am. However, you must remember that he is no longer considered to be *Missing in action*. He is now officially listed as *Killed in action*. He's a ghost now, an SIS ghost."

"Of course," Michael smiled, "I had forgotten that you had seen to that."

"Further, OSS might also be interested in his mother's testimony. It's only a possibility, but it's one I would welcome," Sir Richard said.

"First, then, we need to interview Greta Kimmel to verify everything Brenda just told us. Then, we'll need to inform E.D. of his mother's whereabouts and determine if he's willing to travel here to testify," Michael said.

"Correct," Sir Richard nodded.

"We could also offer the possibility of a reunion with his mother, if we can free her from the camp in Petawawa," Michael said.

"Leave that detail to me, Michael," he smiled. "I can't wait to talk with that commandant again."

Chapter 44

E.D.'s travel by rail from Munich to Geneva was fraught with more Gestapo and SS checkpoints than usual. Twice during the journey, E.D. left the train at busy stations and traveled by other means to the next station, avoiding the Gestapo who continuously moved from car to car, eager to interrogate almost every passenger. On a good day, the trip could be made in twelve hours, but it took E.D. fourteen hours to finally arrive in Lausanne. It would be four more hours before he disembarked in Geneva.

Despite the delays, E.D.'s mind had raced through each hour, trying to balance the needs of his mission with the news Herr Gerber had provided concerning his mother. Rocking in the aging railway car, his memories traveled back in time to his mother, his champion. Powerless to defend herself or her son against her husband's unprovoked rages and beatings, they suffered together, these two. When his father finished beating one, he often sought the other. Only enough liquor eventually sent him to his bed, ending their agonies for one more night.

It was his mother who continually cheered E.D. on, especially after his father went to war. During his years at university, she kept their home alive, making it much more than a place to study and sleep. They became a team, fighting to survive on the money his mother earned from laundering and ironing for their neighbors, as well as the money E.D. made from working at odd jobs. Still, she always made time to ask how he'd spent his day or how he was doing, not because they were routine questions or something a mother should do, but because she genuinely cared. Now, however, she had disappeared across the ocean.

"How will I ever travel that far? If I do, how will I find her?" he said aloud.

As the train from Lausanne approached Geneva, his thoughts turned to Brenda. She was the only other woman who had come close to knowing him. When they first met, he noticed her apparent wariness of men, something he understood better when she eventually shared her story with him. Though they lived closely, he was careful to maintain an almost professional distance from her, avoiding even casual familiarity that might make her uncomfortable. From time to time, they would laugh together, and those moments became more frequent as she grew more at ease with him. In time, they came to realize they missed each other when they had to be apart for more than a few hours. In public, they played lovers, holding hands, whispering in one another's ears, laughing, all to maintain their cover and keep other men away. In time, they might have given up mere acting for something more, but all too soon they were apprehended, arrested, and separated. Under 24-hour observation, E.D. had lost the one person with whom he could talk when the day was done, the one who understood what it was to be alone, even when they were together.

"Higher fields," he said to himself. "Could she really be at Highfield, now?" He closed his eyes, and the memory of her blonde hair, deep blue eyes, and impish grin raised a smile on his face, which only disappeared when the conductor announced the train's imminent arrival in Geneva.

E.D. disembarked, and after a lone Gestapo agent stopped him to examine his papers, he exited the station without further incident. When he arrived at the basement flat a few minutes later, he quickly stepped inside, locked the door, and adjusted each of the blackout curtains before tossing his bag and jacket on his bunk. Moments later, there was a knock on the inner door, and Hugo appeared with several pages of paper in his hand,

"Never had one this long or so complicated in its coding," he said, rubbing his eyes with his other hand. As he turned toward the door, he added, "As usual, it's on flash paper. A single match will make it disappear in a second."

After thanking him, E.D. lit the single bulb next to his bed to read.

Dear Ernst,

I write to you with the name you were given at birth, because I need to communicate with that man. By necessity, you've been known by other names, but I need to speak with Ernst Hoffman now because I require his assistance.

You have earned my admiration, as well as that of many others, although we know you never intended to do so. We recognize you as an overcomer, a man with many gifts and many skills, and a unique survivor. We know that your early years brought you and

your mother a great deal of pain, but they also built a bond between you that remains today. More about that later.

Your experience with the Nazi regime since you were recruited by Hitlerjugend, your education in cartography at the university in Munich, your later studies and expertise in linguistics, your experience as a Nazi Oberleutnant, and your ability to gain US citizenship years before finding your way into the port of Halifax to monitor and direct shipping, remain unparalleled. Any one of these skills, training, and experience would be remarkable feats for most men. You, however, went on to train with the RCAF and RAF, eventually using your university experience in cartography to guide RAF bombers to their targets with greater proficiency than previously thought possible. When your aircraft was shot down, the post you secured with the Resistance has since proven invaluable to us.

Here is where I am asking for your help. The United States Office of Strategic Services has requested our assistance in areas where it lacks expertise, particularly in Eastern Europe. Your eyewitness reports of atrocities ordered and committed at Nazi hands remain only rumors to OSS. We need you to share your firsthand experience of such horrors as an unidentified SIS agent at a meeting between SIS and OSS in Washington, DC. We believe that when representatives from the US intelligence community have an opportunity to see what you have seen, they will redouble their efforts to defeat our heinous Nazi enemy.

Ernst, I am a man who, like yourself, is well-seasoned in the necessity of keeping secrets. Secrets are our stock and trade. However, the monstrous disregard for human life and the systematic extermination of Jews at Nazi hands are crimes that remain veiled in secrecy until eyewitnesses tear those veils away and expose these crimes against humanity.

As one of those eyewitnesses, we offer you a unique reward for your consideration. We recently discovered that your mother, Elke Hoffman, is being held at a Canadian internment camp in Ontario. I am happy to tell you that she will soon be traveling from Ontario under our sponsorship to regain her freedom on Prince Edward Island. Already with us at Highfield is Brenda Kimmel, whose mother and brothers recently joined her after being freed from the same internment camp. Neither your mother nor Miss Kimmel is aware of this communication with you, although I am confident that both are eager to see you again.

If you are willing to accompany me to Washington, I will send immediate instructions to SIS operatives in Switzerland. They are already prepared to secure your passage overland to Marseille, by sea to Spain, and from Spain to Canada by air.

I appreciate your consideration to help meet a need that I consider crucial to our cause.

With my gratitude and deep respect,
R. M.

Chapter 45

With tears on his face, E.D. burst through the inner door of the basement room and down the narrow hall to the closet where Hugo sat hunched over the radio console. He handed Hugo a single sheet with a one-word response to Sir Richard's communique. "YES."

Hugo looked up from the sheet to say, "I decode an epistle, and you answer with a single word?"

"Yes," E.D. said as he turned back toward his room. While Hugo was still shaking his head at E.D.'s one-word response, E.D. turned back to say, "Hugo, expect a rash of short itinerary instructions for me, if you will. I'll need to see them as soon as they come in."

"Short itinerary instructions?" Hugo asked. "Wonderful," he laughed, "just no more epistles, tonight, thank you."

E.D. didn't sleep that night. He packed and re-packed his travel haversack several times, talking to himself all the while.

"I can't believe this is happening. Yesterday I learned from Herr Gerber that my mother left Munich long ago, and that she may be living in Canada. Finding her and ever seeing her again seemed an impossibility. Now, twelve hours later, I know where she is and have been granted immediate passage across the ocean to join her. And Brenda? To find that she is safe and with her family again is another impossibility. All those I hold dear await me in a place I know, and with people I know I can trust. If I never believed in miracles before, I believe in them now."

Accompanied by local SIS resistance operatives, E.D. traveled overland with escorts day and night for three days, reaching a destination in Marseilles. From Marseilles, hidden aboard one local fishing boat after another, he arrived in Barcelona after another three days. From there, as Sir Richard promised, he flew to RAF Gibraltar, then to the UK before flying the North Atlantic Ferry Route that brought him to airfields in Iceland,

Greenland, Labrador, and Newfoundland. He landed in Charlottetown eleven days after leaving Geneva.

When he landed at the airfield in Charlottetown on a Saturday morning in early October, Michael and Sir Richard were there to greet him. Exhausted from almost two weeks of travelling, E.D. was still excited to meet Sir Richard for the first time and to reunite with Michael, who, by now, had become an old friend. Sir Richard kept the conversation brief.

"E.D.," he began, but before he could say anything more, E.D. interrupted him.

"Sir Richard, while I am here among you, I wish to use my given name, if you will. I will be Ernst Hoffman among you until I return to service, if I may."

"By all means, Ernst," Sir Richard said, "Thank you. I want to assure you that we have no itinerary planned for you until we depart for Washington in five days. Michael will be your host at his new home across the road from Highfield. Surely you are anxious to make reunions with those who await you, but feel free to take time to refresh yourself first."

"Thank you," Ernst said. "I'll be happy to bathe and shave and rest for an hour. I have a very limited wardrobe in my bag. If I could beg the use of something clean to wear..."

"By all means," Michael said. "I believe we have everything you might need at home, and, at first glance, it seems we may wear close to the same sizes," he said as he squared his shoulders to match Ernst's frame. "We'll make sure you feel comfortable. Now, let's leave the airfield to itself for the short drive home."

After arriving at Hillside, Ernst slept for nearly two hours before showering, shaving, and enjoying a light meal, as he began to recover from his travel. It was almost three o'clock that afternoon when Michael and Ernst drove to Highfield. Once in Michael's car for the short drive, Ernst spoke freely.

"I haven't seen my mother in years. I fear I'll fall to tears immediately," he said.

"And what is wrong with that?" Michael asked. "Every one of those tears will tell her how much you love her and how much you've missed her. No mother could ask for a more welcome gift."

"When you put it that way, perhaps I can give up all my worries. I suppose I have nothing to prove," he said.

The men were silent for a moment before Ernst said, "Brenda and I have much to discuss. We traveled down some very dark paths together. I hope she won't revile me when we meet again."

"Revile you?" Michael asked. "From what I've heard from her, I think you'll find nothing but relief that you are here and safe."

"I hope so, Michael. Our relationship was always tentative. I felt a need to protect her at all times, but in the end, I failed. We'll have much to rehearse from a dark past," he said.

"And you'll have plenty of time to do so," Michael answered, "but a dark past, once redeemed, can yield a bright future. But more about that later. Here we are."

The Moncrieffs had reserved the east sunroom for Ernst's reunion with his mother, Elke. She was waiting on the settee facing the horizon when Michael brought him to the door. Nervous with anticipation, when she heard their footfall, she stood and turned toward the door as Ernst hurried into her arms. Michael said nothing as he backed away and left them to each other.

"It has been so, so long," she said. "I feared I would never see you again."

"And I as well, Mama," he said. "I searched for you again and again in Munich. It was Herr Gerber who told me you had left Munich for a town called Newstadt somewhere in Canada. I left him in his office at the university when I returned to Geneva."

"Our old friend, Herr Gerber," she smiled as she and Ernst sat, facing each other. "And you came here from Geneva, then?" she asked.

"Yes, Mama," he said.

"I lived in Newstadt, some distance from here in Ontario, for three years. I knew you had spent time in Canada after you left America. The stamps on your letters told me," she said.

"Yes," he replied.

"And I know your father was a prisoner in Canada after the last war," she said, "but he never came home. Did you look for him?"

"I did, Mama," he said. "You should know that he was a war prisoner on this island. He escaped and made a local woman who worked at the prison camp his prisoner. He kept her hostage for many years as he traveled west. She escaped just a few years ago and found her way home here to Charlottetown. He died after her escape."

"So, you never spoke with him?" she asked.

"No, Mama. We never spoke," Ernst said as he looked toward the floor.

"Then he will haunt our dreams no more," she said. "I feared he would find me at Newstadt when I arrived from Germany. Now I will sleep better, knowing I need fear him no more."

"No more," Ernst said, shaking his head. "No more, Mama."

Chapter 46

It was almost an hour before Elke and Ernst stepped into Highfield's front entry to find Michael. After leaving his mother with another kiss and a warm embrace, Ernst followed Michael to the west sunroom on the opposite side of the house. There, sitting on the settee with her back to the doors, Brenda was waiting. When she heard the men's footsteps, she stood, turned, and looked toward Ernst, who rushed to her with open arms.

Brenda was silent, her face buried in his shoulder as she heard him say, "Oh, how I've missed you," surprising himself that he was the first to speak. When she looked up at him, he saw her teary eyes turn into a smile as she said, "All of this seems like a miracle, all because our mothers met by chance as prisoners in Ontario."

With their arms still around each other, Ernst said, "I never took much stock in miracles before, but in the last few weeks I've seen several I cannot doubt."

"Let me look at you," she said as she stepped back and took his hands in hers. "You look just the same," she said through her smile.

"But not you," he said. "You, Brenda Kimmel, are much more of a woman now. You're no longer the little lost farmgirl I met on the platform at the train depot in Ottawa. The change is very impressive," he smiled.

"Well," she said, spinning herself around, letting her skirt reach its full flare, "I am almost twenty now, you know."

"Yes, you are," he laughed, "and I should probably say no more right now. Just know that I like what I see."

Brenda led him outdoors onto the terrace where the sun was resting on the horizon.

"Let's go for a walk," she said as she pulled his hand and led him toward the patio steps.

"Where?" he asked.

"How about going to the fire tower? We can talk along the way," she offered.

"Oh," he said, as his face darkened. "Doesn't that path take us past the sawmill?"

"Yes, but there's no reason to worry about that," she said. "I know how you feel, but everyone here, especially Joseph, the boy we injured, has forgiven us. Though he has never met you, he thinks well of you. The money you provided made it possible for him to attend medical school. You made his dream come true. I talked with him when my own guilt still haunted me, and I assure you, he bears neither of us any ill will. You'll be able to meet him, if you like, tomorrow or the next day. Come on," she said, tugging his hand. "Let's go."

Ernst nodded and followed her toward the path.

The air was cooling after the warmth of the day, and they took their time as they enjoyed the late splashes of light that shone through the trees as the sun moved lower in the sky. In a few minutes, they reached and passed the sawmill, still talking about everything that had brought them back together.

"So," Brenda said, "it was because your mother called my mother *meine kleine taube*. When I heard her use the same pet name you used for me, I could hardly believe my ears. Those three words were my clue."

Ernst shook his head and laughed. "You were *meine kleine taube*. Like that hungry young dove outside my broken basement window in Munich, you had no one," he said. "When I found you, I knew I needed to be the one who'd care for you."

"And you did, Ernst. You found me on the street, and you took me in. You could have left me to fend for myself, but no, you took me in," she said with tears in her eyes.

"And I would do it again," he said.

He wrapped his arm around her shoulder, and she added hers around his waist as they approached the fire tower.

"This is where they rescued me," she said.

"Rescued you?" he asked.

"Yes," she answered. "Michael could tell every time I climbed the stairs to use their radio. See here?" she said as she demonstrated by rocking the bottom step and explaining how the alarm switch worked. Then, as they climbed to the first landing and sat together, Brenda continued.

"While I was using the radio, another man in Charlottetown, Armand, a friend of the Moncrieffs, was monitoring my transmissions. One dark, moonless night, when they discovered I was here, Michael and Susan walked all the way from Highfield to confront me. As Michael neared the top of the stairs, I felt and heard his footsteps. I panicked, sure that I would soon be in handcuffs again and on my way to jail. Instead, they were kind to me, Ernst. Susan spoke with me for almost an hour. She and Michael trusted me to come down from the tower with them, and they took me to a warm cottage where I could spend the night. There were no locks on the doors or windows, Ernst, nothing to keep me from running away. They helped me realize that many things I had long believed weren't true. They didn't catch me, Ernst; no, they *rescued* me. I've been here at Highfield ever since."

Ernst listened intently as tears formed in his eyes. Finally, he said, "Michael did the same for me when I was jailed in Halifax. He told me how he had found some freedom from his angst, the things in his heart that told him he would never be worthy, things that ruled his life. It was then that I began to refuse to believe all the lies my father shouted at me for hours at a time, telling me I was worthless. That was when I found the freedom to go on. Until then, they were the secrets that ruled me. Shortly after that, I escaped the jail at Halifax. But…" he said, as he went silent.

"But what?' she asked.

"It's about another secret," Ernst said.

"Can you tell me about it?" Brenda asked.

Ernst nodded and began, "Two weeks ago, an old professor and family friend of mine in Munich told me something about my family I'd never known. I learned more from my mother only an hour ago. I need to tell you about it."

"Then tell me, Ernst, please," she said.

"When my grandmother," he began quietly, "my mother's mother, died, I was seven years old. She and my grandfather had married in Vienna almost fifty years earlier, long before they moved to Munich. Many years later, when my mother and father met and married, there was something my grandparents never told them."

"What was that?" Brenda asked.

"My grandmother had been born to a Jewish family in Vienna," he said, "and my grandfather told no one until the day of her funeral. That was when he told my mother. Then, about a week later, he sent her a small package wrapped in brown paper. When she opened it, she found some photos of my grandmother at a party when she was a girl. Mama also found this," he said as he reached to his neck to retrieve a delicate gold chain bearing a small six-pointed gold star. "She gave it to me today."

As he handed the pendant and chain to Brenda, he said, "Sometime later, my father discovered the photos and this pendant. He was outraged. He ran to find my grandfather and demanded the truth my grandparents had hidden for so long. Shortly after that, my father's drinking began, along with his rages aimed at Mama and me."

"But why was he so angry, Ernst?" Brenda asked.

"Mama told me it was simply because she and I have Jewish blood in our veins. Many people in Germany hated Jews long before this war began," he said, "and my father was one of them. Mostly, though, I think he felt he had been duped when he married my mother in ignorance so many years before. He couldn't punish an old man like my grandfather, so he turned his hatred toward my mother and me."

Ernst was quiet for a moment before saying, "My grandparents went to church each week at St. Luke's, and often we sat with them. After my grandmother died, though, my father forbade us to go back, in case my grandfather was there. He wanted us never to see my grandfather again."

"So, you did nothing to prompt his rage and the beatings? All the accusations he made were untrue?" Brenda asked.

"That's right," Ernst said. "I never knew why he couldn't bear me until now."

They were silent for a moment before Brenda spoke.

"Then that journey is over, Ernst. You did nothing wrong, and neither have you *been* anything wrong. It's a lot like my family. Even though we had done nothing wrong, the Canadian Minister of Justice interned us solely because we came from German families who arrived here more than a hundred years ago. For both of us, however, something meant for evil has become something good."

"Something good?" Ernst asked.

"Yes," she said. "Those two evils brought us together."

Ernst nodded, but it was another moment before he spoke.

"I need to tell you how badly I've felt about leaving you behind when I escaped. It haunts me even today because I never wanted to hurt you."

"But that chapter has been redeemed, Ernst," she said, "and we're writing a new chapter now. There's a blank page before us. Everything from now on will be new."

Ernst smiled and nodded in agreement, and they started down the stairs together, both pondering what the next chapter would bring. When they reached the bottom, Brenda turned to face him. Looking up into his eyes, she said, "You know, Susan told me that she and Michael shared their first kiss at this tower. From that moment, they knew they were meant for each other."

There was a day when Ernst might have withstood Brenda's thinly veiled challenge, but not on this day. Helpless to resist, but needing to ask her for one thing more, he looked into her clear blue eyes and said, "I need you to wear this for me." He took the chain and star from her hand and placed it around her neck.

"I dare not wear a Jewish star where I'll be traveling in Europe," he said.

"Then I will wear it until the day you return," she whispered in his ear, "and I will pray that day will be soon."

As he drew her close, he said, "Now, about that tradition Michael and Susan began…"

They didn't share just one kiss, but two, and three, and then four before Ernst raised his eyes, looked toward Highfield, and drew Brenda so close they could feel their hearts beating together.

Speaking softly, his lips close to her ear, he said, "I don't want to leave you, Brenda." He paused before correcting himself. "No, that's not true. The truth is, I *never* want to leave you. In a few days, though, I must go away with Sir Richard, but only as far as Washington, DC. There are things I have seen, horrible things, secrets that I must share with those who have the power to stop the evil that perpetrates these horrors. There is so much I can't tell you, evil things I've witnessed in my work, inhuman things, atrocities the Nazis have kept secret."

Brenda leaned back and brought her hands to his cheeks to raise his eyes to hers.

"Ernst," she began, "Sir Richard took time to speak with your mother and me yesterday. He told us about the importance of your work and explained why he needed to take you away for several days."

As Ernst nodded, she continued, "I don't need to know about the things you can't share with me, because those secrets aren't the kind that could ever come between us."

Ernst looked into her eyes again and nodded in agreement, saying, "No, they won't, Brenda. I won't let them."

"There may yet be others, though," she said, "others that *could* come between us, and I'm not sure I could bear that."

Ernst nodded once more.

"Those secrets are secrets of the heart, Ernst," she said. "I've never told you how much you meant to me when you took me in. You saved my life, and despite my fears, I fell in love with a gentle, caring man. At first, I was afraid you might try to take advantage of me, but instead, you honored me. I didn't know that I was falling in love with you then, but I need to tell you now, because the secrets of our hearts should never remain with only one of us, Ernst. I need to share mine with you, always."

Without hesitation, and still looking deeply into her eyes, he said, "And mine will be yours, Brenda Ilse Kimmel, *meine kleine taube*, always."

Two had left Highfield to take a walk earlier that afternoon, but the pair who returned came back a *couple*.

Chapter 47

It had been a week since Sir Richard and Ernst returned from Washington, DC, where Ernst had shared his knowledge and eyewitness experiences of Nazi atrocities in Eastern Europe. His testimony, and especially the photographic evidence he had managed to smuggle out of Poland, although convincing to all, secured no promises of active intervention by US military forces. The men returned to Highfield disappointed but not discouraged. With the help of his network of comrades, Sir Richard had reason to believe a second opportunity to make their case would be forthcoming. Sadly, though, it would not be possible to schedule a second meeting until after Ernst had returned to active service in Europe.

While a guest at Hillside with Michael and Susan, Ernst was happy to help Michael outfit the safe room in the garage basement at Hillside. A virtual twin to the original at Highfield, the room was stocked with supplies of non-perishable food, water, first-aid supplies, and medicines. Sir Richard had helped to procure four Browning M1918 .30 caliber automatic rifles, a Bren LMG, several Webley Mk 1 pistols, a case of No.36M grenades, and a supply of ammunition for each weapon. As at Highfield, there were also three radio sets, complete with antennas, each supplied for their intended locations in the basement, Michael's study, and the attic.

With the help of the new dumbwaiter, Michael and Ernst relocated the weaponry and ammunition from the garage to the north, east, and west elevation attic windows. Before they were finished, they also outfitted the attic with the new radio equipment, installed an antenna at Hillside's center chimney, and located two portable electric generators, one in the attic and one in the basement. When they were finished, Michael felt confident that Hillside was adequately supplied with all the emergency supplies and equipment his family might need.

With the date for Susan's delivery only weeks away, Brenda came to serve at Hillside as a live-in nurse and nanny for Case and Reed. Ernst and Brenda could hardly have been happier to see each other every day at Hillside for his remaining time in Canada. At the same time, Ernst also enjoyed daily visits with his mother at the Kimmel home, where the Kimmel family, so long separated from each other, continued to settle in while enjoying the safety and security of life on Prince Edward Island. The autumn of 1942 became a magical time of peace and joy among the families newly arrived and reunited at Highfield.

On a Saturday morning in late October, Ernst met with Sir Richard in his study at Highfield. Michael joined them with a fresh pot of coffee, and Lois followed with a plate of fresh corn muffins.

"I'm getting used to coffee in the morning," Sir Richard admitted. "Michael introduced me to it, you know. I had started the day with tea for many decades previously."

"Coffee was a staple for us in Germany before the war," Ernst said. "We used to enjoy ours with kuchen."

"Morning coffee, I must say, seems to provide a little extra energy at the start of the day. Nonetheless, in the afternoons, I return to my customary cup of tea," Sir Richard admitted.

After another sip, Sir Richard continued, "I know you are eager to return to your work on the continent, Ernst. To that end, I have arranged for your return flights following the same North Atlantic ferry route that brought you here. We have scheduled your departure from the airfield in Charlottetown three days from now."

"Thank you, sir," Ernst replied. "My departure does not come without regret, of course, for my time here with my mother and Brenda has been a great gift. Perhaps an equal sense of gratitude, however, is the one I feel for the time I have spent with you here at Highfield. Though once your enemy, sir, you have welcomed me without reserve, caring for my mother and me as you would your own family, granting us a reunion we would never have known. I will ever be in your debt."

Rising to offer his hand, Sir Richard said, "And you, Ernst, by a remarkable transformation of your heart, have earned a place in ours, equal to no other. Your service, inextricably linked with ours against a heinous foe, is one as strong as blood. Please, always consider yourself a welcome member of our family."

As the men returned to their seats, Sir Richard opened a folder on his desk, retrieved a travel itinerary from within, and handed it to Ernst.

"Your transport will take you to London," he said, "where we have arranged for you to meet with a man named Jan Molenaar. Long a denizen of the Netherlands, he is studying art at the Royal Academy. He joined the Dutch resistance not long after the Nazis arrived in the Netherlands and has recently become an essential member of our team. He will help to secure your passage across the Channel to those who will assist you in the next leg of your travel to Geneva."

Three days passed quickly, and Ernst left Hillside and Highfield amidst tearful good-byes with his mother and Brenda. When Michael and Sir Richard delivered Ernst to the airfield at Charlottetown, Michael couldn't help noticing a uniformed female passenger boarding the single transport plane on the runway.

As he pointed to her, Michael said, "I believe you'll meet a kindred spirit in that passenger, Ernst. Susan spoke with her several weeks ago. Her father, an RCAF flying ace in World War I, taught his daughter to fly at an early age. Now she's on her way to England to begin transporting aircraft for the RAF in war zones abroad."

"I'm sure she will soon have stories to tell," Ernst said. "Few women would volunteer to enter the man's world of wartime airfields. She sounds like an intrepid woman."

With their good-byes complete, Ernst left Sir Richard and Michael and boarded the aircraft. Once the plane was in the air, Michael drove Sir Richard home to Highfield. Two hours later, however, the telephone in Michael's study rang. Sir Richard was calling.

"Michael," he said in a somber tone, "please join me at Highfield in the study. I have news to share with you."

Chapter 48

When he arrived at Highfield, Michael found Lady Moncrieff waiting with Sir Richard in his study. As Michael closed the door and took his seat, Sir Richard began, "I want you to be aware of some important wartime developments here at home. Hoping to cause Susan no undue upset this close to her delivery date, I decided not to include her in this conversation."

"Thank you," Michael said. "When I returned from the airfield, I found her busily re-arranging the entire nursery, emptying and refilling bureau drawers, folding and refolding linens. I begged her to let it all go and get some rest, but she was unrelenting."

"I believe we could credit that sort of obsession to 'nesting,' Michael," Lady Moncrieff smiled. "Like a mother bird, she's preparing a nest for her little one."

"Ah, is that what it's all about?" Michael smiled. "Well, the delivery date is still two weeks away. She'll have plenty of time to finish the nest. But to your news, Richard."

"Last week, I reported that U-boats had sunk nine merchant vessels in the Gulf of St. Lawrence," Sir Richard began. "Today, however, I am bringing you the sad news of the sinking of the HMCS *Charlottetown*. Nine RCN servicemen, including her captain, perished. Thankfully, fifty-five others survived."

As Michael and Lady Moncrieff sat in silence, Sir Richard added, "This sinking differs significantly from all the others. The *Charlottetown* was not attacked at sea, beyond the Gulf of St. Lawrence, but just one day's sail from Quebec City and," he said pointedly, "an even shorter distance from Prince Edward Island."

"The U-boats are no longer hunting only shipping vessels in the Gulf, then," Michael said.

"Correct," Sir Richard answered. "Now they have the Royal Canadian Navy in their sights."

"In the spring," Michael said, "we spoke of this eventuality. Do you continue to trust that the British treasury accounts in Montreal and Ottawa remain secure?"

"I do, Michael, and for these reasons," Sir Richard began. "I've come to believe that the U-boat attacks we've suffered thus far amount to mere inconveniences when compared to the threats a better-equipped enemy would be able to launch. A successful raid on a land-based target as far up the Saint Lawrence Seaway as Montreal would first require air attacks to neutralize land and airborne defenses, followed by a ground invasion of sufficient numbers to compromise the defensive perimeter and secure the contents of the bank vaults. However, since the war began three years ago, the Kriegsmarine's lone aircraft carrier, the *Graf Zeppelin*, has not seen combat. It has never sailed beyond the Baltic Sea. I believe Hitler would be loath to risk the embarrassment of losing her to the Royal Navy as he did with his prize, the *Bismarck*. Lacking an aircraft carrier, the Kriegsmarine offers no immediate threat to our assets in Canada."

"Thankfully, the Japanese pose no viable threat to us in the Atlantic," Michael said, "but how would you assess the safety of the Allied forces on land and at sea in the Indian Ocean and the Pacific?"

"In many ways, it comes down to numbers." Sir Richard said. "The Japanese military has only 4.5 million in uniform, while the US alone has more than 16 million. When we add Britain's 8.5 million military personnel, one can see that it will be only a matter of time before Japanese personnel losses severely limit Hirohito's ability to defend the territories he seems to have conquered thus far."

"So," Michael said, "you believe that Japan has bitten off more than she can chew?"

"I do," Sir Richard smiled. "Japan's initial victories throughout the Pacific require it to maintain and defend those territories, tasks for which we are already finding its forces unprepared. One by one, they will lose the territories they've gained, and at great cost, as we have already witnessed at Midway. I believe history will tell the story of a small dog in a big fight. Even now, their presence in the Indian Ocean has been compromised. As a result, Boyd is aboard the HMS *Revenge*, sitting safely in port at Mombasa. At the same time, Nigel is sailing aboard the HMS *Formidable*, which will soon sail to Gosport for a refit. The Japanese threat in the Indian Ocean, so intimidating in the spring, has faded. Hirohito's Imperial Navy has abandoned its pursuit of British targets there to respond to more pressing defensive needs in the Pacific theater, where, since Japan's defeat at Midway, United States forces grow stronger every day."

Just then, the telephone on Sir Richard's desk rang. When he answered it, he heard Brenda's voice.

"I'm sorry to disturb you, Sir Richard, but is Mr. Moreland still with you there?" she asked.

"Yes, Michael is here," he answered. "I'll hand him the receiver."

"It's Miss Kimmel," Sir Richard said as he handed the telephone to Michael. "She sounds unusually earnest."

"Yes, Brenda," Michael answered.

The Moncrieffs looked on, trying not to appear too curious as they listened intently to Michael's half of the conversation.

"I see," Michael said. "And the boys? Are they in bed?"

Michael listened for another moment before saying, "Asleep now? Stellar. Of course. I agree. Yes, that would be best. Just five minutes, no more. Certainly. I understand. Thank you. Good-bye."

Without another word, Michael handed the telephone receiver to Sir Richard, and with the hint of a smile appearing on his face, he turned to Lady Moncrieff and bent down to kiss her cheek. Surprised, she turned and looked wide-eyed at Sir Richard as he shrugged his shoulders. With his smile broadening, Michael turned to approach Sir Richard and extended his hand. Puzzled, Sir Richard stood, shook Michael's hand, and watched as his son-in-law strode toward the door, stopped, and turned around.

"You were spot on, Mother," Michael said as he addressed Lady Moncrieff. "Susan *was* preparing the nest, and it seems she completed her task. Brenda called to report that Susan's water has just broken. The hospital is awaiting her arrival as soon as I can drive her there. I'll telephone you when I have news of your third grandchild."

With that, he was gone.

The Moncrieffs turned toward each other, and Lady Moncrieff smiled and said, "I feel quite sure he was not expecting that call tonight."

"So, it appears," Sir Richard agreed. After a moment, he added, "When I think back nearly three decades now, I must say I regret being away for all our children's deliveries. I left it all to you, Angela, I'm sorry to say. I was no help at all."

"It was as it needed to be, Richard. Delivery dates aren't ours to schedule. And don't forget that we were always together for our children's christenings," she said, "all three."

"Ah, yes, the christenings," he smiled, "and the joyous celebrations thereafter. Speaking of which, do you know if Susan and Michael have chosen names?" he asked.

"I've heard Susan mention Christine and Christopher as possibilities, but I've heard nothing definite," she replied.

Turning toward his desk, he asked, "Shall we offer a toast to our newest grandchild?"

At Lady Moncrieff's nod, he reached toward his bottom drawer.

"Oh, Richard," she said, "not the customary Dewars you keep there for the men, if you please. I don't think I'm quite up to that tonight."

"You misjudge me, Darling," he smiled, as he lifted two brandy snifters and a bottle of Harvey's Bristol Cream sherry from the drawer. "I anticipated this eventuality some days ago and re-stocked my office warehouse with one of your favorites."

Smiling and shaking her head as if to say, "You never cease to amaze me," she joined him as he walked toward the fireplace.

Placing a snifter in her waiting hands, Sir Richard said, "A toast - to Christine or Christopher, and to Susan, Michael, Case, and Reed, already the joys of their Moncrieff and Moreland forebears; may they ever share love, faith, and joy, offer others true charity and brotherhood in this life, and find rest and peace awaiting them in the next."

"Hear, hear," Lady Moncrieff agreed as the couple raised their glasses, linked their arms at the elbow, looked fondly into each other's eyes, and enjoyed their first sip, followed by a kiss.

Terms and Abbreviations

Allies—those countries that fought against the Axis powers in World War II, chiefly the United Kingdom, the United States, France, the Soviet Union, and China

Astra 300—a Spanish semi-automatic pistol manufactured by Astra Unceta from 1922 to 1946

Axis—those countries that fought against the Allied powers in World War II, primarily Germany, Italy, and Japan

British Air Transport Authority—British civilian organization during World War II responsible for ferrying military aircraft between factories, airfields, and squadrons

Enigma machine—an encryption device used by Germany to send coded messages

Fleet Air Arm—the Royal Navy's aircraft division operating from Royal Navy ships

Gestapo—the official secret police of Nazi Germany and German-occupied Europe

Hirohito—the Emperor of Japan during World War II

HMS—His Majesty's Ship

Home Guard—an unpaid citizen militia supporting the 'Home Forces' of the British Army during World War II

Kriegsmarine—the navy of Nazi Germany from 1935 to 1945

Leutnant—the lowest junior officer rank in the armed forces of Germany

Low Countries—Belgium, the Netherlands, and Luxembourg

Luftwaffe—the air force of Nazi Germany from 1935 to 1945

Mussolini—the fascist dictator of Italy during World War II

Nazi—the National Socialist Party led by Adolf Hitler that ruled Germany from 1933 to 1945

Oberleutnant—and Upper Lieutenant, the highest lieutenant rank in the German armed forces

OSS—the United States Office of Strategic Services, later renamed the CIA

PEI—Prince Edward Island

RAF—Royal Air Force

RCAF—Royal Canadian Air Force

RCN—Royal Canadian Navy

RN—Royal Navy

SIS—the Secret Intelligence Service in the UK, later commonly known as MI6

SS—Schutzstaffel, a major paramilitary organization under Hitler's Nazi Party, Third Reich

Swizzels—a UK confectionery company founded in 1928

The Abwehr—the German military intelligence service from 1920 to 1944

U–boat—Unterseeboot (under-sea-boat), German submarines used during World War II

Walther PPK—a small, easily concealed semi-automatic pistol often used by SIS personnel

Wehrmacht—the unified armed forces of Nazi Germany from 1935 to 1945

www.ingramcontent.com/pod-product-compliance
Lightning Source LLC
Chambersburg PA
CBHW050400030726
47503CB00006B/1944